WHERE EVIL HIDES

*A Bridget Bishop FBI Mystery Thriller,
Book Three*

Melinda Woodhall

Where Evil Hides Copyright © 2022 by Melinda Woodhall. All Rights Reserved.

All rights reserved. No part of this book may be reproduced in any form or by any electronic or mechanical means including information storage and retrieval systems, without permission in writing from the author. The only exception is by a reviewer, who may quote short excerpts in a review.

This book is a work of fiction. Names, characters, places, and incidents either are products of the author's imagination or are used fictitiously. Any resemblance to actual persons, living or dead, events, or locales is entirely coincidental.

Melinda Woodhall
Visit my website at www.melindawoodhall.com
Printed in the United States of America
First Printing: July 2022
Creative Magnolia

CHAPTER ONE

Lucky stood in the cabin cruiser's cockpit and piloted the sleek boat through the icy water of the Chesapeake Bay. With less than an hour until sunset, the sky overhead was darkening with impending snow, and the temperature was falling with every passing minute and every nautical mile.

Skimming along the water at full throttle, the experienced sailor was oblivious to the frigid wind whipping in through the open sunroof, protected by his sturdy fisherman's rain suit, thick-soled deck boots, and thermal fleece balaclava, which covered his head and face.

As the forty-foot yacht approached Point Charity, Lucky pulled back on the throttle and looked toward the shore with impatient eyes.

The once lush green landscape had faded into the bleaker shades of winter, and the terrain was now barren and topped with ice and snow.

A flock of snow geese soaring overhead in a V formation was the only sign of life on the Bay, but Lucky took no notice of the birds as they beat the sky with their black-tipped wings.

A thrill of anticipation rolled through him as his eyes settled on a large Cape Cod house set back from the water.

Reaching for the high-end marine binoculars hanging around his neck, he held them to his eyes, eager to see if his target had arrived according to plan.

He focused the binoculars on the large kitchen window, pleased to be able to view the warm, cozy room in stark, intimate detail, then released a soft grunt of satisfaction as Harmony Baxter stepped into view.

Pulse quickening, he studied the young woman with a possessive gleam in his eyes. His gaze lingered on the long dark hair that fell halfway down her back and the gentle curves visible beneath her silky pink blouse and slim black pants.

As Harmony turned toward the window, Lucky adjusted the binoculars, zooming in on her relaxed, unguarded face.

She was still wearing the Cherry Dream lipstick she'd applied before leaving the office. It was holding up well.

His eyes narrowed as she began to unpack a bag of groceries, which she must have purchased before leaving the city.

She looks ready to move in. Too bad she'll never get the chance.

Checking his watch, Lucky calculated how much time he had left, then slowly accelerated toward the dock, mentally rehearsing his story in case he was seen or confronted.

But few people braved the Bay on such a cold day, and he was left in peace as he allowed the bow to drift closer to the dock before putting the boat into reverse.

Deftly aligning the stern to the dock, he moved quickly to

wrap the lines around the cleat and secure the boat.

Now, there was just one thing left to do.

The most important part of his plan.

Crossing to the companionway, he descended into the yacht's galley where a slim leather case rested on the teak countertop. Lucky smiled as he opened the case to survey the knives within.

Originally containing five knives of varying sizes, the case now held only three.

Removing the largest of the knives, he ran a gloved thumb over the familiar image engraved on the steel.

Time to give the devil his due.

Careful not to cut himself with the razor-sharp blade, he slid the knife into the sheath hanging from his belt.

Still smiling, he climbed the stairs, emerging onto the deck just as a gust of freezing wind whooshed past. Adjusting his balaclava to cover as much of his face as possible, he jumped onto the wooden dock and walked quickly toward the house.

Circling around to the front door, he was no longer aware of the passing time and the approaching snowstorm. His mind was focused solely on the task at hand.

Undisturbed by the presence of the security camera above the door, he looked around to make sure he was alone, then punched the four-digit password into the keypad with one gloved finger. Turning the brass handle, he pushed gently on the big wooden door and slipped inside.

The large foyer was warm and welcoming compared to the miserable conditions outside. Soothing classical music drifted out of the kitchen and down the hall.

Lucky stood still and listened, then raised an eyebrow.

When did she add Mozart's Serenade No. 13 to her playlist?

He knew all the music Harmony liked. She preferred the kind of whiny pop music that made his skin crawl.

Either her tastes are changing, or she's trying to impress someone.

Based on what he knew about the woman in the kitchen, which was pretty much everything, he decided it was the latter.

Perhaps she was preparing for her potential role as wife to one of the richest men in the country. Planning a future full of all the good things life had to offer.

She doesn't know there is no future. At least, not for her.

Drawing the heavy knife from its sheath, Lucky was already moving toward the kitchen when he heard Harmony's voice.

"Monty should be here within the hour."

The words were accompanied by a giggle.

"I talked him into a quiet weekend on the Bay," she added smugly. "Just the two of us. That man will be down on one knee before the weekend's out."

Her shrill laugh set Lucky's teeth on edge, and his grip tightened on the handle of the knife as he realized she must be speaking to someone on the phone.

Leaning forward to peer through the kitchen doorway, he saw the woman he'd come to kill.

Holding a slim cell phone between her ear and her shoulder, Harmony Baxter was arranging bottles of mineral water onto the top shelf of the stainless steel, French-door refrigerator, unaware that anyone was behind her.

"And once his divorce is finalized, I'll become the new Mrs. Montgomery Montclair so fast it'll make his head spin," she boasted. "But look, I gotta go. I want everything to be perfect when he gets here."

With another earsplitting giggle, she disconnected the call and set the phone on the counter.

"You've been a naughty girl, Harmony."

Harmony spun to face Lucky, his menacing words prompting a startled scream.

"Playing around with a married man is always a bad idea."

Her eyes widened as she took in the balaclava and the knife, which was already slashing toward her. Its razor-sharp blade sank into her chest with surprising ease.

They both looked down as a gush of blood spread over the pale pink silk of her blouse, staining it a deep, garish crimson.

Before she could move, Lucky lifted his free hand and grabbed her by the throat.

Tightening his grip on the slippery knife, he sliced down with all his strength, feeling flesh and bone give way under the ice-tempered, high carbon steel blade.

Harmony tried to speak but managed only a few gurgled words before blood spilled over her cherry-colored lips.

"Help...me...Scarlett..."

The hair on the back of his neck stood on end as Lucky made out the garbled words and saw Harmony's glazed eyes staring past him to focus on a spot over his shoulder.

Jerking his head toward the back door, he saw a face staring in through the glass inset.

The woman outside gaped at him in horror.

With a vicious final twist, Lucky ended Harmony's pointless struggling, then turned back to face Scarlett Montclair, who was still standing on the back porch looking in as if frozen in place.

Wrenching the knife free, he dropped Harmony onto the floor and charged toward the back door, intent on reaching the unexpected witness to his crime before she could escape.

A slick pool of blood at his feet sent him slipping and sliding across the room. Crashing against the cabinet, he banged his elbow hard on the granite countertop, then fell back onto the hardwood floor as the knife flew from his hand.

The small devil's face engraved on the steel blade turned around and around as the knife spun across the floor.

Scrambling back to his feet, Lucky flung open the back door and ran after Scarlett, but Monty Montclair's estranged wife had already jumped into her sleek white Mercedes and was squealing out of the driveway and onto Windwalker Way.

Lucky skidded to a stop in the frozen yard, his mind spinning, unsure if Scarlett had recognized him behind the balaclava, wondering how long he had before the police would arrive.

As he turned back to the house, the skies opened, and the

snow that had been threatening all day finally started to fall.

CHAPTER TWO

The predicted snowstorm arrived just before dark, covering the parking lot outside the Wisteria Falls Forensic Psychology office with a delicate layer of white powder, sending a ripple of dismay through Bridget Bishop as she looked up from her computer.

The psychologist had planned to be out of the office before the storm hit, hoping to avoid an evening commute complicated by slick roads and tired drivers, but her afternoon session had run over, and the follow-up report she was writing had taken longer than expected.

Switching on her desk lamp to combat the darkness descending outside her window, Bridget looked down at Hank, who was napping at her feet, his shiny mahogany coat gleaming in the lamplight.

The Irish setter was tired and ready for home, and she couldn't blame him. It had been a very long day for them both, and it wasn't over yet.

As she pushed back her chair and stood, gingerly stretching her aching back and stiff neck, Bridget berated herself for agreeing to have dinner with Terrance Gage that evening.

WHERE EVIL HIDES

I should have known I'd be shattered by Friday night. Especially with the Montclair case coming to a head.

After declining several recent invitations from her ex-boss at the FBI's Behavioral Analysis Unit in Quantico, she'd finally given in and agreed to meet, eager for an update on the BAU, and on Russell Malone, Gage's foster son who had recently moved into his big house in Stafford County.

But now Bridget was tired and emotionally drained after the long day and part of her wished she could just write up the notes from her two tense sessions and go home.

Checking her reflection in the window, she lifted a hand to smooth back her wavy, chestnut-brown hair, then looked down at her plain, slightly rumpled suit.

She glanced at her watch, stirring the little voice in her head.

Don't even think about it. There isn't time to go home to change, and Gage won't care what you're wearing anyway.

The little voice was probably right, as usual.

Although Gage was selective about the clothes he wore, dressing in expensive tailored suits and hand-crafted leather shoes, he was unlikely to comment on her own attire.

More likely he'd dispense with the small talk altogether, jumping right in to ask about her recent private practice work before raising his true objective: her return to the BAU.

While Gage had been agreeable to using Bridget's consulting services on several serial homicide cases since she'd left the Bureau, he'd been persistent in his opinion that she was wasting her time in private practice.

But Bridget had left her role as a profiler and behavioral analyst for a reason, and the nightmares that had started after the Backroads Butcher case still plagued her, along with troubling memories of the killers she'd interviewed and studied before the premature end to her career with the FBI.

She'd hoped to regain a semblance of balance and order in her life by working on less violent and disturbing cases for her current employer, a private forensic psychology practice with clients involved in criminal or civil court cases.

And for the last few months, ever since the SOS Shooter case had been solved, she had taken a much-needed break from work involving dead bodies or psychotic killers.

Unfortunately, Bridget had discovered that psychopaths and serial killers weren't the only ones out in society causing pain and grief to innocent people.

This sad fact had been highlighted during her morning session with thirty-eight-year-old Scarlett Montclair, and then again at an afternoon session with Scarlett's soon-to-be ex-husband, sixty-year-old Monty Montclair.

The warring couple was involved in a high-profile, mud-slinging divorce that had devolved into accusations of infidelity, child abuse, and neglect.

The presiding judge had ordered psychological evaluations of both parties prior to making a final decision on custody of their only child. Both Scarlett and Monty were seeking sole custody of sixteen-year-old Cassidy Montclair.

However, after evaluating both adults in the impending divorce over multiple sessions, Bridget wasn't sure if either one of them was mentally or emotionally fit to parent the shy, quiet teenager.

As Bridget shut down her computer and picked up her bag, Dr. Gary Zepler appeared at her office door.

Her boss made a show of looking at his watch, then peered over his glasses, and smiled through his full white beard.

"Based on that snowstorm out there, I'd say it's quitting time, although I suspected you might still be here."

He rested his hands on his substantial midsection.

"Does that mean your sessions with Montgomery and Scarlett Montclair ran over?" he asked. "Was there an issue?"

"Not with the sessions, no, but I can say unequivocally that both Monty and Scarlett have issues," Bridget replied with a wry smile. "Which is to be expected. Otherwise, Judge Kimble wouldn't have mandated that they meet with me."

Looking down at the copious notes she'd taken during the last eight hours, she pushed back a wave of fatigue.

"If I had to write my final evaluation today, I'd have no choice but to report that Monty is a textbook narcissist and that Scarlett achieved a perfect score on the borderline personality disorder questionnaire. It's a wonder their marriage has lasted this long. It sounds like they've put each other and their daughter through hell."

Gary tutted and gave a world-weary shake of his head.

"I've seen it play out time and again," he drawled in his fatherly voice. "Two people once deeply in love become obsessed with destroying each other. As the immortal Shakespeare once said, Love is a *devil*."

Before Bridget could respond, Aubrey March's tall, slim frame appeared in the doorway behind Gary.

"There's a call for you," the receptionist said, adjusting the purse strap over her shoulder. "A detective with the Charity Point P.D. said it's urgent. I'll transfer it before I head out."

Wondering why a detective from the little bayside town of Charity Point would be calling her, Bridget raised her eyebrows and reached for the phone on her desk.

She picked up the receiver as soon as the call came through.

"This is Dr. Bridget Bishop," she said. "How can I help?"

"Dr. Bishop, thank you for taking my call."

The woman on the other end of the connection spoke in a brisk, no-nonsense voice.

"I'm Detective Peggy Quinn with the Charity Point Police Department. I was hoping to confirm your whereabouts this afternoon around four o'clock."

Bridget's blue eyes widened at the request.

"My whereabouts this afternoon?" she repeated, earning a questioning look from Zepler, who still stood in the doorway. "Well, I was here in my office. In Wisteria Falls. I haven't left since lunchtime. Why?"

"I'm sorry to have to ask, but who were you with during that time, Dr. Bishop?"

WHERE EVIL HIDES

A knot of worry formed in Bridget's stomach.

"I'm sure you know I'm a psychologist, Detective Quinn," Bridget replied warily. "I can't divulge-"

"Let me cut to the chase," the detective interrupted. "Montgomery Montclair has been detained for questioning in relation to a homicide. He claims you're his alibi."

Bridget gripped the receiver against her ear, momentarily stunned into silence by the blunt statement.

"So, let me ask you again. Did you meet with Mr. Montclair this afternoon? Did he leave your office around four?"

"Yes," Bridget finally managed to reply. "Yes, I did meet with Mr. Montclair this afternoon, and I'd say he left here a few minutes past four. I can check our security cameras if you need the exact time."

By this time Gary Zepler had stepped further into the room, his forehead twisted into a concerned frown.

"Unfortunately, I need more than that," Quinn said, suddenly sounding as tired as Bridget felt. "I need you to come out to Charity Point and give a full statement. As it stands, he's my number one suspect in a homicide investigation, and you're his alibi."

"Whose homicide?" Bridget asked, her heart dropping. "Was it his wife? Has Scarlett been-"

"No," Detective Quinn said. "Mrs. Montclair isn't the victim. In fact, she's right here at the station. She's the one who reported the crime. You can probably hear her if you listen. She's pretty upset."

The faint sound of a woman sobbing somewhere in the

background reached Bridget as she tried to process what the detective was saying.

"Okay," Bridget finally said, mentally calculating how long it would take her to get to the bayside town. "I'll be there as soon as I can, but with the snow and the rush hour traffic, it may take me a couple of hours."

After she hung up, her eyes flicked to the window, then back to Gary Zepler, who was staring at her, his eyes wide with curiosity behind his glasses.

"Scarlett Montclair witnessed a homicide and Monty's been detained for questioning by the Charity Point police," Bridget said in a stunned voice. "Apparently, he gave me as his alibi. They want me to go give a statement."

Zepler blinked.

"Go to Charity Point? Over on the Bay?"

Bridget nodded.

"Monty has a vacation house out there," she said. "That must be where it happened. They're fighting over that, too, from what Scarlett said."

Reaching for her coat, she looked toward the window but could see only the dark sky and swirling snow. She turned to Hank, who was following her toward the door.

"Come on, boy, we're going on a road trip. I just hope we get out to Charity Point before this snowstorm gets us."

CHAPTER THREE

Special Agent Charlie Day strained to see the road ahead through the swirling snow and darkness. The headlights of her big, black Ford Expedition illuminated the slick white blanket that lay over the asphalt, forcing her to keep her speed down and her windshield wipers on.

The storm had arrived just as she'd gotten the call from the Charity Point Police Department, and even in her haste to respond, she'd had the sense to stop long enough to slip into her warmest woolen coat and to pull a thick knit cap over her golden blonde hair.

She turned up the heat in the Expedition to full blast, but it didn't help. The chill of discovering the Devil's Blade Killer had taken another victim had already seeped under her skin and into her bones.

Shivering, she used the hands-free controls to call Special Agent Tristan Hale's number, not wanting to make the ninety-minute drive out to Charity Point on her own, telling herself he'd want to know that they'd finally gotten a lead on the homicide investigation which had frustrated them for months.

As a high-pitched b*uzz, buzz, buzz* filled the roomy vehicle, Charlie realized he wasn't going to answer, and she couldn't pretend she was surprised.

After all, she'd seen Hale exiting the FBI's Washington field office hours before. He'd snuck out earlier than usual without telling anyone he was leaving, and she suspected he had a hot date.

She also suspected he'd been seeing someone new and based on his change in attitude and frequent absences, she figured the relationship must be serious.

Ignoring the pang in her stomach at the thought, she focused on the road ahead and the possibility that she was about to break her case wide open.

And if I have to do it on my own, so be it.

What other choice did she have? She couldn't pass up a hot lead at this stage in the investigation.

Not after months of dead ends and no progress.

Not when we've finally caught a break and have a genuine lead.

She could hardly believe forensic evidence had been found directly linking a fresh crime scene to the two open homicides.

Their months-long investigation had previously provided little in the way of leads or suspects after Esme Dupree's body had been found in her Baltimore apartment.

The pretty young sales manager had been sliced open from neck to groin. Fingerprints lifted from a knife still embedded in the victim's body had gotten a hit in the national Automated Fingerprint Identification System, also known as AFIS.

And when detectives in Baltimore had seen that the prints on the murder weapon matched latent prints from a Jane Doe homicide in D.C.'s Rock Creek Park the summer before, they'd called in the FBI.

Thus far, Charlie and Hale had failed to identify Jane Doe, and they had no viable suspects in Esme Dupree's brutal murder, but they knew the homicides had to be linked.

If the matching prints hadn't convinced Charlie that the same killer was involved, then the matching murder weapons would have done the trick.

Both women had been eviscerated with high-end imported knives sold under the Devil's Blade brand in the US.

Since taking on the case, Charlie had started thinking of the two homicides as the Devil's Blade murders, and she and Hale privately referred to their unsub as the Devil's Blade Killer.

She'd spent many nights during the last few months lying awake, wondering why a vibrant young professional such as Esme Dupree had been so violently killed.

As she'd tossed and turned, Charlie had often wondered who Jane Doe had been, and if there was anyone else out there looking for her, too. Anyone vainly hoping for her safe return.

Although Charlie had worked on over a dozen serial cases in the past and had seen the battered bodies of many young women like Esme Dupree, it never got any easier.

If anything, with each senseless act of violence and each

victim she encountered, it got harder for her to handle, harder for her to remain objective.

And as she sped down the snow-slicked highway, heading away from D.C., Charlie found herself gripping the steering wheel with a mixture of dread and determination.

She'd likely be forced to witness the grisly crime scene of the killer's third victim, but perhaps this time he'd made a mistake. Perhaps she would finally find out who had wielded the Devil's Blade knives, and why.

* * *

Charlie hurried into the small Charity Point police station an hour later, brushing the snow off her coat and wiping her boots on the thick rubber doormat.

Looking toward the sergeant's desk, she braced herself for the usual pushback from the locals, prepared to stand her ground if they tried to block her from participating in the initial investigation.

While Detective Quinn had proactively contacted her about the latent prints in AFIS, the call had most likely been an attempt to gather evidence rather than a request for help, and Charlie doubted Quinn would want the Bureau jumping into the local homicide straight away.

"Agent Day?"

A small, wiry woman with frizzy hair and kind, worried eyes stood in the lobby next to a message board filled with *Most Wanted* posters and legal notices.

"I'm Detective Peggy Quinn."

Holding out a small hand, the woman stepped forward eagerly, and Charlie had the impression that she'd been waiting for her.

Charlie shook the offered hand, noting the firmness of Quinn's dry, calloused grip, estimating that the detective wasn't yet forty although at first glance she'd appeared a good deal older.

During her career working with police departments around the country, Charlie had noticed that homicide detectives seemed to age faster than the rest of the population.

She'd come to believe that the emotional burden of finding dead bodies and comforting grieving families took its toll on even the most hard-boiled detectives.

"I'm glad you made it," Quinn said, nodding toward the door. "That storm out there's tied the traffic up all along the Eastern Shore. Wasn't sure you'd get through."

Charlie relaxed at the unexpectedly warm welcome, relieved that she wouldn't have to argue her case.

"Let's go in the back and I'll fill you in," Quinn said, leading Charlie down a narrow hall. "My partner is on maternity leave and I've been running the investigation on my own so far."

The detective waved Charlie toward a tiny office.

"I've worked plenty of accidental deaths and drownings, along with the occasional suicide, but we haven't had a homicide in these parts for years," she admitted as she shut the door. "Not since I made detective."

Charlie was beginning to understand why Quinn had

been glad to see her. The detective was running a one-woman show.

"We've got a young woman dead out on Windwalker Way," Quinn continued. "She's been tentatively identified as Washington D.C. resident Harmony Baxter."

She turned to a battered printer beside her desk and collected several pieces of paper off the tray. After a quick glance at the top sheet, she slid the paper across the desk toward Charlie.

Looking down at the paper, Charlie resisted the urge to grimace or turn away. Instead, she forced herself to study the gruesome crime scene photo.

The image showed a woman crumpled on the hardwood floor of a large kitchen. Her pink silk blouse, stained red with blood, had been slit down the front to reveal a grisly glimpse of the fatal injury beneath it.

"How did you find her?" Charlie asked, the calm question belying her inner wince of horror.

"The owner of the property, a Mrs. Scarlett Montclair, ran in here like a bat out of hell about five o'clock screaming that she'd seen a woman get killed and that we needed to get out to Windwalker Way before the *crazy bastard* got away. Her words, not mine."

Quinn made no attempt to hide her impatience with Scarlett Montclair's hysterics.

"After we got her to calm down, she said she'd arrived at the house, pulled around to the back, went to open the kitchen door, and saw a masked man through the window. Claimed he stabbed the victim right in front of her."

"So, she caught him in the act," Charlie said, leaning forward with interest. "Did she recognize the assailant? Has she made an identification or provided a description?"

Shaking her head, Detective Quinn held up a hand.

"I'm getting there, Agent Day," she said. "It's not that simple. You see, Scarlett Montclair saw the assailant, but maintains that he was dressed in heavy outerwear and wore a ski mask. She said he looked familiar but wasn't sure why."

Before Charlie could jump in with the barrage of questions that sprang to mind, Quinn continued.

"Our responding officers arrived at the scene to find her husband Montgomery Montclair standing in his kitchen next to the victim," she said. "He was covered in blood."

Charlie opened her mouth, then shut it again as she processed the information.

"Mr. Montclair claimed he had been attempting to give the victim CPR when the officers arrived."

Quinn didn't sound convinced.

"Officers recovered a sizable knife that appears to be the murder weapon," she added. "I had our CSI tech print it at the scene and run the prints through AFIS right away. I thought maybe if we were quick enough, we could put out an APB on our guy before he got too far."

The detective's quick work impressed Charlie. She might be a one-woman show, but she was sharp and determined.

"We got results back within the hour, which is a pretty good turnaround in my experience, but it didn't give us a suspect. Just indicated the prints matched latent prints found at two other crime scenes. That's when I saw those were your cases."

Detective Quinn slid another of the printouts toward her.

"I also saw a note in the record about some sort of devil's head engraving on the murder weapon. Is this the one?"

Charlie stared down at the steel blade in the photo, her gray eyes resting on a grinning devil's head encrusted with blood, and nodded.

"This makes three," she said in a grim voice. "The Devil's Blade Killer has done it again."

"Is that what you're calling him?" Quinn asked.

Charlie shrugged as she pictured the big knife protruding from Esme Dupree's body. It had been identical to the one in the photo in front of her. And according to Quinn, the prints had matched, too.

"Where's your suspect?" she asked, sitting up straight. "We need to find out if he's our guy as soon as possible."

"We brought Mr. Montclair down here to the station for questioning while our CSI tech and the medical examiner are working the scene," Quinn said. "We've kept him and Mrs. Montclair separated so they can't collaborate on their stories."

Grimacing at the thought of the local CSI tech trying to work the bloody scene alone, Charlie calculated the possibility that Roger Calloway would be willing to mobilize an FBI evidence response team on a snowy, Friday night.

The special agent in charge wouldn't be pleased to get her call but after his usual bluster he'd likely figure out how to get a team out there if she explained who their prime suspect was.

"Mr. Montclair is refusing to say much," Quinn continued. "When I asked the old boy to voluntarily submit his fingerprints or DNA, he clammed up and asked for a lawyer."

Charlie wouldn't have expected anything less. The billionaire pharmaceutical CEO probably had a team of lawyers on his payroll just waiting to do his bidding.

"We're still working out the timeline, of course," Quinn said. "Mr. Montclair claims Harmony Baxter was dead when he arrived, and his wife said she'd seen the murder take place a good thirty minutes before that. We'll have to see what we can verify. We'll look at phone records, traffic cameras..."

"What about the house? Does it have a security system? Cameras?"

Quinn's forehead wrinkled into a frown.

"There are cameras, but they appear to have been deactivated," she said. "Maybe Mr. Montclair can fill us in on why they were deactivated when his lawyer shows up."

"Have you officially arrested him?" Charlie asked.

The detective looked startled.

"Oh no, I want to question him first and check his alibi," she explained. "Thought I'd wait for his lawyer to arrive and see what he has to say. You're welcome to sit in."

Charlie nodded, agreeing with the detective's cautious approach, especially when dealing with a wealthy, influential suspect like Monty Montclair who probably belonged to the same country club as half the judges in the state.

Besides, something about the series of events Scarlett Montclair described didn't sit right with Charlie.

"While we're waiting for Mr. Montclair's lawyer, I'd like to talk to the other person of interest in the case."

Quinn looked confused.

"Scarlett Montclair," Charlie clarified. "According to her statement, she was present during the commission of a murder. It would be helpful to walk through her version of events. I'd like to see if her story holds up."

CHAPTER FOUR

Scarlett Montclair bent her head to sip from the mug of lukewarm coffee Detective Quinn had provided in response to her request for a latte. Lifting a shaky hand, she brushed back several long strands of auburn hair that had spilled over the shoulder of her cashmere sweater.

She'd been huddled in the metal folding chair for almost an hour waiting for Quinn to return to the tiny interview room, and she wasn't good at waiting even at the best of times.

Her teachers had labeled her hyperactive, always fussing at her to stop squirming and fidgeting, as early as kindergarten.

But Scarlett couldn't help it if she grew restless easily. She'd been born that way. And it wasn't her fault the classes were so dreadfully boring.

When her behavior had been deemed disruptive enough to warrant summoning her mother to the school for a meeting with the principal, Shirley Lafferty had assured the stern educator that her daughter was just going through a phase and that she'd soon grow out of it.

But Scarlett had heard the hint of sadness in her

mother's voice and had known then that she'd never be what everyone wanted her to be. After that, she'd been determined to prove herself right.

Her rebellious approach to life and her stunning good looks had led Scarlett into a short-lived modeling career, followed by a tumultuous affair with a married man who was old enough to be her father.

The man just happened to be Monty Montclair, a billionaire in the making who coveted only the finest things money could buy. When he'd set eyes on gorgeous twenty-year-old Scarlett Lafferty, he'd been sold.

Within two years Monty had divorced his first wife and moved Scarlett into a world of luxury homes, cars, and yachts.

Their life together over the last sixteen years had been unconventional and unpredictable, just as Scarlett preferred it.

Monty's busy business schedule often conflicted with the constant round of parties, fashion shows, and holidays Scarlett enjoyed, so the couple had spent much of their marriage apart, which had suited them both just fine.

Things hadn't started to fall apart until the year before when she'd learned that Monty had been romantically involved with several young women who'd worked for him.

At first, she'd tried to ignore the evidence presented to her, wanting it all to just go away, but her pride and her sense of self-preservation had taken over when she remembered that Monty's first wife, Mimi Montclair, hadn't yet turned forty when he'd left her for a younger woman.

Considering the amount of money at stake, Scarlett had prepared for a protracted divorce and custody battle but had underestimated how ugly things would get.

She never predicted she'd end up huddled in the Charity Point Police Department's interview room being questioned about the murder of her husband's latest mistress.

And why didn't I tell Detective Quinn the truth about what I saw?

Hearing footsteps in the hall, Scarlett's pulse quickened.

She turned green eyes toward the door as it swung open to reveal Peggy Quinn's small figure. The detective was followed into the room by an attractive woman with golden blonde hair and striking gray eyes.

"Mrs. Montclair, this is Special Agent Charlie Day with the FBI. She'd like to ask you a few questions."

Scarlett's heart skipped a beat.

Is lying to a federal officer a misdemeanor or a felony?

Watching warily as the blonde woman took a seat across from her, Scarlett wondered why the FBI was involved. In the movies, they usually only chased after bank robbers, kidnappers, or serial killers.

"I'm sure you must be tired and upset, after what you've been through today," Charlie said, lowering herself into a chair across from Scarlett. "And I know you've already told Detective Quinn what you witnessed, but I'd like to hear it for myself. Would that be okay with you?"

Scarlett swallowed hard and nodded, reminding herself to stick to the same story she'd told Quinn.

"I drove out to Charity Point this afternoon," she began. "I got to the house around five o'clock, and then-"

Charlie held up a hand to stop her.

"Let's slow down and back up a bit."

A curious frown creased the agent's forehead.

"First of all, where were you coming from?"

"Wisteria Falls," Scarlett said. "It's my hometown. I moved back a few months ago. After my husband and I separated."

"Okay, and what was the purpose of your trip to Charity Point?" Charlie asked.

"Our vacation home is on the Bay, and so I-"

"It doesn't seem like vacation weather," Charlie interrupted. "What made you come out in the storm?"

Scarlett hesitated, not sure how to explain.

She thought back to the call she'd received that morning and all her pent-up indignation and rage returned to fill her voice.

"I wanted to confront Monty," she admitted. "I'd received a phone call from Jagger Yardley telling me that Monty was going to be at the house with *her*."

The frown on Charlie's forehead deepened.

"Jagger Yardley? The private investigator?"

Nodding, Scarlett tried not to look surprised, but she wondered how Charlie knew Jagger.

"Yes, my lawyer retained his services when I decided to file for divorce," she said. "He's been watching Monty and his...*friends*. He found out that my husband was planning to spend the weekend in Charity Point."

Scarlett wrinkled her delicate nose in disgust.

"He had the nerve to cancel plans with Cassidy over the weekend," she fumed. "Can you imagine? He fobbed off his own daughter so that he could see that...*woman*."

She remembered Harmony Baxter was dead just in time to swallow back the derogatory word she'd intended to use. After all, her mother had taught her never to speak ill of the dead.

"Cassidy was heartbroken when she found out her father had canceled their plans," Scarlett continued. "It just made me so mad. I jumped in the car and drove out to the house without thinking. I do that sometimes."

"Do what?" Charlie asked.

She looked up, poising her pen over the folder on the table.

"I get mad and do stuff without thinking," Scarlett replied with a shrug. "Anyway, when I got to the house, I went around to the back door. That's when I saw the man in the kitchen."

Picturing the black mask over the man's face, she shivered.

"I wasn't sure what he was doing so I watched through the window. I couldn't believe it when he lifted the knife and brought it down," she said, her voice cracking. "He *stabbed* her. It was horrible. He looked back and saw me. For a minute I couldn't move. Then suddenly I was running for my car."

"And did you recognize the man with the knife?"

Scarlett shook her head, perhaps a little too quickly.

"You told Detective Quinn earlier that something about the man seemed familiar," Charlie said. "Can you explain what you meant? What was it that was familiar?"

"I don't know," Scarlett said, dropping her eyes to her coffee cup. "As I told Detective Quinn, I can't explain it. I just felt like I'd seen the man somewhere before."

Charlie jotted something in her folder, then looked up.

"Could the man have been your husband?" Charlie asked. "Could that be why there was something familiar about him?"

Feeling as if all the air had suddenly left the room, Scarlett pushed back from the table. The room was closing in on her.

"I guess so...but I'm not sure," she gasped out, slapping her hand down hard on the table. "It could have been Monty. It could have been him or someone else. I mean, the guy had one of those ski masks on and a big coat and gloves..."

"The man was wearing gloves when he was holding the knife?" Charlie asked, ignoring Scarlett's obvious distress.

Scarlett closed her eyes and tried to picture the scene through the kitchen window. She replayed the moment the man had lifted the knife in the air.

"Yes," she finally said. "He had on black leather gloves."

Charlie nodded in satisfaction, as if an important fact had been established, and wrote another note in the folder.

"And what did you do next?" she asked. "After the man saw you, what did you do?"

"I ran, of course," Scarlett said. "I ran to my car without

looking back and drove straight here."

She knew what was coming next.

"Did you call 911?" Charlie asked. "Did you alert them that Harmony Baxter had been stabbed? That she needed immediate medical attention? Did you explain that a man in the area was armed and dangerous?"

"No," Scarlett snapped. "I'm not sure why I didn't think of it. I just drove straight here. I guess I was scared and in shock. I just...panicked."

Charlie leaned forward and propped her elbows on the old wooden table.

"Do you know why the security cameras had been deactivated?" Charlie asked. "Did you turn them off?"

"Of course not," Scarlett said, wondering for the first time if she should have requested a lawyer. "Monty must have deactivated them."

Her answer caused Charlie to pause and study her.

"I understand that you and your husband have been going through a divorce," she said softly. "That must be hard."

"Yes, it is."

Scarlett blinked back sudden tears.

"Apparently, my husband was chronically unfaithful, only I was the last one to find out."

Charlie handed her a tissue.

"I mean, we had our problems like anyone else, but I thought we were going to last. And then..."

She paused to blow her nose.

"Last summer I got a message claiming Monty was

having an affair. I didn't want to believe it," she said. "But turns out it wasn't just one affair. He'd been seeing different women for years."

Wadding the tissue into a ball, Scarlett threw it in the trash and looked at her watch.

"I'm sorry, but I really need to get home," she said. "My daughter will be waiting for me and-"

"Do you know a woman named Esme Dupree?"

Charlie's unexpected question stunned Scarlett into momentary silence.

How the hell does she know about that bimbo?

Scarlett cleared her throat.

"I now know that there were lots of women circling around Monty," she said stiffly. "They were like vultures waiting for our marriage to die. I don't know their names."

Glancing up at the agent's somber face, Scarlett decided she might as well tell the truth. It was sure to come out eventually.

"However, right before we split up, a woman named Esme called me. She said she worked in sales at Montclair Biotech. She said she wanted to talk to me about Monty. To tell me something. But I hung up and...she never called back."

Charlie leaned forward, clearly shocked by the information. Scarlett wondered if she'd said too much.

"So, Esme Dupree used to work for Montclair Biotech?" Charlie asked. "And you think she had a relationship with your husband?"

"You'd have to ask her because you certainly couldn't

trust Monty to tell you the truth," Scarlett said. "I made that mistake and see where it got me."

Her words were followed by a rap on the door.

Quinn opened it to reveal a uniformed officer.

"Bridget Bishop is here," he said, sounding excited. "You know, the FBI profiler from the news. I put her in your office."

Scarlett jumped to her feet as Charlie turned to Quinn.

"What's Bridget doing in Charity Point?" Charlie asked.

"She's my psychologist," Scarlett said before Quinn could respond. "Monty must have called her, and I want to talk to her, too. I want to talk to Dr. Bishop right now."

CHAPTER FIVE

Bridget unbuttoned her coat and tugged off her hat before dropping into the chair across from Detective Quinn's desk. She looked down at Hank, who sat at her feet regarding her with dark, curious eyes. She couldn't blame him for wondering why they'd driven two hours through a snowstorm just to sit alone in a small windowless room.

"Sorry, Hank," Bridget murmured, scratching the soft fur over the Irish setter's ears. "Hopefully this won't take long."

Her phone buzzed somewhere nearby, and she reached for her coat, digging through the pockets until her fingers found the slim, sleek device.

Pulling it out, she saw a text from Gage on the display.

Where are you? We're still here waiting.

She winced as she remembered their dinner plans, then quickly tapped out an apology.

Sorry, something urgent came up. Breakfast tomorrow instead?

As she dropped her phone back into her pocket, wondering who had been waiting at the restaurant with Gage, the office door opened.

A small, tired-looking woman appeared, her hair frizzy and her lips chapped as if she had spent too much time on the Bay.

"It's good to meet you, Dr. Bishop," the woman said, sticking out a hand. "I'm Detective Peggy Quinn, and I have to say I feel like I already know you after everything I've seen on TV and read in the papers."

"Well, don't believe everything you read," Bridget replied with a tired smile, standing to take the offered hand. "The press has been known to sensationalize a story. They usually make my life sound much more interesting than it actually is. And please, call me Bridget."

Before she could retake her seat, a familiar voice spoke from the hall.

"Don't buy into her humble routine, Detective Quinn. Bridget has faced more than one deranged serial killer in her time. I'd say that counts as interesting to most people."

Looking past Quinn, Bridget was startled to see Charlie Day.

She hadn't seen the FBI agent since they'd wrapped up a serial homicide investigation over the summer.

"What are you doing here?" Bridget asked.

Her initial pleasure at seeing a familiar face quickly gave way to concern. Why was the FBI involved in a local homicide?

What had Monty and Scarlett gotten themselves into?

"It seems two unsolved homicides I've been working on are linked to the death of a young woman in Charity Point," Charlie explained. "Which is why I'm here. And I believe the prime suspect in that homicide is claiming you as his alibi. Which I'm guessing is why *you're* here."

Bridget looked to Detective Quinn.

"All I know is I'm here to give a statement regarding Monty Montclair's whereabouts this afternoon," she said. "And I was told Monty's a suspect in a homicide his wife witnessed."

"That's right," Quinn said. "The victim was Monty's new girlfriend, a D.C. resident named Harmony Baxter. The couple planned to spend the weekend at Monty's house on the Chesapeake Bay, and apparently that pissed-off Scarlett Montclair since he'd canceled plans with their daughter."

Bridget could imagine Scarlett's fury. The woman's personality disorder made it hard for her to regulate her emotions, and she would have likely perceived Monty's actions as a betrayal of both her and Cassidy.

"Scarlett claims when she arrived at the house, she witnessed a masked man stab Harmony," Charlie chimed in. "Instead of calling 911, she drove to the Charity Point police station to report the murder. By the time the responders arrived, Monty Montclair was standing in the kitchen covered in blood."

Quinn picked up a printout off the desk and handed it to Bridget, who stared down at the eviscerated woman in horror.

"This is how we found Harmony Baxter," Quinn said. "Monty claimed to have attempted CPR unsuccessfully before the officers arrived. He insisted he'd just gotten there, and that he'd been at your office in Wisteria Falls until four."

"Which would have made it difficult if not impossible for him to have reached the house in Charity Point by five when Scarlett claims to have witnessed the murder," Charlie added.

"How is all this linked to your open cases?" Bridget asked, looking to Charlie.

Reaching toward the desk, Charlie handed Bridget a printout bearing the image of a long knife covered in blood.

"Fingerprints on the presumed murder weapon match latent prints recovered from the two homicides I've been investigating," Charlie said. "And all three women were killed with a Devil's Blade knife."

Bridget tried to get her head around what she was hearing.

"So, Monty Montclair is a suspect in a *series* of homicides?" she asked. "You think he's a *serial killer*?"

"You don't?" Quinn asked, cocking her head.

The detective sounded genuinely curious.

"Mr. Montclair told officers you performed a psychological evaluation on him just this afternoon, and you're a criminal profiler. If he's capable of murder, you should know, right?"

"It's not that simple," Bridget protested. "Yes, Monty Montclair was in my office in Wisteria Falls until at least four o'clock this afternoon, and we have security cameras in the building to back that up. But as far as determining if he's capable of serial murder…"

She shook her head, thinking back to the hours she'd

spent interviewing Monty over the last few weeks.

Nothing he'd said or done indicated he was psychopathic or capable of extreme violence.

"Why were you meeting with Monty anyway?" Charlie asked, her eyes narrowing. "I thought your private practice work involves forensic cases for the court."

Bridget nodded, deciding her court-ordered role in the case didn't impose doctor-patient confidentiality privileges.

"That's right. I've been retained by the Commonwealth of Virginia as part of a litigious child custody case. The judge ordered psychological evaluations of both Monty and Scarlett," she admitted. "I haven't completed the evaluations yet, although I've collected enough information to build their initial psychological profiles, and I wouldn't say either one of them presents a danger to anyone, at least not physically."

Of course, she knew both Monty and Scarlett were more than capable of causing substantial emotional harm to the people around them if it suited their purpose, but Bridget wasn't sure that unpleasant fact was relevant in this situation.

Prompted by the overly cautious voice in her head, she decided a disclaimer would be wise.

"I should point out that I'm not acting as a doctor or therapist to either Monty or Scarlett. I'm conducting an evaluation, not providing treatment," she stressed. "They've been warned by their lawyers anything they tell me during the evaluation can be revealed in open court if deemed relevant."

"So, you're saying it's likely they haven't been completely open or honest with you?" Charlie said.

Bridget shrugged.

"I'm saying I can't guarantee one or both of them isn't capable of violence," she clarified. "But if they are secret psychos, they've done a good job of hiding it."

"Scarlett has requested to see you," Quinn said. "Or perhaps *demanded* to see you would be more accurate."

Looking down at Hank, who was dozing off at her feet, Bridget hesitated. She'd had enough of Scarlett Montclair and her drama for one day.

Then her eyes fell to the photos on the desk. As she studied Harmony Baxter's body and the knife with the grinning devil's head engraved into the steel blade, she gave a reluctant nod.

* * *

Scarlett was pacing back and forth like a caged animal by the time Bridget followed Detective Quinn and Charlie Day into the small interview room where she'd been waiting.

"I need something for my nerves," Scarlett demanded when she saw Bridget. "I saw a woman get killed you know."

She held up her hands, displaying long red fingernails and a huge solitaire diamond ring.

"See how I'm shaking?"

Her voice verged on hysteria.

"I probably have PTSD," Scarlett insisted. "I need Xanax,

or Valium, or *something.*"

"I'm not a psychiatrist and I can't prescribe medication," Bridget explained in an even tone that belied her exasperation. "Now, where is Cassidy while all this is going on?"

As part of the evaluation process, Bridget had met with Scarlett's teenage daughter several times and had sensed the deep emotional stress the girl was under.

In her initial shock at hearing about Harmony Baxter's murder, and seeing the gory crime scene photos, Bridget had almost forgotten about Cassidy.

Now checking her watch and seeing the late hour, she was suddenly worried for the girl, who had become little more than a pawn to her warring parents.

"She's at home," Scarlett said defensively. "A sixteen-year-old doesn't need a babysitter. Besides, what was I supposed to do when Monty canceled their weekend plans at the last minute?"

"When we talked this morning, you planned to stay as far away from Monty as possible," Bridget pointed out. "You said you moved back to Wisteria Falls to get away from him. So, why drive all the way out to Charity Point to see him? What did you hope to accomplish?"

Scarlett's frustration instantly deflated into despair. She sank into a metal folding chair, her shoulders sagging.

"I hired a private investigator to find dirt on Monty."

Her voice was thick with self-pity.

"When Jagger told me about the romantic getaway Monty planned to have in our house...after he said he was too busy to have his daughter for the weekend...I just lost it. The next thing I knew, I was driving through the snow. I didn't know what I was going to do when I got to the house, I just wanted to make the cruel bastard pay for everything he's done."

Studying Scarlett's downcast eyes, Bridget suddenly wondered if either of Cassidy's parents actually wanted to spend time with their daughter. She had long suspected their custody battle was driven by spite rather than love for the girl.

"I never thought Monty could be capable of *murder*," Scarlett said, dabbing at her eyes and looking sideways at Charlie as if gauging the impact of her tears. "But it looks as though I've been wrong about a lot of things."

Charlie stepped forward and spoke for the first time.

"You were wrong to hire Jagger Yardley, that's for sure," she said. "He's got a reputation as being a troublemaker. And it looks like you have enough trouble already without him."

But Scarlett wasn't interested in advice. She was too caught up in her own melodrama to listen to reason.

"You want to know how wrong I was? I actually trusted Monty when he promised to take care of me until death do us part. I believed that he was a good man. But now...*this*," she said, turning to Bridget. "You're a criminal profiler like those men on TV, right? Did you know he was capable of *murder*?"

Bridget met Scarlett's eyes, trying to assess her state of mind. Borderline personality disorder played havoc with emotions, causing extreme highs and debilitating lows, and increasing suspicion and paranoia in relationships.

"Most people are capable of murder under the right, or perhaps I should say, the *wrong* circumstances."

Bridget spoke slowly, trying to choose the right words.

"If someone finds themselves in a highly stressful situation, the fight or flight instincts are triggered. It's impossible to predict how a person will react in every situation."

Knowing she hadn't answered the question, Bridget thought back to the notes she'd written in Monty's file only a few hours before as she'd confidently documented her findings.

Monty Montclair was a textbook narcissist, of that she had no doubt, but could he also be a cold-blooded serial killer?

CHAPTER SIX

Monty Montclair sat upright, careful not to allow his custom-made suit to touch the sticky metal table bolted to the interview room's concrete floor. He lifted a soft, well-manicured hand to smooth back his hair, which was still unexpectedly dark and thick even though he'd recently celebrated his sixtieth birthday.

A combination of medications, the occasional discreet implant procedure, and weekly appointments with his barber, had kept Monty's hair looking as if it should belong to a much younger man.

The CEO's physique had also been kept in impressive condition thanks to regular workouts with a personal trainer and a low-calorie diet prepared to perfection by his long-time private chef.

Only the baggy pouches beneath his eyes and the loose skin around his jawline hinted at his real age. He'd seen the disturbing consequences of botched plastic surgery on too many faces at his country club to risk going under the knife, and thus far had stuck to Botox, fillers, skin peels, and expensive face creams to combat the signs of aging.

Checking the Rolex on his tanned wrist, he sighed.

How dare they detain me? How dare they keep me waiting?

The local police were obviously too ignorant to know who he was, and more importantly, who his friends were.

And where the hell is Sutler?

Based on the fact that he'd been sitting in the inhospitable room for several hours, it was clear to Monty that the legal counsel for Montclair Biotech was in no hurry to earn his exorbitant paycheck.

What am I paying that hack for, if not for a moment like this?

Of course, he had to admit he'd kept the lawyer busy over the last few years, but that hadn't really been his fault.

He couldn't help it if certain women became vindictive when a workplace fling came to its inevitable end.

Whoever wrote hell hath no fury like a woman scorned must have known some of the women I've dated.

And recently, Erwin Sutler and the company's other top executives had been tied up with more pressing matters, such as keeping certain damaging information from going public.

And now we'll have to waste time proving I wasn't the one who killed Harmony when what we're working on could be a matter of life or death for thousands of patients.

Monty felt a rare flutter of unease.

The company he'd founded and built into a multi-billion-dollar business would be ruined if they didn't find a way to hide and resolve the issue with their latest wonder drug.

Vixenzia was the new CDK4/6 inhibitor the company had spent a hundred million dollars developing, and it had been touted to the market as a near-miracle, one that could rapidly shrink tumors in early-stage breast cancer patients.

Unfortunately, recent trials had not only proven that Vixenzia was ineffective but there had also been numerous reports of unpleasant side effects.

The situation had reached a crisis point last week when the doctors managing the trial reported several unexplained deaths linked to the drug.

Determined to save the company from sinking stock prices and ruinous lawsuits, Monty had done what needed to be done to keep the news out of the press, although he wasn't sure how long they had before someone leaked.

And now he would have to take Sutler off the Vixenzia issue to help him with something far more personal.

Pushing all other thoughts from his mind, Monty forced himself to focus on his present predicament.

He needed to convince Detective Quinn that he'd had nothing to do with Harmony Baxter's murder.

I tried to save her for God's sake, not kill her. I really did try.

The memory of hovering over Harmony's gutted body flashed through his mind, prompting a shudder of revulsion.

Fortunately for his new suit, he'd attempted to perform CPR while wearing the same type of heavy-duty raincoat he wore aboard his yacht during inclement weather.

Unfortunately for Harmony, the only thing Monty knew about CPR was what he'd seen in the movies and on television, and he'd quickly given up the effort altogether when he'd caught sight of the grisly mess under her blood-soaked blouse.

The distasteful memories were interrupted by voices in the hall. By the time Erwin Sutler stepped into the interview room, Monty had arranged his face into a mask of injured innocence.

"Finally," Monty said, pinning the lawyer with a reproachful stare. "What took you so long?"

The lawyer shrugged off his coat, his body thick and hard under his expensive but ill-fitting suit, his high forehead already beading with sweat in the overheated room.

Smoothing back his thinning hair, Sutler shrugged.

"Traffic was a bitch," he said irritably, tugging at his collar. "You're lucky as hell I made it here at all."

He swung around to face the two women who'd trailed him into the room. Monty recognized Detective Quinn, but he hadn't seen the blonde before.

"Mr. Sutler, now that you're finally here, can we get started with the interview, please?" Quinn asked, waving him toward the chair next to Monty. "Special Agent Charlie Day with the FBI will be joining us."

Monty's eyebrows shot up.

"FBI? Why is the FBI involved?" Sutler asked, voicing Monty's question. "Am I missing something here?"

"I thought I was conducting the interview, Mr. Sutler," Quinn said. "How about I ask the questions?"

Ignoring her sarcasm, Sutler persisted.

"On what grounds are you detaining my client?" he barked. "Mr. Montclair has suffered a traumatic experience today and based on what he told me over the phone, you should be praising him for trying to save a young woman's life, not making unsubstantiated accusations against him."

Monty kept his face devoid of expression as he studied the two women, wondering how they would respond to Sutler's standard offense-as-defense routine.

The local detective was starting to rise to the bait, but the FBI agent was unfazed.

"We'll nominate Mr. Montclair for his good citizenship award later," Charlie said, taking a seat across from Sutler. "But for now, we need him to tell us how he ended up at the scene of a homicide covered in the victim's blood."

A stab of alarm knifed through Monty as he met the FBI agent's steely gray eyes over the table.

She seriously considers me a suspect. She thinks I killed Harmony.

Jumping up from his chair, he stared down at her.

"You do know who I am, don't you?" he demanded. "You do know I'm the founder and CEO of Montclair Biotech, and a major donor to the governor's re-election fund?"

Charlie Day waited for him to finish, her stony expression unchanged, her hands folded casually on the table.

A slow simmer of resentment started up in Monty's gut.

Why shouldn't she be relaxed? The cold bitch hasn't got anything to worry about, has she? It's my ass on the line here.

He allowed Sutler to pull him back into his chair, just wanting it to all be over.

"Look, I already told the officers at the house. I drove over to meet Harmony and she was there on the floor when

I got there," he gritted out. "It was like a scene out of a horror movie. It was…awful."

Shaking his head, he exhaled in frustration.

"I tried to perform CPR, but it was too late. When I got up to call 911, the police were suddenly there. I'm not sure who called them, but they came in and…I told them what happened, and then they brought me here. That's all I know."

"Did you turn off the security cameras at the house on Windwalker Way?" Charlie asked. "Before you arrived?"

Monty frowned.

"No, have you checked them?" His pulse started to thump. "Maybe we can see who-"

"We already tried that," Quinn cut in. "The cameras were all shut down just before five o'clock this afternoon. Just before Harmony Baxter arrived."

Her words hung in the air for a long beat.

"But I didn't arrive until well after five," Monty sputtered. "I was in Wisteria Falls until four, and I have an alibi that can prove it. Talk to Dr. Bishop and she'll tell you. There's no way I could have gotten to Charity Point so quickly."

"We talked to Bridget Bishop, and she confirmed that you were in her office in Wisteria Falls until four," Quinn said. "But we're still working through the timeline. Still figuring out who could have done what and when."

Charlie leaned forward.

"We did find fingerprints on the murder weapon," she said softly. "If you agree to give us your prints, we could be one step closer to eliminating you as a suspect."

Sutler put out a hand to stop Monty from responding.

"I think we need to stop right there," he advised, unable to hide the look of alarm on his face. "If you have enough evidence to arrest my client, then do so, otherwise..."

Monty glared at the lawyer.

"Are you out of your mind? Why would they arrest me?" he demanded. "I haven't done anything wrong."

"Mr. Montclair, I'm giving you a chance to assist in our investigation," Quinn said in a weary voice. "Now, it's getting pretty late, so if we can just take your prints and a DNA sample, we can all..."

Before she could finish her sentence, Sutler made a show of getting to his feet and walking to the door.

"Let's go, Monty," he said gruffly. "They don't have enough to arrest you, and now they're grasping at straws."

"Mr. Sutler, we found your client standing over his dead girlfriend covered in blood and within reach of the likely murder weapon," Quinn snapped.

Her patience was clearly wearing thin.

"We can either arrest him and take his prints and DNA during booking, or he can volunteer to give them to us willingly. It makes little difference to me, but I'm assuming you'd like to avoid having his mugshot plastered on the news."

"My prints are going to be on the knife, Detective," Monty said in a tight voice. "If it's the same one I saw on the floor it most likely came from *my* collection. My son gave me two sets to mark the launch of a new drug. Special order from Japan. I kept one set in my kitchen and one in my boat."

Groaning, Sutler held up his hand again, desperate to stop Monty from saying any more.

"You keep Devil's Blade knives on your boat?" Charlie asked, her cool mask finally slipping.

"Yes, the Devil's Blade brand is the best there is," Monty said with a hint of smugness. "They use ice-tempered, high carbon steel to-"

"What boat?" Quinn interrupted.

"*Monty's Mojo*. She's a forty-foot cabin cruiser," he boasted as if discussing the boat over beers at the country club. "She's at the dock on Windwalker Way. You can't miss her."

Quinn raised a skeptical eyebrow.

"We didn't find a boat," she said.

Monty hesitated, momentarily flustered, then nodded.

"Oh, yes, that's right, I forgot. I arranged for her to be wintered at the marina in Alexandria," he said.

Making a sudden decision, Monty turned to Quinn.

"Go ahead and take my fingerprints and DNA if you want. If my prints are on the knife, all it proves is that it's my knife, not that I used it to kill Harmony, or anyone else."

Refusing to look at Sutler, he ignored his lawyer's protests.

"In any case, I want to be cooperative," Monty insisted. "I want to help find whoever used that knife to kill Harmony."

WHERE EVIL HIDES

* * *

Within the hour Monty had been fingerprinted by a taciturn uniformed officer and promptly returned to the same interview room where Erwin Sutler sat stewing.

Detective Quinn and Charlie Day returned minutes later. The FBI agent carried a manila folder in one hand.

Dropping the folder on the table between them, she opened it to reveal a full-page headshot of an attractive woman with dark eyes and shoulder-length hair the color of warm caramel.

Monty's throat constricted as he tried to swallow.

"Have you ever met this woman, Mr. Montclair?"

Charlie's dry tone made it clear she already knew he had.

"Yes, that's Esme Dupree," he said stiffly. "She's a former sales rep at Montclair Biotech."

His mind spun with the implication of the photo.

Does she know about the affair? Does she know about the others?

Picking up the top photo, Charlie revealed the one beneath it, eliciting a gasp from Monty.

"This crime scene photo was taken after Ms. Dupree was discovered in her Baltimore apartment. She'd been stabbed to death with a Devil's Blade knife."

Monty gaped at the graphic image, unable at first to believe what he was seeing.

"She's *dead*?" he finally stammered. "I mean...I can see she's dead, but...I didn't know. She just *disappeared* a few months ago. The best salespeople do that...they jump ship when the money's right somewhere else."

"And you'd thought she'd just *jumped ship?*" Charlie asked, sounding incredulous. "You didn't bother looking for her?"

Swallowing back a cynical laugh, he thought of Randolph Hildebrand's angry outburst when Esme had demanded a payout. His second in command had thrown a fit, raving about optics and shareholder confidence.

Teddy had been there, too. But Monty's son had remained quiet, his look of reproof the only sign of his displeasure.

They'd all breathed an audible sigh of relief when one day Esme simply hadn't shown up at the office.

The women Monty had gotten involved with in the past had often resigned once the affair had been discovered and ended. And the keepers around him tended to run off the best ones.

Although he'd long suspected payouts had been used to resolve certain situations, he'd never seen any hard evidence of hush money going through the business accounts.

No, that type of expenditure might be noticed by the Board.

Looking up, Monty realized that Charlie and Quinn were still waiting for his answer.

A knock at the door gave him a temporary reprieve.

Quinn went to the door, then slipped outside to speak to a uniformed officer. The same one who'd taken Monty's prints.

When she returned with the officer, she whispered

something to Charlie, who nodded, then turned to Monty.

"Montgomery Montclair? You're under arrest. Your prints match the knife recovered–"

"This is bullshit," Sutler yelled, cutting off Quinn's words. "That knife was taken from Mr. Montclair's property. Of course, his prints are going to be on it since he'd used it recently. You implied if my client provided prints, you wouldn't arrest him."

"We aren't sure where that knife came from," Quinn reminded him. "And I'm not arresting him for *Harmony Baxter's* murder. At least not yet."

She turned back to Monty.

"Mr. Montclair, your prints have been matched to latent prints recovered from a Devil's Blade knife used in the commission of a homicide. Thus, I'm arresting you on suspicion of the murder of Esme Dupree."

Quinn put a firm hand on Monty's upper arm as the officer clicked handcuffs on his wrists.

"No more talking...no more statements," Sutler ordered as they led Monty toward the door. "Say nothing without me."

Catching Charlie Day's hard gray eyes on him, Monty shook his head in outrage.

"I didn't kill Esme or Harmony," he ground out between gritted teeth. "I've never killed anyone. And I'm going to have all your jobs for this once I prove it."

CHAPTER SEVEN

Special Agent Terrance Gage stood in a patch of morning sunshine knotting his tie and studying the thick coating of fresh white snow on the driveway below his bedroom window. Turning at a faint buzzing from his bedside table, he walked over to read the text message from Bridget Bishop.

May be a little late. Sorry about last night.

Tapping in a quick reply, Gage dropped the phone in his pocket, then crossed to the mirror to check his reflection.

Running a big hand over his deep bronze, clean-shaven head, Gage leaned closer to inspect his face, looking for new lines or wrinkles.

Satisfied with what he saw, he patted aftershave on his cheeks and nodded. He'd done all he could do.

Heading down the hall, he stuck his head in Russell's room to confirm the teenager was still sleeping, then made his way downstairs and into the kitchen.

"Hey, Sarge, you staying inside today?"

The tiger-striped tomcat blinked up at him with blatant disinterest. As Gage poured food into his bowl, Sarge snuggled deeper into the new cat bed Russell had picked out, making no move toward the door, which rattled under a gust of icy wind.

The air in the garage was frigid as Gage climbed into his Navigator. He immediately turned the heater on high before backing out of the driveway and heading toward the highway.

His phone buzzed just as he was merging into the heavy stream of weekend traffic flowing into the city.

Groaning at the name on the display, he tapped a reluctant finger on the hands-free control to accept Anne's call, assuming she wanted to nag him about Russell again.

His younger sister had condemned his decision to take Russell in from the start, unmoved by the teenager's need for a safe place to stay while his mother served out her jail time.

"Sorry, Anne, but I'm working today," he announced without a greeting. "Can't talk now."

"It's Saturday," she said as if he didn't have the sense to know what day of the week it was. "Does that mean you're leaving that boy all alone in your house?"

Gage sucked in a deep calming breath, just as his therapist had suggested, determined not to let her get under his skin.

"His name is Russell, and he's Kenny's *son.*"

His heart squeezed at the thought of his late friend.

"He's a good kid, so stop your nagging. He needs me."

"Maybe, but what do *you* need? You aren't getting any younger, Terry," Anne warned him. "And having a convict's kid living in your house isn't going to help you attract the right kind of woman."

Rolling his eyes, Gage resisted the urge to raise his voice.

"God save me from finding the right kind of woman if she's anything like that last psychopath you set me up with," he replied between clenched teeth. "The woman had the nerve to ask me how much life insurance I carried. I figured that was a good indicator I should walk away...while I still could."

"She owns an insurance company," Anne refuted in her typical I-can't-believe-my-brother-is-such-an-idiot voice. "And she's very successful at what she does. But I'm sure she doesn't want to take on some other woman's troubled child."

A band of tension tightened around his chest and Gage automatically lifted his hand to his sternum and began to rub.

Ever since Russell had become his responsibility, Gage had started noticing a recurrent feeling of pressure in his chest more and more often.

He was beginning to think maybe it wasn't such a bad thing that he hadn't met someone and started a family after all these years. He wasn't ready to change who he was for any woman, and he didn't know how to be a good father.

"If you won't put that boy in a proper home, you should at least bring him to church tomorrow," Anne said with a put-upon sigh at Gage's silence. "Show him how decent, law-abiding families spend their weekend."

"We've got plans," Gage snapped, horrified at the image of Russell being scrutinized by Anne and her condescending friends. "Now, as I said, I'm at work."

Ending the call with a satisfying jab of his thumb, he merged into the far lane, noting his exit ahead, and let his thoughts shift to less stressful matters, like building a team capable of profiling and identifying serial killers.

He'd been trying to arrange a meeting with Bridget Bishop for over a month, eager to share the news about the new analyst he'd recently added to the BAU's team of profilers.

Bridget had worked with Argus Murphy before, and although they'd butted heads in the past, Gage felt sure the two would end up getting along, eventually.

The sign for the Sunnyside Up Diner appeared on the horizon as Gage contemplated Bridget's possible reaction. He had to admit that on the surface, Bridget and Argus appeared to be opposites in every way.

Well, every way but one. They are both highly effective profilers.

Their previous experience working together on the Backroads Butcher investigation had been contentious at times to say the least, although back then, Argus had been working for the National Center for the Analysis of Violent Crime as a profiler coordinator.

He'd been tasked with coordinating the requests for BAU assistance from several FBI field offices, including the office in Washington, D.C., and he'd managed to bump heads with Bridget on more than one occasion.

But the role had allowed Argus to make a lasting impression on Gage, and when a behavioral analyst position had opened up at Quantico, Argus had immediately come to mind.

Steering the dark gray Navigator into the parking lot, Gage could already see the BAU's newest profiler waiting by the front door.

Argus Murphy was hard to miss, even at a distance.

His close-cropped, neatly styled hair was a bright, carroty orange that shone like a beacon in the morning sunshine and matched the faint smattering of freckles across his cheeks.

As Gage jumped out and crunched over the icy parking lot toward the entrance, Argus lifted his arm to check his watch.

"You're right on time," the analyst said, sounding impressed, "while I've been standing outside for the last twenty minutes. My calculations of historic traffic patterns indicated a sixty-two percent risk of congestion in and around the city, so I left home early."

"Sometimes you have to rely on experience rather than statistics," Gage said, suppressing a smile as he followed Argus into the diner. "Although I usually just go with my gut."

Gage asked the server for his usual table by the window, enjoying the analyst's shocked expression as they settled into the old-fashioned red vinyl booth.

He knew Argus considered himself a data scientist. He prided himself on being driven by data rather than emotions, and the thought of making any decision based only on gut instinct baffled him.

"I hope you don't mind having to eat with me twice in a row," Gage said, not bothering to pick up the familiar menu. "I know Bridget felt bad about missing our dinner last night."

Clearing his throat, Argus nodded stiffly toward the door.

"And I hope you don't mind I invited someone to join us."

Argus' bright, amber eyes looked past Gage, who turned around just as a striking blonde woman in a blood-red parka entered the diner.

Charlie Day shrugged off her coat, hung it on a metal coat rack by the door, and headed toward their booth.

"She said she has an update on the Devil's Blade murders," Argus added in a hushed tone. "I'd thought you'd want to hear it as soon as possible."

"Maybe we should wait for Bridget to get here," Gage said.

He looked out the window toward the parking lot, then lifted his wrist to check his watch.

"I'm hoping to talk her into working on the profile with you," he admitted, earning a startled stare from the analyst. "Maybe a little good news would help persuade her."

"Who has good news?" Charlie asked.

Her eyes were grim as she slid into the booth next to Argus.

"You do," Gage said, with a grin. "At least that's what my new profiler was telling me."

"I said I had an update on the investigation," Charlie said. "I didn't say it was a good one."

The grin faded from Gage's face.

"We have another victim," Charlie added. "Another young woman was stabbed to death yesterday. We've managed to keep it quiet so far, but it'll make the news sometime later today. Especially considering who our new suspect is."

Picking up the menu, she studied it, leaving Argus and Gage to stare at her with expectant eyes.

"I'm starved," she said, waving to the server. "Let's order."

"Hold on, we should wait for Bridget," Gage said. "She should be here any minute."

Charlie shook her head.

"I thought she told you. She's running late. Can't say I blame her. Neither of us got home until well after midnight."

She stifled a yawn.

"Let's order, and while we eat, I'll tell you all about it."

CHAPTER EIGHT

The snow plow had briefly woken Bridget just after dawn as it worked its way down Fern Creek Road, but she'd rolled over and gone back to sleep, not waking again until Hank had started scratching on the front door to go out.

Now that the Irish setter had been walked and fed, she was on her way to drop the tired dog off at her father's house, where he could spend the day unwinding after their late night in Charity Point.

Wishing she could have gotten a few more hours of sleep, Bridget glanced at the clock on the dashboard of her Explorer, realizing she was going to be later than she'd expected for her breakfast with Terrance Gage.

But after canceling their dinner plans the night before, she didn't have the heart to stand him up again.

And now that Charlie Day had called and said she'd be joining them to give Gage an update on last night's events, Bridget was curious to see the profile the BAU had worked up on the Devil's Blade killer so far.

I'll bet the profile doesn't suggest the killer is a successful, ultrarich narcissist such as Monty Montclair.

Turning the Explorer onto Maplewood Drive, Bridget pulled into Bob Bishop's ice-coated driveway and crunched to a stop.

She climbed out carefully, then opened the door to the back seat, allowing Hank to jump down and bound toward the front porch, his paws punching deep holes in the snow as he went.

Bridget followed more slowly, not wanting to slip. She rapped twice on the door, then let herself into the warm foyer.

"Dad? You here?"

Footsteps responded to her call, and Bob Bishop's lined but still handsome face appeared in the hallway. He bent to ruffle Hank's cold fur.

"I'd have thought you'd want to stay inside where it's warm on a day like this," Bob said, studying her with narrow eyes. "You must be working on a new case."

Not wanting to get into a conversation with her father about the Devil's Blade murders, Bridget pretended not to hear him as she continued down the hall.

Bob Bishop had worked as a detective on the Wisteria Falls police force for decades before a stroke had prompted his unwelcome retirement several years earlier.

Bridget wasn't sure why she always felt a little guilty when she told him about working on the same kind of investigations her father had handled back when she'd been a little girl.

She sometimes imagined he had passed on the investigative torch to her, but the thought of leaving him behind and in the dark didn't bring her comfort.

Moving toward the kitchen door, she stopped at the sound of a familiar voice on the other side.

"Is that who I think it is?" she asked her father.

"Yep, that's Chase Grafton," he said with a grimace. "Paloma likes to listen to the *Chasing Killers* podcast while she makes breakfast."

Bridget could see her father wasn't a fan of the true-crime podcast that seemed to have everyone in town hooked, including her stepmother.

She winced as Chase Grafton's words spilled through the door and out into the hall.

"Our episode today focuses on the shocking revelation that billionaire Monty Montclair was arrested last night and charged with murder in the stabbing death of twenty-eight-year-old Esme Dupree. My guest will be..."

Straining to hear if Chase Grafton knew about Harmony Baxter's death, or the Devil's Blade knives, Bridget jumped when her father's big hand fell on her shoulder.

"You sure you're feeling okay, honey?" he asked, staring down into her blue eyes with concern. "You look awful tired."

"I'm fine, Dad," she insisted. "And I really appreciate you watching Hank for me. I'll try to pick him up by dinnertime."

The retired detective didn't look convinced. He wasn't willing to let the matter drop so easily.

"Should you really be driving around half asleep?" he asked, cocking one thick eyebrow. "The roads are dangerous enough out there already with all that snow."

But Bridget was already halfway out the door, not wanting to discuss the Devil's Blade investigation or her possible role in it when she wasn't sure herself.

If Gage already has an analyst working up a profile, he won't need me giving my two cents. Although maybe when he hears Monty Montclair is involved...

Pushing the thought away for later consideration, Bridget climbed back in her Explorer and flipped on the radio. Some lively music might help her shake off the last of her fatigue.

But as she navigated down Landsend Road and onto I-66, the radio was full of news about Monty Montclair's arrest, and the homicide at his vacation home on the Chesapeake Bay.

She should have known the news would spread quickly. Small town forces like the Charity Point PD weren't meant to hold secrets. Her own hometown of Wisteria Falls had certainly taught her that lesson over the years.

When Bridget finally pulled off the exit and turned into the Sunny Side Up Diner's parking lot, she was relieved to see Charlie sitting beside Gage at a table by the window.

They'd waited for her.

"Sorry I'm late," Bridget said, slipping into the booth next to Charlie. "Did you all already eat something?"

"The pancakes were delicious," Charlie said, nodding down at her empty plate. "So good in fact that I didn't save you any."

Before Bridget could reply, a man spoke beside her.

"Um, that's where I was sitting."

Bridget looked up to see Argus Murphy.

The man's freckled face pinkened as he pointed to a glass of water with a slice of lemon on the table in front of Bridget.

"And that's my water," he added. "I can move over if-"

"No," Bridget said quickly, picking up her purse. "That's fine, I'll move over."

Wondering what Argus was doing there, she stood and moved to the other side of the booth, sliding in beside Gage.

She gave her ex-boss a questioning look.

Gage cleared his throat.

"Bridget, I want to introduce you to the BAU's newest behavioral analyst," he said, gesturing toward Argus. "He's already been working on a profile for two linked homicides Charlie and Hale are investigating."

"Uh, actually it's three homicides, now," Argus corrected. "Based on what Charlie just told us. But I guess you already know all about the Devil's Blade murders, Bridget. You got a whirlwind introduction last night from what I understand."

All eyes at the table turned to Bridget.

"Yes, I got called in by the Charity Point police. Seems like it's going to be a challenging case," she said, swallowing back an unexpected pang of disappointment. "And congratulations on the new role. You must be excited."

Forcing herself to look at the menu, Bridget realized she hadn't eaten since lunchtime the day before.

When the server stopped beside the table, she ordered

French toast with warm maple syrup, orange juice, and coffee.

She looked up to catch Gage studying her with a thoughtful, calculating frown as if he could read her mind. Could he sense her doubts about Argus?

Does someone with zero empathy or understanding of human emotion have what it takes to be a profiler on a serial homicide?

Deciding it wasn't up to her to answer that question, she watched the server set a steaming mug of coffee in front of her.

"Argus was actually one of the main reasons I was eager to see you, Bridget," Gage said as she took a sip from her mug. "I want you on this Devil's Blade case. You and Argus would make a good team. And working together on the profile, you'd get the job done in half the time."

Bridget winced as hot coffee burned her tongue. Lowering the mug, she sucked in a deep breath.

"I've already got a job."

She felt her back stiffen despite the little voice in her head advising her to stay calm and to keep an open mind.

"In fact, that job was why I was called out to the Charity Point police station last night when the new suspect in the investigation got arrested."

"Yes, I know you're raking in the big bucks in private practice," Gage replied, seemingly unfazed by her prickly response. "But I also know you have a history with the BAU...and a future with the unit if you want one."

He lifted his hands in surrender.

"I know, I know, we've been through this before. But I

can't believe you aren't interested in the case after what you saw last night," he persisted. "With your ability to understand and predict human behavior, and Argus' skill at analyzing data and statistics, you guys would be a huge asset to the investigation if you teamed up."

Glancing over at Argus, Bridget saw a glint of dismay and doubt in his pale, amber eyes.

So, he's not a fan of Gage's bright idea either.

Charlie's phone buzzed on the table before Bridget could formulate a response.

"It's Calloway," Charlie said. "He's finally given approval to send an evidence response team out to Charity Point. I've got to call Detective Quinn and get out to the crime scene."

Grabbing the phone, she waved Argus out of the booth so she could stand. As she hurried toward the door, Gage also got to his feet.

"I'll take that as my cue to leave as well," he said, checking his watch. "I've got to go check on Russell."

He turned to meet Bridget's eyes.

"Think about joining the investigation and let me know," he said. "But don't wait too long. I have a feeling this case is about to blow wide open."

Bridget watched Gage stop to take care of the bill, then push through the door into the snowy parking lot.

She hadn't even gotten a chance to ask about Russell.

As she started to turn back to Argus, who now sat alone in the booth, her phone let out a soft chime.

It was the ring tone she'd assigned to Vic Santino.

"Sorry," she mouthed to Argus as she gestured to the phone and accepted the call, eager to hear Santino's voice.

Bridget and the U.S. deputy marshal had been officially seeing each other for several months, and she'd been feeling pretty good about the relationship lately, although they never did seem to get to spend as much time together as she would have liked based on Santino's haphazard schedule.

He could be called out on a case at any minute with little advance notice, which meant planning romantic meals or weekends away was often risky.

But Bridget knew better than most how unpredictable law enforcement could be. After graduating from the FBI Academy, she'd worked first in an FBI field office and then as a behavioral analyst in the BAU, before the high-profile Backroads Butcher serial homicide case and her father's sudden stroke had convinced her to try private practice.

"Morning!" she said into the phone, unable to keep a smile from spreading over her face as she heard Santino's deep reply.

Glancing over her shoulder, she saw that Argus had pulled on his coat and was walking toward the exit, his head down and his hands thrust into his pockets.

The little voice in Bridget's head tutted.

Where's your empathy now? Remember, he's only taken on the job you willingly gave up. So why feel threatened?

She bristled at the idea she was feeling threatened by Argus or anyone else.

"Bridget? You still there?"

Looking down at the phone in her hand, she realized Santino had asked her a question.

"Are we still spending the day together?" he repeated. "Or do you need to work?"

She knew Santino wouldn't blame her for calling off their plans if she needed to focus on a case.

After all, he'd been forced to do the same plenty of times. But she was eager to see him, and she thought she might be able to take care of her craving to see Santino as well as her inclination to follow up on the events of the prior evening.

"You know how you've been wanting to take me to the Eastern Shore to meet your mother? Well, I was thinking maybe today should be the day."

"It's a bit cold to go on the Bay," Santino protested. "Besides, my boat's been shrink-wrapped and docked for the winter. It'd take some effort to get her water worthy."

"Then we'll just have to go the long way and take the Chevy," she said, warming to the idea. "Oh, and I'll need to make a little detour on the way home."

* * *

Bridget sat forward in her seat, suddenly nervous as she saw the white wooden sign with the words *Sofia's by the Shore Bed & Breakfast* painted in eggshell blue.

A woman stood on the long wooden porch that ran across the front of the elegant two-story house. As Santino's red Chevy pickup drew closer, the woman waved and hurried down the stairs, wearing a wide smile.

"It's freezing out here, Vic," she laughed, drawing a thick jacket around her willowy frame as Santino climbed out. "Leave it to you to pick the coldest day of the year to bring your friend for a visit."

Lifting her head, she accepted a kiss on each cheek from her son, then turned to Bridget, who was shivering next to Santino.

"It's good to meet you, Bridget," the older woman said, offering her a gloved hand. "Although, Vic didn't give us much notice you were coming, and we aren't prepared to host guests. We close the B&B down during the winter months."

Bridget clasped the woman's hand, noting that she had the same hazel eyes and dark hair as her son, although Sofia Santino's eyes were framed by a delicate web of lines, and she had a generous sprinkling of silver in her hair.

"It's a beautiful house," Bridget said, following Sofia inside. "Has it always been a bed and breakfast?"

"Oh, no," Sofia said. "It's been in my family for many years, but after Vic's father died, it was too big and too expensive to keep just for us. So, I turned it into Sofia's by the Shore!"

She came to a stop in a large dining room which looked out onto a snow-covered terrace. Bridget gasped in pleasure as she saw the calm water of the Chesapeake Bay beyond the gently sloping lawn.

"How lovely it is," she said. "You must want to just sit here all day and enjoy the view."

"Yes, but when we're open for business, I rarely have

time," Sofia replied. "Although now that all the kids are grown, and all but one are gone, it's not such a madhouse."

Santino helped his mother pull off her jacket before removing his own.

"My mother was a widow with five children running a B&B on her own," he said with a laugh. "She didn't sit around looking out the window very often from what I remember."

"Well, I did have five built-in helpers," Sofia teased, meeting Bridget's eyes. "Vic was the oldest and the only boy. His sisters drove him crazy, but now the oldest three have moved to all corners of the country. Only Luna is left at home."

Footsteps sounded in the hall.

"Did I hear my name?"

A young woman appeared in the doorway. She wore a colorful apron over jeans and a long-sleeved t-shirt.

She had her brother's dark hair and hazel eyes.

"Yes, I was just telling Bridget that you are the only one who hasn't run off and abandoned me," Sofia said, crossing the room to put an arm around the girl's narrow shoulders.

"Bridget, I'd like you to meet my baby sister, Luna," Santino said with a mock bow. "And Luna, this is my friend Bridget."

Returning Luna's shy smile, Bridget tried not to let Santino's introduction ruin her mood.

But the little voice in her head must have sensed her disappointment.

Why should he call you his girlfriend? Sure, you've been dating for a while, but you haven't discussed being exclusive yet, have you?

Bridget ignored the question, focusing instead on what Santino's mother was saying.

After they'd all enjoyed a lively chat over warm cups of coffee and a freshly baked pecan pie, Luna offered to show Bridget around the sprawling bed and breakfast.

She stopped in each room to point out a nice view of the Bay, a unique painting, or some other feature that made it special.

By the time they made it out to the terrace, Bridget had decided she liked the young woman's friendly, open attitude, but she'd gotten the impression that Luna was fiercely protective of both her mother and her big brother, and she wasn't sure she'd managed to earn the young woman's seal of approval.

Standing on the terrace, looking out toward the water, Luna appeared to be impervious to the frigid air around them.

She cleared her throat and kept her eyes on the Bay.

"You're the first woman my brother has brought home since Maribel died," she said quietly. "You must be special."

Bridget stared at her in surprise.

"I don't know about that," she said. "Your brother and I are just...friends."

She stumbled over the word. It felt like a lie. At least to her.

"I see how he looks at you," Luna said. "And I've heard him talk about you. His feelings for you are obvious."

A small glow of pleasure lit in Bridget's chest, but Luna's next words extinguished it.

"The loss of Mirabel and their unborn daughter almost killed my brother," Luna said. "I never thought he'd allow himself to get close to anyone again."

A sick ache started up in Bridget's stomach as she realized what Luna was telling her.

Santino hadn't just lost a wife. He'd also lost a child. The family and the life he'd planned had been taken from him in one cruel blow.

"My brother's been through hell," Luna said, her voice thick with emotion. "But seeing him with you today...well, he seems more like the old Vic, so maybe he's starting to heal."

Her next words were as soft as a whisper.

"Just don't hurt him, Bridget. I couldn't bear it."

Unanswered questions about Mirabel and her untimely death swirled through Bridget's mind as footsteps sounded behind them, and suddenly Santino was there.

"Come on inside," he urged, taking Bridget's hand. "It's cold out here. What are you two talking about anyway?"

Bridget looked toward Luna, but Santino's sister had turned to stare out at the water.

"We were just admiring the view," Bridget said, summoning a weak smile. "But I think we better get going. I want to stop by Charity Point before it gets too late."

CHAPTER NINE

Charlie Day glared up at the useless security camera over the front door, then turned her eyes to the crowd of reporters and onlookers gathered along Windwalker Way. The morning news about Monty Montclair's arrest had exploded across the Chesapeake Bay area, mobilizing the press, and sending shockwaves throughout the quiet bayside community.

The FBI's evidence response team had cordoned off the entire perimeter of the Montclair property, from the street all the way back to the boat dock.

News crews with high-powered camera lenses had taken up positions on the side of the road, shooting videos of the crime scene as local reporters provided breathless commentary.

Harmony Baxter's homicide was the first murder that had taken place in Charity Point for over a decade.

The picturesque town served as a striking setting for the lurid story of a young woman's violent death at the hands of her billionaire lover, and the press was making the most of it.

Catching sight of a familiar figure hovering on the other

side of the crime scene tape, Charlie ducked back into the house.

She didn't want to attract Chase Grafton's attention. The man was a persistent pest, always sneaking around trying to uncover information on the crimes he featured in his *Chasing Killers* podcast.

"What's got you rattled?" a deep voice asked as she closed the door behind her. "You look like you've seen a ghost."

Special Agent Tristan Hale stood in the foyer wearing protective booties over his shoes. His dark hair was disheveled, and his square jaw was covered in a night's growth of stubble.

"It's just the press," Charlie said with a shrug. "They're having a field day, acting like it's a carnival out there instead of a crime scene."

Expecting Hale to make one of his usual sarcastic comments, Charlie felt a pang of unease when he only nodded. Something was definitely off.

While Hale had arrived at the scene freshly showered and smelling of his usual cologne, he seemed tired and distracted.

As she filled him in on the key details of Harmony Baxter's homicide, his eyes flicked down to check his phone.

Before Charlie could finish the update, she heard Peggy Quinn's raised voice coming from the kitchen. The normally unflappable detective sounded flustered.

"This is a protected crime scene," Quinn cried out as

Charlie hurried down the hall. "You can't come in here."

Expecting to see Chase Grafton skulking around the backdoor, she was startled to see Scarlett Montclair standing on the porch, accompanied by a teenager Charlie assumed was her daughter, Cassidy.

"This is my house and I want to know what's going on," Scarlett protested, not budging from the open doorway. "Have you really arrested my husband like they said on the news?"

Charlie glanced toward the teenager standing behind Scarlett. A flush of embarrassment reddened the girl's cheeks.

Cassidy Montclair looked like a younger, less brittle version of her mother, with soft auburn hair and a shy, self-conscious demeanor. She dropped her eyes when she saw Charlie watching her.

"Get back behind the tape like everyone else," Quinn snapped at Scarlett. "You'll be notified when we're done with our investigation, and once you can return to the house."

Feeling Hale come up behind her, Charlie didn't take her eyes off Scarlett, who shook her head at Quinn's order.

"I'm not going anywhere until I know where Monty is," she insisted. "If he's out there killing women who have pissed him off, I need to know about it. I need protection."

"Come on, Mom," Cassidy said, reaching out a small hand to grasp at her mother's coat sleeve. "Let's go."

Scarlett spun to face her daughter, then hesitated.

Bridget Bishop was hurrying up the driveway, her blue

eyes wide with worry, her boots slipping on the icy pavement.

"What in the world are you doing bringing Cassidy here?" Bridget asked, skidding to a stop next to Scarlett. "This is a *crime scene*. It's no place for a teenager."

She pointed back at the news vans lined along the street.

"And those cameras are recording all of this," she scolded. "Do you want your daughter to be on the evening news?"

Charlie had rarely seen Bridget so agitated.

Stepping forward to stand next to Quinn on the porch, Charlie motioned toward the road.

"Go on, Mrs. Montclair," she urged. "Get back behind the crime scene tape. Or better yet, go home."

As if realizing she was outnumbered, Scarlett turned away, but before she could leave, a black Range Rover with dark tinted windows squealed to a stop beside one of the news vans.

Two men jumped out, quickly ducking under the yellow crime scene tape to charge up the driveway toward the house.

Charlie recognized the older of the men as Monty's lawyer, Erwin Sutler. The man with him looked vaguely familiar.

As they approached, Detective Quinn put her hand on the butt of her gun and called out in a loud voice.

"Stop right there, you're trespassing at a crime scene!"

The men stopped and looked at Quinn in shock.

"I'm Teddy Montclair, and this is my father's house,"

the younger man called out. "We're here to pick up some of his things to bring to the jail. We'll be heading there next to try and bail him out."

Studying Teddy's features, Charlie saw his resemblance to his father, with a tall, svelte frame, and thick brown hair, although his voice carried none of Monty's arrogance.

She strode past Quinn, nearly slipping as she made her way down the porch steps toward Teddy and his companion.

"No one is allowed inside, Mr. Montclair, and nothing can be taken away," she said, keeping her voice firm but neutral.

There was no need to escalate an already tense situation.

"Then what's *she* doing up there?"

Sutler pointed to Scarlett, who remained stubbornly standing by the back door.

"If she can be here, then-"

"Mrs. Montclair was just leaving," Quinn said, taking Scarlett's arm and propelling her down the steps. "And I'd suggest you all do the same."

Charlie turned to see Cassidy trailing silently behind Quinn and her mother as Hale kept watch from the porch.

"I'd think you would know better than to trespass at an active crime scene, Mr. Sutler," Charlie said. "Now, get your client back in the car and go."

Sutler scowled at Scarlett when she passed by, watching as she and Cassidy climbed into a sleek white Mercedes.

"Monty's right," he muttered. "Scarlett's unfit to be a parent and she knows it. She also knows that fingering

Monty as a killer is the only way she's going to get custody."

He turned and prodded Teddy toward the road.

"Come on, let's go get your father out of jail."

It wasn't until both the Mercedes and the Range Rover had gone that Charlie looked back to see that Hale had gone, too.

* * *

Charlie didn't hear from Hale again until Monday morning.

Her cell phone began to vibrate just as she stepped onto the small porch of the rowhouse she owned near Logan Circle.

She smiled at an elderly couple walking by with a small dog dressed in a bright red sweater and reached into her pocket. As the trio disappeared around the corner, her fingers settled on the phone.

"You got the court order?"

Hale's voice was gravelly as if he'd just woken up.

"Good morning to you, too," she said, unable to keep the sarcasm out of her voice. "And yes, I have it."

Descending the steps, she walked along the slick sidewalk, heading toward the black Expedition parked along the curb.

"I'll pick you up on the way to deliver it if you're ready."

"I'm ready," he said. "I'll be waiting outside."

When she pulled up outside his apartment twenty

minutes later, Hale looked uncharacteristically rumpled.

Is he wearing the same clothes he had on yesterday?

The thought that he must have spent the night out hit her somewhere below the solar plexus.

As he slid into the seat beside her, she heard a faint ding from his phone. Her eyes automatically flicked to the device in his hand and registered the name on the display.

Someone named Beatrix had sent him a text.

Thank you for the flowers.

Averting her eyes, Charlie pushed away an unwarranted surge of jealousy. She had no right to begrudge Hale his new romance. She was the one who hadn't been ready to jump into a workplace relationship.

Merging into the heavy morning traffic, she assured herself she'd made the right call.

Sure, it's hard to resist his musky cologne and that stupid curl of hair that keeps falling over his forehead, but it just isn't a good idea.

The last time she'd gotten involved with someone in law enforcement, it had ended badly, and she'd sworn off dating fellow agents and officers in the future.

Of course, that vow made it hard to find a suitable match, since what civilian would ever accept her lifestyle?

After all, she'd chosen to have a career as an agent, and the FBI pretty much dominated her life.

Hunting down dangerous criminals and catching the occasional serial killer was what she did for a living. A normal man would expect her home every night in time to make dinner and tuck in the kids. It just wouldn't work.

Any way she looked at it, she was destined to end up alone.

Her brooding thoughts matched Hale's quiet mood as they worked their way through the busy streets of downtown D.C., finally arriving at Montclair Biotech's corporate headquarters.

The tall, modern building was all steel and glass.

Pulling into the attached parking garage, Charlie thought it looked as cold and unwelcoming as the gray day outside.

Her impression didn't change as she and Hale passed through a stark lobby with minimalist furniture and a modern sculpture of what looked to Charlie like a giant teardrop.

They rode up to the tenth floor in a glass elevator, stepping out onto the smooth marble floor of the executive wing.

A soft ding announced their arrival, but the reception desk was empty. Charlie looked toward Hale, who cocked his head, then pointed down a wide corridor.

Faint voices could be heard from an open door near the end.

"Come on," Hale murmured. "Let's show ourselves in."

Stopping outside the spacious boardroom, Charlie's eyes widened at the spectacular view of the city visible through the floor-to-ceiling windows.

A dozen men or so sat around a long, rectangular table.

As she stepped into the room behind Hale, Charlie recognized Teddy Montclair and Erwin Sutler among them.

Although she'd never seen the man sitting at the head of

the table, she could tell by his demeanor that he was leading the crisis meeting the men appeared to be having.

The man stood when he saw the two agents appear at the door, his stocky frame rigid, and his eyes anxious under thick black eyebrows.

"Sorry to interrupt," Hale said quickly. "No one was at the reception desk. I'm Special Agent Hale with the FBI and this is Special Agent Day."

Holding up his badge, he stepped further into the room.

"We're conducting a homicide investigation and have a court order compelling Montclair Biotech to turn over certain evidence pertinent to the investigation."

He looked down at the document in his hand.

"Basically, we need to have Montgomery Montclair's computer, access to his electronic correspondence, and the personnel records of a former employee named Esme Dupree."

The man standing at the head of the table grew pale but managed to reply in a measured tone.

"I'm Randolph Hildebrand, the company's Chief Financial Officer," he said solemnly. "I guess you could say I'm Monty's second-in-command."

Before Hildebrand could continue, Erwin Sutler jumped to his feet. As the lawyer began to protest, Hale handed him the court order, and Charlie waved away his objections.

"A judge has signed the order allowing us to seize Mr. Montclair's laptop and cell phone," she said to the men gathered around the table. "The warrant also compels you to provide us with emails on the Montclair Biotech server, as well as certain employee files."

Teddy Montclair looked at Sutler with the helpless, frustrated expression of a thwarted child, but as the lawyer finished reading the document, he shook his head and exhaled.

"We have to comply," Sutler gritted out between clenched teeth. "They have the right to take Monty's laptop and access his emails and other correspondence on the company's servers."

Teddy took the court order from Sutler's hand and read it, then quickly passed it on to the man seated beside him as if they were playing a game of hot potato.

"You're the compliance officer, Cliff. Are you okay with the FBI rifling through our confidential records?"

"If they have a court order, there's not much I can do about it," the man replied with a shrug, scanning the document, and then looking up at Charlie. "But we'll need to get a copy of the order and we'll need you to document all files you access."

Charlie nodded, relieved they hadn't gotten more resistance.

She turned back to Randolph Hildebrand.

"Alright," he said. "If Legal and Compliance both say it's okay, then I guess it's okay."

He looked at the executives around the table. Charlie noticed without surprise that they were all men.

"I guess we need a system administrator to access the server?" Hildebrand said uncertainly.

He looked toward a young man at the end of the table

who was typing energetically on the keyboard of a tiny laptop.

"Tariq, can you get Agent Day access to the files she needs?"

The man looked up distractedly as if he'd forgotten other people were in the room.

"Haven't you been listening? The FBI has a court order requiring us to provide them with Mr. Montclair's computer and his emails stored on the server."

Hildebrand leveled a stern look at the young man.

"Can you see that they get what they need?"

Tariq nodded and closed his laptop, then jumped to his feet.

"Sure, I can help you with that."

He offered Charlie a tight smile.

"Give me a minute. I'll be right back."

"I'll come with you," Hale said.

His tone invited no argument.

As he followed Tariq out of the room, Charlie looked down at her notepad, then over at Hildebrand.

"I also need any records related to the employment of Esme Dupree," she said.

She pointed to the document on the table before any of the men could object.

"It's all there in the court order."

Hildebrand sighed and looked at the faces around the table.

"Who can show Agent Day to HR and get her the records?"

The compliance officer reluctantly lifted his hand.

"Very good," Hildebrand said, relieved to have it all settled.

Charlie waited as the compliance officer stood and buttoned the jacket of his expensive suit, which appeared to have been tailored to accentuate his broad shoulders and trim waist.

Straightening his tie, he gestured for Charlie to precede him through the door. Once they were in the hall, his face relaxed into a cautious smile.

"I'm Cliff Finley, by the way," he said, walking next to her down the marble hall. "I head up the compliance department."

"Yes, I did manage to catch that bit," she replied, giving the handsome man a sideways glance, wondering how much information she could get out of him. "Is Randolph Hildebrand always so nervous? He seems...uptight."

Finley shrugged.

"Randy's alright. It's just that he's got a lot riding on his shoulders right now with all this going on. It's tough."

Charlie resisted the urge to roll her eyes.

She felt like telling the executive he should save his sympathy for Harmony Baxter's family, then decided not to bother. Finley would find out the gory details soon enough, along with the rest of Montclair Biotech's executives, the company's shareholders, and the rest of the world.

Stopping outside a glass door with the words *Human Resources* stenciled in elegant lettering, Finley pushed the door open and waited for Charlie to step inside.

A woman with spiky, platinum blonde hair and silver-framed glasses sat at a glass-topped desk.

"Morning, Fran," Finley said, sounding hesitant. "I hate to interrupt your schedule on a Monday, but we've got a bit of a situation and I need to borrow you for a minute."

The woman's eyes widened as he explained who Charlie was and what she needed.

"I need all files pertaining to Esme Dupree's employment," Charlie emphasized. "Even the ones considered confidential or sensitive."

Fran nodded and turned to her computer.

She seemed flustered as Finley stared over her shoulder for a long beat, but she began to tap on the keyboard as he turned away to take a call.

"There was some trouble," Fran said quietly once Finley had stepped into the hall. "You see, Esme filed a complaint before she quit. She claimed that Mr. Montclair...the *older* Mr. Montclair...behaved *inappropriately*."

Looking nervously toward the door, she leaned closer to Charlie, as if fearful someone might be listening in.

"We've been warned to keep it quiet," she said. "We've been warned to keep all the complaints quiet."

"All the complaints?"

Charlie cocked her head.

"Esme Dupree wasn't the only one who filed a complaint?"

"Oh, no," Fran said, raising both eyebrows to stress how ridiculous it was to think Esme's had been the only complaint.

Biting her lip, she sighed.

"It'll take a while to pull everything together," she said. "And some of it might have been deleted or archived. But I'll work on it. If they let me."

Looking over Charlie's shoulder at the closed door, Fran appeared to be checking that Finley hadn't returned.

"You seem nervous," Charlie said. "Is it Mr. Finley?"

"No, he's okay, I guess. But he reports to Mr. Montclair, doesn't he?" she said. "And I don't want to lose my job."

The fear wasn't completely unjustified, Charlie knew. Although Fran was required by the court to provide the requested information, she could be unfairly blamed for simply following the order.

"So, who warned you not to say anything about the complaints?" Charlie asked, taking out her notebook.

"Mr. Hildebrand, mainly," she said with a grimace. "He's always talking about optics and shareholder confidence. Although all the executives know what Monty's like."

Fran looked as if she was about to say more when the door opened and Finley stepped back into the room, followed by Hildebrand.

"I wanted to check that Fran was being helpful," the CFO said. "We do want to cooperate of course, although sometimes files can get deleted or overwritten."

He stared down at Fran with an innocent expression.

"That's why we have forensic technicians who can help recover deleted files," Charlie said, her voice cold. "Any attempt to block us from getting the files we need will be considered an attempt to interfere with an investigation."

Hildebrand's face didn't change, but his eyes hardened.

"Well, get on with it then, Fran," he said curtly, before turning to leave the room.

Charlie watched him disappear into the hall, then turned back as Fran typed Esme Dupree's name into the system.

Perhaps the system held the clue to what had happened to the young woman and why.

Maybe the killer's name is in there, too.

CHAPTER TEN

Lucky lifted his phone and tapped on the app linked to the security cameras at the house on Windwalker Way. Using facial recognition to bypass the login screen, he navigated to *Live Feed One*, before sitting back in his chair.

He half expected the mounted camera on the front porch to have been disabled or even dismantled, but instead, he saw a live stream of the front walkway and part of the driveway.

A policeman in a heavy black jacket stood guard next to the crime scene tape that cordoned off the scene. A news van drove past the house, followed by a delivery truck.

Switching to *Live Feed Two*, Lucky was suddenly looking into the living room, watching as an FBI crime scene tech searched through the bookshelf against the wall, examining every item with care before moving on to the next.

He was impressed with the FBI's diligence. In fact, he'd performed a similar search of the house before deciding to go through with his plan to kill Harmony there.

It was never a good idea to go into a mission without knowing exactly what you were getting yourself into.

Switching to *Live Feed Three*, Lucky saw the backyard, the dock, and the Chesapeake Bay beyond. Two agents stood talking by the water. One pointed south as the other looked east.

So, they're starting to suspect I arrived by boat. About time. But it's clear they still don't have a clue who I am, or where I am now.

Navigating to the *Recent Activity* mode, Lucky scrolled through the recordings he'd saved from the day before.

He stopped on a recording of Scarlett and Cassidy standing on the back porch and shook his head in disgust.

What kind of screwed-up mother drags her kid to a crime scene?

The following recording showed Cassidy putting a hand on her mother's arm, trying to get her to leave without causing a scene.

Zooming in on Cassidy, Lucky studied the teenager. She certainly did look a lot like her mother. And at a distance, the two could almost be mistaken for sisters.

He wasn't sure that was such a good thing.

If someone doesn't teach her any better, the little bitch will probably turn out to be a money-grubber just like her mother.

Of course, maybe now that Harmony was gone, he'd have more time. Plenty of time to teach both Scarlett and her lookalike daughter a lesson if he got the chance.

And he knew just what kind of lesson he would teach them. The same as he'd taught the others.

Feeling a familiar restlessness, Lucky closed the app and threw down the phone, allowing the sensation to wash over him, knowing it was pointless to resist it.

The only way to stop his craving was to satiate it.

But hadn't he intended Harmony to be his last? After all, he couldn't go on like this forever, could he?

If I do, eventually I'll get caught. I'll end up in jail like Monty.

He wasn't really sure how it had all started in the first place.

What had started out as a simple mission had turned into an all-consuming obsession. And once he'd taken the first one...

They say you never forget the first time.

Closing his eyes, Lucky allowed his mind to drift back.

Irina Jensen's eyes didn't meet his as they both waited by the elevator, although Lucky thought he saw her lips twitch in amusement as her long, slim fingers fidgeted with the sleeve of the simple blouse she'd paired with navy blue pants and matching pumps.

Was she flirting with him, or laughing at him?

She had recently been brought in as Monty Montclair's temporary PA, and the stunning woman hadn't had the time or opportunity to get to know the rest of the staff yet.

But Lucky knew her. In fact, he knew everything about her. He'd made it part of his mission to find out every intimate detail.

He'd even seen what she'd been doing with her CEO boss the night before, watching every minute of their fumbling encounter through the secret cameras installed throughout the executive wing.

A hot rush of excitement rushed over him at the memory, and he looked up to find Irina staring at him.

But her eyes darted away as the elevator doors opened to reveal two female lab workers from the seventh floor.

The women looked at him and ceased their discussion.

He figured they had been gossiping about the issue with the latest trial drug. The news would make its way around the building like wildfire if these two big-mouthed troublemakers got hold of it.

Originally intending to step off the elevator on the second floor to grab a cup of coffee from the cafeteria, he changed his mind when he saw the car keys in Irina's hand.

He already knew she owned a ten-year-old Nissan hatchback, but perhaps, if he walked out through the parking garage, he could find out where she went when she left the building.

Why did it always take her an hour to get home?

Lucky waited as the elevator stopped at the second floor, watching as the lab workers stepped out to leave him alone with Irina.

He imagined he could smell her perfume and feel her body heat.

She was so very lovely. At least on the outside.

As he was just about to speak, a deep voice called out.

"Hold the elevator."

A trio of men from the marketing department bounded inside the small elevator and pressed the Ground Level button.

Impulsively pushing his way off the elevator with a muttered, "excuse me" just before the doors slid shut, Lucky jogged down the stairs to the garage, emerging from the stairwell just in time to see Irina climb into her battered hatchback.

The little car fought the traffic all the way to Rock Creek Park with Lucky tailing behind.

Parking at a distance, he pulled out his binoculars and trained them on the bench where Irina had stopped to switch her pumps for tennis shoes and pull her long blonde hair into a ponytail.

As she started to jog away, Lucky rolled up his sleeves, revealing the red and black tattoo on his right forearm.

His eyes rested momentarily on the devil's horns and snarling teeth. He felt his hand reach toward the passenger's seat. The hand moved on its own accord. As if possessed by the hot rage inside him.

He wasn't sure what he planned to do with the heavy knife until he slid it into its sheath and attached the sheath to his belt.

Opening the door, he stepped out onto the ground, moving toward the path with well-practiced stealth.

Before he knew it, he was jogging along behind Irina on the otherwise empty path, his work shoes pinching his feet as he gained speed and closed the distance between them.

Looking around, Irina saw him running up behind her. She let out a startled yelp. Their eyes met, and he saw her fear.

Something in his expression must have warned her.

She accelerated, her legs pumping over the uneven ground with unexpected speed, but she was no match for him.

Lucky caught up to her just as she stumbled over a rut in the dirt and tumbled into the underbrush along the path.

Skidding to a stop, Lucky tackled her before she could scramble to her feet. He felt the Devil's Blade in its sheath against his thigh and reached for it without hesitation.

The knife rose and fell, and rose and fell, driven by an unseen force within him, sinking into soft flesh again and again until the *rage subsided, and he fell way, panting in exhaustion and relief.*

As reason returned, he looked around, knowing he had to hide the evidence of what he'd done. Dragging Irina's limp body deeper into the undergrowth, he saw the matted trail of bloodstained grass and leaves left behind.

He hesitated for an instant, then kept going, knowing better than to panic. That would solve nothing and end up getting him caught.

Although he had momentarily given into his baser instincts, he was back in control, and now he needed to cover his tracks.

Concealing Irina under a pile of fallen leaves and branches, he stopped to wash the blood off his hands and clothes the best he could in the nearby pond, then hurried back to his car.

He didn't remember the knife until he was halfway home, looking down at the empty sheath with a start.

"It's okay," he muttered to himself as he rolled down his sleeve, once again hiding the tattoo on his arm. "Maybe that's how it was meant to be. Maybe the Devil's Blade is the key."

Lucky's phone buzzed, rousing him from his memories and bringing him back to the matter at hand.

The first kill had both horrified and enthralled him, and the unseen force that had possessed him had thus far led him to use the Devil's Blade on two other occasions.

But with each subsequent kill, the transcendence he felt when wielding the knife wasn't as strong as the first, and the release that came over him afterward wasn't as intense.

He'd told himself Harmony would be the last, but as he looked down at his phone and read the message, he smiled.

WHERE EVIL HIDES

His mission wasn't over yet.

CHAPTER ELEVEN

Bridget added a log to the fire and lowered herself onto the small, braided rug in front of the fireplace, trying not to spill the cup of warm chamomile tea she held in one hand. Feeling Hank's warm body nestled in beside her, she closed her eyes and inhaled deeply, trying to settle her nerves.

She'd spent most of the day in a quandary about how to complete her evaluations of Scarlett and Monty Montclair now that the situation had been thrown into limbo by Harmony Baxter's homicide, and the rest of the time had been spent brooding over Gage's invitation to consult with the BAU on the Devil's Blade murders.

Her mind kept returning to Argus Murphy and the dejected set of his shoulders as he'd left the Sunnyside Up Diner the day before. She tried to shut out the doubts swirling through her mind without success.

Are my reservations about Argus joining the BAU really just a projection of my own insecurity?

Thinking back to the conflict they'd had working on the Backroads Butcher case, she could see now that she'd made very little effort to see things from his point of view or to resolve their differences.

At that time Argus had been working as a liaison between the BAU and various FBI field offices. But he'd been determined to be in on the case, which had mesmerized the country.

He'd spent weeks compiling stacks of lists, charts, and reports, insisting there had to be a pattern to the killer's heinous actions, determined to find some sort of rhyme or reason behind the killings.

In hindsight, Bridget could see his input had been invaluable. There had been a pattern, although at the time she'd been too engrossed in the case to see it.

He'd been right. At least partially. And I didn't want to admit it.

The quiet crackling of the fire and the soft, flickering flames had just begun to calm her nerves when the phone in her pocket erupted with a jarring buzz.

Without checking the display, she silenced the noise by accepting the call. Too late she realized Chase Grafton was on the other end.

"I hear you were in Charity Point on the day Harmony Baxter was killed," the podcaster said, not bothering with a greeting. "So, I'm guessing that means her homicide has been conclusively linked to the other Devil's Blade murders?"

Before she could respond, he continued.

"What's the connection between the victims? Have the cops managed to identify Jane Doe yet?"

Bridget thought of the picture she'd seen of Harmony's

dead body and the grinning devil's head engraved on the steel blade of the murder weapon and silently cursed small-town police departments.

"I know you couldn't have gotten your information from Daphne, because I haven't spoken to her at all over the weekend," Bridget said, ignoring his questions. "So, it must be someone at the Charity Point Police Department."

"I have my sources, and your best friend isn't one of them," Chase replied. "Although Mrs. Finch does make a mean apple pie. I grabbed a slice when I dropped Daphne off last night."

Bridget held back the sharp reply that hovered on her tongue. The podcaster was trying his best to get a sound bite out of her that he could use on his next episode.

But she wasn't going to take the bait.

It wasn't her business if her childhood friend was dating Chase Grafton, and as long as the true-crime podcaster didn't interfere with her or her work, she didn't care how much of Mavis Finch's apple pie he consumed.

The little voice in her head readily agreed.

Daphne never did have any sense when it came to men.

"Look, I'm busy, Chase, and I can't...no, I *won't*...tell you anything. So, I suggest you call your other sources."

She tapped *End Call* before he could protest, pleased to have gotten off the phone without divulging any new information.

Lifting the cup of tea to her lips, she was just about to take a sip when the phone buzzed again.

Convinced it would be Chase Grafton calling back, she

was about to answer the phone and tell him to stop stalking her when she saw Scarlett Montclair's number on the display.

Bridget heard soft sobs as she held the phone to her ear.

"What's wrong, Scarlett? What's happened?"

The sobs stopped as Scarlett blew her nose.

"It's Cassidy," she said in a tearful voice.

Bridget's heart dropped.

"What about Cassidy?" she asked, gripping the phone to her ear. "Is she alright?"

"I don't know," Scarlett said, sniffling into the phone. "We had an argument about her father, and then she just…had a meltdown or something. She's locked herself in her room. I don't know what she might do. Can you come talk to her?"

Looking down at Hank sleeping peacefully by the fire, Bridget contemplated the cold, miserable weather outside and hesitated.

"Dr. Bishop?" Scarlett asked again. "Will you come?"

* * *

The headlights of Bridget's old Explorer illuminated the driveway as she pulled up to the house on Coventry Lane.

An icy gust of wind whipped dark tendrils of hair around her face as she climbed out and walked up the front path, wondering how she'd let herself get talked into going out on such a dismal night.

Scarlett Montclair's cozy house in Wisteria Falls was less

grand than the palatial home the woman had lived in during her last sixteen years as a billionaire's wife, but it was well maintained and adorned with graceful columns and a wide veranda.

Bridget considered it far more charming than the mammoth D.C. mansion near Embassy Row she'd visited while conducting Monty's court-ordered evaluation.

The judge's order had required Bridget to observe Cassidy Montclair's homelife and her interaction with her parents and extended family, thus several trips to both of her parent's homes had been arranged.

Bridget had even gotten a chance to meet Scarlett's parents, a quiet, polite couple named Shirley and Roy Lafferty who had seemed devoted to their granddaughter.

Knocking on the front door, she wondered why Scarlett hadn't called on her own parents for help in calming down their granddaughter.

The distance Scarlett kept between her daughter and her parents didn't make much sense to Bridget, who had been dismayed to learn that Scarlett restricted Cassidy's visits to her grandparents' house to once a month under the premise of needing more alone time with her daughter.

But it hadn't taken Bridget long to see that Scarlett's decision had less to do with wanting quality time with Cassidy than it did with her being embarrassed by Roy and Shirley Lafferty's humble background and simple lifestyle.

Scarlett had escaped her modest beginnings by marrying Monty and moving away from Wisteria Falls.

Perhaps she was now scared of sliding back into the life

she had once discarded as readily as last year's fashion.

From what Bridget had observed, separating herself from the calming influence of her parents had been one of Scarlett's biggest mistakes.

Her marriage to Monty, a blatant narcissist with an eye for attractive young women, had only compounded the problem.

And as she'd witnessed the pampered life of excess that both Scarlett and Monty enjoyed, Bridget couldn't help but notice the estranged couple's shared tendency to manipulate their daughter and take advantage of Cassidy's timid and unassuming nature.

Pulling her coat tighter around her, Bridget knocked again on the door, feeling her irritation rising.

She couldn't blame Cassidy for finally exploding with anger. The teenager had every right to be scared and frustrated by her parents' escalating feud and her father's arrest. And expressing anger and unhappiness wasn't necessarily a bad thing, although she doubted Scarlett would see it that way.

Bridget suspected Scarlett would see her daughter's outburst as an act of personal betrayal which in turn could throw the woman into a rage or send her spiraling into a depressive episode.

Bridget's fears were confirmed when Scarlett finally opened the door wearing a short, silky robe loosely tied at the waist as if she hadn't been expecting guests.

Lifting a hand to her auburn hair, which had been twisted into a messy knot on top of her head, Scarlett swayed slightly on her feet and waved Bridget inside.

A heavy scent of alcohol hung in the air, making Bridget's eyes water as she followed Scarlett down the hall.

"Where's Cassidy?" Bridget asked, looking toward the hall in concern. "Is she okay? Is she still in her room?"

"She hasn't come out," Scarlett said. "Won't say a word."

Crossing to the bar, she poured a long splash of whiskey into a shot glass and downed it in one quick gulp.

"What happened to make her so upset?" Bridget asked as Scarlett again lifted the bottle.

"She's upset about her *father*."

Scarlett spit out the word as if it was a curse.

"We were watching a show and one of those special bulletins came on," she said. "Breaking news, they said. But it was the same old thing about Monty getting arrested."

Averting her eyes, Scarlett shrugged.

"She said her father shouldn't have been arrested. That there was no way he would ever kill anyone, and I just told her the same thing you told me."

Bridget frowned.

"What did I tell you?"

"You told me that you never can tell what somebody might do when they get into a certain situation," she said. "I told her that she didn't really know her father and she just...exploded."

Tipping the whiskey bottle over the shot glass, she sighed.

"I told her that I'm not going to have my daughter speak

to me that way and that she was grounded."

When only a few drops of golden liquid trickled out, Scarlett set the bottle back on the table with a loud *thud*.

"She ran to her room and slammed the door, still yelling. After a few minutes, she just went quiet. Wouldn't answer me at all. I didn't know what to do, so...I called you."

"And what is it you thought I could do?" Bridget asked.

Her voice was cold as Scarlett began searching through the bottles on the shelf above the bar.

"She likes you...she told me so," Scarlett said.

Apparently not finding the bottle she'd been looking for, she turned to face Bridget.

"Maybe she'll believe *you* if you tell her why her father is in jail," she said, her voice edged with resentment. "She certainly won't listen to a word I say."

Biting her lip, she gestured toward the hall with a long-suffering sigh.

"Maybe you can get through to her. God knows I've tried."

Exasperated by Scarlett's unwarranted self-pity, Bridget struggled to keep her emotions under control.

Don't let her get to you. You aren't here for her in any case. You're here for Cassidy. She's the innocent one in all this.

Allowing the little voice in her head to soothe her frazzled nerves, Bridget inhaled deeply and moved toward the hall.

Cassidy needed to hear a voice of reason to help her get through this latest trauma in her life, and currently, Bridget was the only one available.

"Cassidy? It's Dr. Bishop," she called when she reached the closed door. "Can I talk to you for a minute?"

She waited, listening for any sound from the teenager's room, then knocked softly on the door.

"Cassidy? I know you have some questions about your father, and I'm here if you'd like to talk."

There still was no sound from inside.

A sudden sense of unease fluttered to life in Bridget's chest.

Just how upset had the girl been? Could she have done something foolish? Maybe tried to harm herself?

Knocking harder, Bridget raised her voice.

"Cassidy, I need you to answer me so that I know you're okay," she called. "Otherwise, I'm going to have to come in."

A heavy silence followed Bridget's words.

She tried the knob, but the door was locked.

"Do you have a key?" Bridget asked, turning to look at Scarlett, who stared at her with a vacant expression before shaking her head. "How about a nail file? A metal one?"

Scarlett nodded and left the room. Seconds later she was back holding out the requested file.

Taking it in a shaky hand, Bridget inserted the file in the lock and twisted it until she heard a faint *click*.

She turned the handle and pushed open the door, bracing herself for whatever she might see.

The window was open, and the room was empty.

"Cassidy's gone," Bridget said as Scarlett came up behind her. "She must have climbed out the window."

Moving across the room, Bridget leaned out and looked into the backyard. The back gate was open. It swung ominously in the chilly air.

Bridget took out her phone and shone the light down toward the ground under the window, looking for any sign of footprints. Any sign that someone else had been there.

Did Cassidy leave on her own? Or was she taken?

The plush grass gave her no answers.

She thought back to Scarlett's words about Cassidy yelling in her room before going quiet, then pushed away the thought.

The window had obviously been opened from the inside without force, and the screen had been pushed out and set neatly against the wall.

Looking around the girl's room, she saw no sign of a struggle. Nothing had been disturbed.

"Is anything missing?" Bridget asked, looking up at Scarlett, who was staring around the room in shock.

"My *daughter* is missing," she snapped as anger flashed into her eyes. "And her backpack and phone. I can't believe it!"

Bridget reached out a hand, but Scarlett shoved it away.

"The ungrateful brat has run away!" she yelled, stomping to the window, and sticking her head out into the dark night beyond. "Cassidy! Get back here!"

Wincing at the high-pitched shriek, Bridget again reached for Scarlett and pulled her back into the room.

"Does she have a phone?" Bridget asked, keeping her voice low and calm. "Can you call her?"

Scarlett reached into her pocket and pulled out a small phone. She tapped on the display and held the phone to her ear with a trembling hand.

"Voicemail!" she cried, throwing the phone to the floor.

She turned to Bridget and grabbed her arm in a vice grip.

"What if he's got her?" she demanded, her green eyes wide.

"Who do you mean?" Bridget asked, pulling her arm away. "What are you talking about?"

A guarded expression fell over Scarlett's face.

"I...don't know," she stammered, dropping her eyes. "I'm not sure, really. I'm just worried for my little girl."

Bridget shook her head, trying to think. Based on everything she'd heard and seen, it seemed most likely that Cassidy had gotten fed up with her parents and run away.

"Where would she go?" Bridget asked, forcing herself to ignore Scarlett's outburst and think rationally. "If Cassidy got mad and decided to run away?"

She thought of Shirley and Roy Lafferty.

"Would she go to her grandparents' house?" Bridget asked.

Scarlett frowned and shook her head.

"If she wanted to worry me, she'd never go there," Scarlett insisted. "She knows my parents would call me right away and then send her home."

"Okay, so think," Bridget urged her. "Where else would she go? Who else would she turn to for help?"

Squeezing her eyes shut, Scarlett appeared to be thinking.

"She has taken an Uber into the city before a few times to see her father," she finally said. "But since he's in jail...maybe she'd go see Teddy? She knows he hates me, so he'd probably let her hide out there."

Scarlett's eyes slowly narrowed.

"Cassidy always did have a soft spot for him. She thinks he's some kind of hero, although I never could see why. He's a two-faced liar in my book."

"Should we call him and ask if Cassidy's there?" Bridget suggested, ignoring the hostility she heard in Scarlett's voice.

But Scarlett was already walking toward her bedroom.

"You think I'm going to give that creep fair warning?" she called over her shoulder. "And give him a chance to hide Cassidy away? No siree. I'll show up unannounced and take my daughter home. Just wait a minute while I get dressed."

Bridget opened her mouth to protest but Scarlett had already disappeared down the hall.

Minutes later she was back, dressed in tight jeans and a black leather jacket as if she were on her way to a rumble.

"Let's go," she said, slinging a big leather purse over her shoulder and striding toward the door. "I'll drive."

Bridget didn't move. She just stared at Scarlett in shock.

"Look, you've gotta go with me, because if she is there, she won't want to talk to me," Scarlett said. "You've got to talk some sense into her. Besides, Teddy won't dare lie to you."

Following Scarlett out of the house, Bridget wondered

just what she was getting herself into.

But she couldn't let an angry, tipsy Scarlett drive into D.C. on her own to confront Cassidy, could she?

Someone could get hurt, or worse.

"I'll go on one condition," Bridget said. "*I drive.*"

CHAPTER TWELVE

Scarlett Montclair leaned her forehead against the Mercedes' passenger's side window and closed her eyes, trying to stop the car from spinning. She wasn't sure how many shots of whiskey she'd had, but it felt as if the whole bottle was now sloshing around inside her stomach.

Opening her eyes, she squinted out at the street beyond, surprised to find that they were already nearing Teddy's townhouse near Capitol Hill.

She hadn't been back to her stepson's neighborhood since she'd split up with Monty, but some things and some places never seemed to change.

"I think we're about there," Bridget said, glancing at the navigation system's display. "Where should I park?"

Scarlett lifted a hand and gestured toward the curb.

"That's Teddy's place over there," she said, pointing to a white brick townhouse with dark blue shutters. "Just find anyplace along the street. We won't be here long."

Bracing herself against a sudden wave of nausea, she threw open the door before Bridget had even turned off the engine and pushed herself up and out of the car. The burst of cold air against Scarlett's face made the nausea subside.

She looked up at the dark windows of the townhouse, unimpressed with the neat, well-maintained exterior. It was nothing special compared to Monty's nearby mansion.

Although Teddy claimed he enjoyed living a much more modest and low-key lifestyle than his father did, Scarlett knew that Monty controlled his son's salary and thus held the purse strings, curtailing the younger Montclair's spending.

Teddy had still been a teenager when she'd come into Monty's life, and she hadn't been much older. During her marriage, she'd heard plenty of arguments over money between father and son.

In fact, she could hardly remember them arguing over anything else. The only thing either one seemed to care about was money or the family business, and the two subjects were inexorably linked.

Scarlett had eventually come to realize that Monty enjoyed wielding power over the people in his life, including his long-suffering son, and while her husband was more than willing to spend lavishly to fulfill his own needs and desires, he was tight-fisted when it came to giving money to anyone else.

"Come on, Scarlett," Bridget called, suddenly appearing on the sidewalk to take her by the wrist. "Let's go see if he's home, it's freezing out here."

Allowing herself to be pulled up to the front door, Scarlett felt the effect of the alcohol fading away.

By the time Teddy appeared in the doorway, she felt

stone-cold sober and unsure what they were even doing there.

"What's going on?" Teddy asked as he stared out at the two women with a confused frown.

"We're here to speak to Cassidy," Bridget said, startling Scarlett with her confident tone. "She left home without permission, and her mother's been quite worried."

Teddy hesitated, then stepped back and gestured for them to follow him inside.

"She's not here," he said, closing the door behind them as they stepped into the warm foyer. "Although she did call me earlier asking about our father. She sounded quite upset until I told her Monty would be out on bail later tonight. That cheered her up."

Anger bubbled up in Scarlett's chest at the confirmation of her daughter's betrayal.

"So, she didn't tell you she'd left home?" Bridget asked. "She didn't want to come here?"

Scarlett watched Teddy's face closely, looking for any sign of deception, sure he was hiding something.

"No, she just said she was worried and wanted to know how her father was doing," he repeated. "Are you saying that she's left home? That she's missing?"

His face creased with instant worry. For a minute, Scarlett even believed it was genuine.

Then a skeptical voice spoke up inside her head.

He's just putting on a show for the high and mighty Dr. Bishop. Cassidy is probably in there right now laughing at me.

Pushing her way past Teddy into the living room, Scarlett

looked around for any sign of her daughter.

"You said your father's getting out on bail tonight?" Bridget asked as she and Teddy followed after Scarlett. "Could your sister have gone to his house?"

"Half-sister," Scarlett blurted, suddenly sure Teddy was playing them both for fools. "Cassidy is Teddy's *half-sister*."

Bridget glanced at her in surprise, and Scarlett thought she saw a quick flash of disapproval on the psychologist's face.

She thinks I'm crazy. She's on Monty's side...just like Teddy.

The thought solidified in Scarlett's mind as Teddy spoke.

"I just got back from my father's place, and I can assure you that Cassidy wasn't there," he said stiffly. "But I'm sure she'll show up eventually. Once she's cooled down."

The patronizing tone in Teddy's voice set Scarlett's nerves on edge. He was probably enjoying this.

He's always hated me. Always blamed me for what happened to his mother. Always thought I was trash compared to Saint Mimi.

Scarlett looked toward the mantel over the cold, unlit fireplace. The picture of Mimi Montclair was still there, just where it had always been.

Teddy's mother gazed out from the past with a beatific smile that spoke of better days. Days before Scarlett had arrived on the scene to steal away her unfaithful husband.

Back then I was little more than a child myself. How foolish and naïve I must have been to trust Monty when he'd been so eager and willing to abandon his first wife and his only son.

Catching Teddy watching her, Scarlett held his gaze.

"If I find out she's here, I'm going to-"

"She's not," Teddy said with finality. "Now, please leave."

He made no effort at niceties as they walked to the door.

"If Cassidy contacts you, please let Scarlett know," Bridget said, hesitating in the doorway. "And I'd like to know, too. I met Cassidy during the evaluation and could see she's a very sensitive girl. I worry about her being out there on her own."

Teddy's face softened as he looked down into Bridget's worried blue eyes.

"Of course, if I hear from Cassidy, I'll call right away."

He didn't look at Scarlett as he closed the door.

Hurrying back to the Mercedes, Scarlett narrowed her eyes in Bridget's direction. Anger and fear competed in her chest.

What the hell is the good doctor playing at?

The question swirled through her head as she wrenched open the car door, slumped back into the passenger's seat, and fastened her seatbelt with an angry *click*.

She waited until Bridget had pulled the sleek white car back into traffic, then turned on her with clenched teeth.

"You've been working against me this whole time, haven't you?" she demanded. "How much is he paying you?"

Bridget gaped at her in astonishment.

"How much is *who* paying me?" she asked. "Teddy?"

"No, not Teddy," Scarlett snarled. "Monty. How much has Monty been paying you? Because I'll double it!"

Pulling the Mercedes alongside the curb, Bridget put the car into park and turned to face Scarlett.

"The only one who has paid me anything related to my involvement with you and your husband in the past is the Commonwealth of Virginia."

Bridget spoke in a slow, soft voice as if addressing a child.

"I'm here now as a favor to *you*, and out of concern for your daughter. I expect, and would accept, no payment for my efforts tonight."

Before Scarlett could spit out an angry response, Bridget held up a hand to stop her.

"And I will give you some free advice, which I hope you will seriously consider," she continued. "Of course, it's up to you if you take it or not."

Glaring at the psychologist, Scarlett cocked her head.

"Okay, go ahead, give me your best shot."

"I suggest you seek counseling," Bridget said. "To help you with your mood swings and emotional outbursts. It's possible you have a behavioral disorder, although that will be up to you and your therapist to figure out."

Scarlett blinked.

"Behavioral disorder?" she said numbly. "What are you talking about? I don't have a *disorder*."

"You may not," Bridget conceded. "But based on my evaluation for the court, you exhibit a range of behaviors associated with borderline personality disorder."

Shaking her head, Scarlett refused to listen to any more of the psychologist's lies.

"You're just trying to make me think I'm crazy," she yelled. "I know all about that. It's called *gaslighting* and Monty used to do that to me all the time."

She produced an angry laugh.

"He tried to make me think I was paranoid when I'd accuse him of cheating on me," she fumed. "I lived with that man for almost sixteen years before someone did me a favor and gave me the evidence needed to prove to myself and everyone else that I wasn't insane!"

"I'm sorry you had to go through that," Bridget replied quietly. "It must have been very painful. But I'm not Monty, and I'm not gaslighting you. I'm here to help find Cassidy."

At the sound of her daughter's name, Scarlett's anger vanished as quickly as it had come.

My little girl is out there in the cold, dark night on her own. Who knows what could happen to her, or who she might meet?

Scarlett knew she had to get Cassidy to come home. Then she'd have to make sure she stayed home and stayed safe.

"Now that Monty's been arrested, the judge is bound to give me custody, right?" Scarlett asked, forgetting about the accusations she'd made only moments before.

"I'm not sure what will happen," Bridget admitted. "I assume the case will be postponed until the charges against Monty are resolved, one way or the other. But our priority right now needs to be finding Cassidy."

Turning to look out the window, Scarlett hesitated. Maybe it was time to tell the truth about what she'd seen the day Harmony Baxter had been killed.

"Do you think Cassidy could be in danger?" she asked as

a horrifying possibility took root in her mind. "If the man who killed Harmony finds her before we do…"

Fear pierced her as she thought back to the man she'd seen through the kitchen window.

"Think of it. He already found our house once, didn't he? He was fit and strong. Poor Cassidy wouldn't stand a chance."

Her voice faltered as she saw Bridget's expression change from one of sympathy to one of stunned comprehension.

"You know Monty didn't kill Harmony," Bridget said, no hint of doubt or question in the statement. "But that's not what you told Detective Quinn or the FBI."

She shook her head in disbelief.

"You said you didn't get a good look at the guy. That you didn't see any distinguishing characteristics. That was a lie."

Scarlett dropped her head, still picturing the man wielding the knife, imagining it slashing down with brutal force.

"I told Detective Quinn there was something familiar about the man," she murmured, more to herself than to Bridget. "That was true. But I didn't tell her the man wasn't Monty."

"How can you be sure?" Bridget asked.

It was too late to back out now, so Scarlett plowed on.

"The man in the kitchen…the killer…was strong and fit," she admitted. "Monty is still fit, but he isn't exactly muscular. And he isn't as tall as the man I saw."

Bridget didn't look convinced.

"I'm sure," Scarlett insisted. "After sixteen years of marriage, I should be able to recognize the shape of my husband's body, shouldn't I?"

"But that's not what you said the night it happened," Bridget reminded her. "Why did you lie? And why are you telling me the truth now?"

Scarlett shrugged, knowing she had no choice. She had to come clean. She had to make sure the police knew that a killer was still out there. That he might find Cassidy or some other vulnerable girl. That someone else might end up dead.

I should never have let it go on so long.

When she'd implied that the man she'd seen in the kitchen could have been Monty, she hadn't really thought it through.

She'd just wanted Monty out of the picture. And she'd wanted him to get what he deserved for being unfaithful and for trying to take her daughter away.

"I'm going to call Charlie Day with the FBI, and then Detective Quinn," Bridget said, taking out her phone. "You need to tell them exactly what you've seen. They need to know the real killer is still out there."

* * *

The long drive back from D.C. was spent in tense silence, with Bridget keeping her eyes on the slick highway ahead as Scarlett stared out at the passing cars.

Her coat pocket vibrated just as the Mercedes turned onto

Coventry Lane. Glancing down at her phone, she felt her pulse jump at the name on the display.

Letting the call roll to voicemail, she darted a quick look at Bridget, then sat up straighter in her seat and tried to think.

What do I do if Cassidy doesn't come home tonight? Do I just sit around and wait? Do I tell him I can't come over?

It wouldn't be right for her to go see her lover while her daughter was technically missing, would it?

"I'm sure Cassidy will come home when she gets cold enough," Scarlett said in Bridget's direction. "I'll go inside now and call all her friends. She's got to be somewhere..."

Bridget nodded, but her face was solemn.

"Let me know if she shows up or you hear anything," Bridget replied. "And don't forget what Detective Quinn said. You'll need to go to Charity Point and give an updated statement tomorrow."

Scarlett nodded noncommittally, then opened the door and stepped out into the cold. Her pocket began to vibrate again as she circled the car to stand beside Bridget's old Explorer.

Ignoring the call, she plucked the keys to the Mercedes from Bridget's hand and hurried up the walkway without another word, knowing that the man on the other end didn't like to be kept waiting.

She also knew he was growing increasingly impatient with the whole secret romance situation.

While he had agreed to hide their involvement, at least until her divorce was finalized, his ego wouldn't allow him to skulk around in the background for long.

Scarlett's gloveless hands were cold and trembling as she punched the security code into the door lock keypad.

Turning as the Explorer's headlights lit up the front porch, Scarlett watched Bridget back onto the road and then disappear into the dark night.

With a suspicious frown, she pushed open the door, wondering if the psychologist was already on the phone with her FBI buddies again, plotting against her.

She shut the door behind her, then turned to lean her forehead on the cool, smooth wood, suddenly exhausted from all the stress of the day, not to mention the dozen shots of whiskey she'd thrown back.

"Where the hell have you been?"

Two big hands settled on Scarlett's shoulders. Jerking her backward, the hands held her against a rock-hard body.

"Have you been screwing around on me already?"

The question was delivered in a dangerous whisper that sent a thrill down Scarlett's spine.

She wasn't sure if it was a thrill of fear or anticipation.

Allowing herself to relax against the man behind her, Scarlett waited for her heart to stop thumping in her chest, then slowly turned to face Jagger Yardley.

"I said, *where have you been?*"

The P.I. towered over her, glaring down with a gleam in his dark eyes that could pass for either suspicion or desire.

Scarlett thought that perhaps it was a bit of both.

Either way, she was drawn to the bare, muscular chest in front of her, which narrowed into a slim waist.

"What are you doing in here half-dressed?" Scarlett asked in a breathy voice that revealed the effect he was having on her. "How did you get inside?"

She stared at Jagger, her mind whirring through the possibilities even as she admired his square, clean-shaven jaw, which was clenched around a set of straight, white teeth.

The private investigator had a reputation in D.C. as a troublemaker. People who worked with him soon found out that he had a huge chip on his shoulder and a temper to match.

But he was also known to take on the type of shady cases most other private investigators wouldn't touch, so he was in constant demand.

Scarlett considered herself lucky that he'd agreed to take her on as a client, and she'd grown to trust him despite the rumors of blackmail and extortion that followed him around.

She knew better than to care what other people said or to be put off by his bad reputation. She knew better than most what it felt like to be talked about behind her back.

None of the people out there throwing stones really knew her, and they probably didn't know Jagger either.

"Cassidy is missing," she said, taking a step back when she saw that both his hands were fisted. "We had an argument about Monty, and she ran off. I was out looking for her."

He pulled her toward him with an unhappy scowl.

"Well, I've been waiting here most of the night," he

complained. "I wanted to see you."

Scarlett felt her body involuntarily respond to his even as she tried to wiggle away, hurt that he didn't seem even remotely worried that her daughter was gone.

"I said, Cassidy is *missing*," she repeated, turning away.

"The kid has probably found herself a boyfriend," Jagger said, his voice softening. "She's sixteen already. It's about time she got her own life don't you think?"

Shrugging, Scarlett tried to think back to what she had been doing when she was Cassidy's age. The image of herself sneaking out of her bedroom window to meet up with older boys didn't reassure her.

"If she's not with her friends, then she's probably with her father," Monty said. "The reason I came over here in the first place was to tell you that Monty was granted bail. He's out."

"So, you really think Cassidy could be with him?" she asked.

Jagger stared down at her and smiled.

"I think it's likely," he agreed. "She's either there or hanging out with a friend. Either way, she's fine."

Wanting to believe he was telling the truth, Scarlett nodded and allowed him to pull her closer.

"And now, since we've got the house to ourselves..."

Jagger's words faded as he lowered his head to hers, overriding all her objections and momentarily erasing all thoughts of her missing daughter.

CHAPTER THIRTEEN

Terrance Gage sat back in his chair and glanced at his watch, hoping Russell had made it to school in time to take the chemistry test he'd been stressing over. His own morning commute had been delayed by streets slick with melting snow and ice, and he'd been late for his morning update with Argus Murphy.

Sucking in a deep breath, Gage sat up straight and tried to focus on what the behavioral analyst was saying.

"We've made progress in our analysis of the data provided by Montclair Biotech's HR department," Argus said. "Based on a review of the files we feel sure that-"

The phone on Gage's desk buzzed and they both looked down to see Bridget Bishop's name on the display.

Argus rolled his eyes as he again lost his boss' attention.

"Bridget," Gage said, his voice cheerful. "How's it going? You enjoying the fine weather out there?"

"I'm calling about the Devil's Blade case," Bridget said, sounding serious and in no mood for small talk. "Do you have a minute?"

Looking at Argus, then back at the phone, Gage hesitated, then shrugged. It was time they all started getting along, whether they wanted to or not.

"Argus Murphy is here with me," he said briskly. "Let me put you on speaker."

Without waiting for her response, he tapped the speaker icon and set the phone on the desk.

"Okay, so what's up with the Devil's Blade investigation?"

Bridget cleared her throat.

"Scarlett Montclair admitted last night that the man who stabbed Harmony Baxter couldn't have been Monty," Bridget said. "She claims the man was bigger and stronger than her husband."

"So, she's changed her story?" Gage asked.

He leaned forward in his chair to get closer to the phone and saw that Argus had done the same.

"Apparently, she'd gotten a better look at the man than she originally admitted," Bridget said. "She didn't immediately clear up the doubt about Monty because she wanted him out of the way. She thought it would help her custody case."

Gage and Argus both shook their heads in disbelief.

"If she's telling the truth now, she has impeded an investigation, leaving our killer on the loose," Gage said, shocked by the woman's irresponsible behavior. "What made Scarlett Montclair suddenly admit what she'd done?"

"Cassidy is missing," Bridget said. "The girl snuck out of her bedroom window and ran away last night. As far as I know, she never came home."

Gage frowned, not sure he understood the connection.

"So, Scarlett thinks her daughter's disappearance has something to do with Harmony Baxter's death?"

"Scarlett suspects the man who killed Harmony was watching the house," Bridget explained. "She's worried he may get hold of Cassidy. I guess that possibility scared her into admitting she lied about what she'd seen and that the real killer is still out there."

Furiously scribbling notes on the folder in front of him, Argus hesitated, then looked up.

"So, if Monty Montclair didn't kill Harmony, that means he probably didn't kill Esme or Jane Doe, either," he said. "Which cancels out all the work I did on the profile over the weekend."

Bridget spoke up before Gage could respond.

"I'm not sure how far you'd gotten on the profile of our unsub prior to Harmony's homicide," she said. "But at least now you know that Esme Dupree had previously worked for Montclair Biotech, as did Harmony Baxter. So, I'm guessing Jane Doe did as well."

Her words brought a small smile to Gage's face.

"Okay, I heard you say *our unsub*. Does that mean you're accepting my offer to work the case with us?"

"I guess it does," Bridget said. "If that's good with Argus."

Noting the deflated look on Argus' face, Gage could see it was anything but good with the BAU's new analyst.

"He's fine with that," Gage said, hoping his words would soon be true. "And I'm ecstatic. We're gonna need your help."

"Good," Bridget said, sounding relieved. "I don't believe Monty is a serial killer, but I do think he or his company holds the key to finding our unsub."

Gage nodded while Argus sat in stoic silence.

"The murders do seem to center around Monty," Gage agreed. "Now we just have to figure out *why*. Maybe that will lead us to our *who*."

"We'll need to act quickly," Bridget said. "If my suspicions are correct, our unsub kills to satisfy an urge he can't control. Then once he takes a victim, he's satiated, at least for a while."

Her voice hardened as she continued.

"But he was interrupted during his last kill. Scarlett's sudden arrival may have stopped him from achieving whatever release he was after. If so, he could be out there now looking for his next victim."

The thought sent a small shiver through Gage.

"Okay, then," he said. "Let's help Charlie and Hale find this psychopath before anyone else gets hurt."

He was about to end the call when Argus spoke up.

"I was just about to give Gage an update when you called, Bridget," he said, sounding resigned. "I do have some progress to report if you'll give me a few minutes to explain."

Nodding to show his approval, Gage sat back in his chair.

"Charlie Day gave me access to all the emails the Bureau received from Montclair Biotech's IT department," Argus said. "As well as the personnel files and relevant information from the HR manager."

Argus opened the file in front of him.

"Tariq Green in their IT group was very helpful. With a little prodding, he sent us all records of hirings, firings, and disciplinary actions and complaints for the last two years."

He paused, as if for dramatic effect.

"I think I've identified our Jane Doe."

Picking up a photo from the folder, Argus slid it across the desk toward Gage, who stared down at a pretty woman with long blonde hair and sad eyes.

"Irina Jensen worked as a temporary PA for Monty Montclair about six months ago," Argus said. "She wasn't there very long. Just a few weeks."

Argus produced a printout of an email from a temporary staffing agency.

"She was released from the temp contract early after she failed to show up for work without notice. No one at the temp service or at Montclair Biotech heard from her again."

He frowned down at the folder's contents.

"Although no one has reported her missing, I believe Irina Jensen may be our Jane Doe."

"Good work," Gage said, sliding the photo of the blonde woman back toward Argus. "Get with Bridget and share what you've got, and I'll let Charlie know what you've uncovered."

Checking his watch again, Gage absently rubbed his chest, deciding to reschedule his doctor's appointment.

There was too much going on. He couldn't afford to waste an afternoon hanging around in a waiting room.

"Charlie's going to be glad we finally have a name for

Jane Doe," he said with approval.

"It's all about the data," Argus said as a pink flush of pride colored his cheeks. "You follow the data, no matter where it leads, and eventually you'll get to the truth."

CHAPTER FOURTEEN

Opening the front door, Bridget stepped onto the porch of her red brick house and looked up and down Fern Creek Road. As she buttoned her woolen coat and pulled a black hat over her hair, her breath escaped from her mouth in ghostly clouds that soon vanished into the frosty air.

A fresh mantle of snow had fallen overnight, coloring the entire street a delicate, wintery white.

Hank trotted beside Bridget as she headed toward the Explorer, his paws moving quickly over the frozen ground.

After ushering the Irish setter into the backseat, she used a plastic scraper to clear the ice off the windows before climbing behind the wheel.

Holding her breath as she turned the key in the ignition, she prayed that the old car would start.

When it did, she looked back at Hank with a smile, waiting for the engine to warm up as she pulled out her phone.

She was hoping Cassidy had returned during the night, but when Scarlett answered her call on the first ring, sounding jumpy and anxious, her hopes faded.

"No, she hasn't come home or called," Scarlett said, confirming Bridget's fears. "I even called Monty's number, but there was no answer, so I left a message."

Asking Scarlett to let her know as soon as she heard anything from her daughter, Bridget disconnected the call and dropped her phone into her coat pocket, then backed out of the driveway and headed toward Faye Thackery's place.

The therapist had a home office not far away, and Bridget drove the familiar route on autopilot as she tried to imagine where Cassidy Montclair could be.

As she pictured the teenager's delicate features and shy smile, Bridget's mind flashed back to their initial meeting at Monty Montclair's opulent mansion.

The uniformed housekeeper led Bridget down a long marble hallway, then hesitated outside an open door.

"Miss Montclair is waiting in the sitting room," the woman said in a hushed tone. "Poor girl doesn't seem to be herself lately."

Making a mental note of the comment, Bridget stepped into the richly appointed room. Looking around, she registered the high ceilings, expensive furniture, and fine artwork as her eyes were drawn to a small figure by the window.

Cassidy Montclair sat on a plush sofa, her head down and her silky auburn hair falling forward, partially concealing her face as she kept her eyes on the thick oak coffee table before her.

"Cassidy? Can I come in?"

Looking up in surprise, the teenager appeared to be a smaller, softer version of her mother. When she didn't respond to the question, Bridget tried again.

"I'm Dr. Bridget Bishop. I think your mother told you I was coming to see you. Is this a good place to talk?"

The girl looked around as if considering the appropriateness of the location, then nodded mutely.

"Very good," Bridget said, lowering herself into a chair across from the teenager. "As you may have been told, I'm a psychologist working on behalf of the judge presiding over your parents' divorce. I'm sure you're wondering why I wanted to talk to you."

Cassidy shrugged. She lifted her eyes to Bridget, who saw that they were the same shade of green as Scarlett's.

"My father said you're here to make sure I'm not being abused."

The girl's voice held reproach.

"Well, if you were, you could tell me, and I'd help you," Bridget said as she met and held Cassidy's suspicious gaze. "Is anyone here mistreating you?"

"No, of course not." Cassidy shook her head. "My father's a good man. He wants what's best for me."

Bridget nodded as she took out a notepad and pen.

"Alright, then that's settled," she said, making a show of writing something on the top sheet. "You are not being abused or mistreated. Now perhaps we can move on. I'd like to ask you a few other questions if that's okay."

The tension in Cassidy's face softened, and again she nodded.

"Good, then I won't waste time speaking to you as if you were a child," Bridget continued. "You're practically a young woman and it's your future the judge is going to decide, so it's best for us *to talk openly and practically if possible."*

Cassidy's eyes widened.

"Fine with me," she said, lifting her delicate chin. "I don't know why everyone treats me like a kid anyway."

"Okay then, let's start with your parents' divorce. Is it hard for you to talk about, or are you feeling okay with it?"

Bridget kept her voice as light and non-judgmental as possible as she began asking a series of questions that would help her understand Cassidy's current frame of mind.

She needed to determine if the girl was being pressured to choose sides and if she preferred to live with one parent over the other, and why. They were sensitive questions that aroused complex emotions, and Bridget took her time, allowing Cassidy to express herself in her own way and at her own pace.

Quickly establishing that Cassidy was unexpectedly mature for her age, Bridget could see the teenager was aware of the turmoil swirling around her and her parents.

She was reserved at first, but as she started to relax, Cassidy's natural, easy-going nature was revealed, and Bridget sensed a quiet strength of will and resilience under the girl's mild demeanor.

The only spark of real anger came when Bridget asked her what she considered to be her parents' strengths and weaknesses.

Immediately defensive, Cassidy jumped to her feet and paced to the window, wrapping her arms around herself.

"I know my mom can be impulsive sometimes, and she can come across as self-centered and shallow...but she has a good heart," Cassidy insisted as if Bridget had said otherwise. "And some people may call my dad arrogant and materialistic, but he's

just ambitious and successful. That's not a crime."

"No, of course, it isn't," Bridget agreed.

She sensed the girl's inner conflict and sympathized. Cassidy wanted desperately to remain loyal to her parents even as she was a front-row witness to their many flaws.

"They both mean well," Cassidy said, her voice losing some of its steam. "And they both love me, in their own way, although..."

A wistful expression fell over her face, and she turned away, as if ashamed of whatever emotion she was feeling.

"Although what?" Bridget prodded, hearing the sadness under Cassidy's words. "What is it that's upsetting you?"

"It's just, sometimes I feel as if I don't belong," Cassidy admitted. "Sometimes I feel like I ended up in the wrong family."

Bridget pulled herself back into the present moment as the turnoff to Faye Thackery's cozy bungalow came into view. She tried to shake off an uneasy feeling that Cassidy was in danger.

Pulling into the driveway, she jerked the Explorer to a sudden stop, narrowly missing Faye, who stood in front of her holding a heavy shovelful of snow.

The therapist was bundled into an enormous parka. Faux fur framed her elfin face, which was pink with exertion, and knee-high snow boots added several inches to her tiny frame.

She threw the shovelful of white powder toward a lopsided pile behind her, then turned to face Bridget.

"Come on in!" she called, lowering the shovel.

Bridget released Hank from the backseat, smiling as he

bounded up the sidewalk in search of the treats Faye was known to dole out to her four-legged guests.

Following Faye around to the side of the bungalow, Bridget stopped outside the entrance to the therapist's office and wiped her boots on the *Namaste* door mat.

Entering the small reception area, Faye pulled off her parka and hung it on a hook by the door as she ran a tiny hand through her silvery pixie cut.

"Make yourself at home," she called over her shoulder, waving Bridget and Hank into the peaceful room where she held her sessions, before disappearing into the back.

Bridget sank onto a wide, comfortable sofa while Hank settled onto the soft Moroccan rug at her feet.

She jumped up when Faye reentered carrying a tray laden with two cups of coffee and two slices of warm carrot cake.

Taking the tray, Bridget set it on the table as Faye bent to offer Hank his much-anticipated treat.

"Nothing like a little exertion first thing in the morning to increase your circulation and improve your mood," the therapist said as she collapsed onto a nearby chair.

Bridget smiled as she poured them each a steaming cup of coffee and took a bite of the cake.

Her smile dimmed as the bright orange hue prompted thoughts of Argus Murphy.

"There's a new analyst at the BAU," Bridget said without thinking. "But we don't really get along."

Faye raised her eyebrows as she picked up a notebook and pen off the table.

"Are you consulting on a new case?" she asked, cocking

her head. "I thought you were enjoying your time away from the Bureau. That it was helping with the nightmares."

"It was," Bridget said, averting her eyes.

The statement wasn't technically true. The nightmares hadn't gone away. Maybe they never would.

"But I couldn't just walk away once I found out what was going on. You see, one of my private practice cases has gotten tied up with a serial investigation. Three women have already been killed, and..."

Faltering as she saw a look of dismay flicker across Faye's face, Bridget decided not to go into the gory details of the Devil's Blade murders.

Faye knew she was still haunted by the serial killers she'd profiled and investigated in the past. The therapist wouldn't be thrilled to find out she was involved with yet another subject of future nightmares.

"Anyway, what I was saying is that I've been partnered up with a new analyst and we're on very different wave lengths."

Fidgeting with her cup, Bridget wondered why she was even telling Faye about Argus. He wasn't the real problem, was he? She was the one who had the issue.

She just wasn't sure what the issue was.

"He approaches his work from a totally different place than I do," Bridget said, trying to explain her frustration. "He challenges anything that can't be proven by empirical data and discounts any sort of instinct or intuition. When I was working on the Backroads Butcher investigation, he kept sticking his nose in. I got the feeling he thought I was conjuring up crazy theories over an Ouija board."

Faye grinned at the idea.

"Maybe you're the yin to his yang," she said, raising a delicate eyebrow. "Working with two conflicting philosophies can be difficult, but it's also an opportunity for growth. You two might prove to be good sounding boards for the other if you can get past the competitive instinct and start cooperating."

Bridget nodded. She knew in theory Faye was right, but she wasn't sure Argus would agree.

"I'm sure with time you can work through your issues with the new guy," Faye said. "I'm more concerned about you getting too emotionally involved in another investigation."

She studied Bridget with an assessing stare.

"You said the case is related to your private practice work?"

Lifting her coffee cup to her lips, Bridget took a long sip, trying to decide how to respond.

"This case wouldn't happen to involve Monty Montclair, would it?" Faye prodded, her eyes narrowing as she began to make connections. "You mentioned a high-profile divorce case last time we met, and Chase Grafton said-"

"Please don't tell me you've been listening to the *Chasing Killers* podcast like everyone else in this town," Bridget said, unable to hide her frustration. "He's sharing confidential information that could put lives at risk."

Faye ignored the reprimand.

"So, you're profiling the Devil's Blade Killer?"

Seeing the concern on Faye's face, Bridget was tempted to deny it. But as a psychologist herself, she knew better than most that there was no point going to therapy if you weren't going to tell the truth.

"Yes, I'm consulting with the BAU on the case," she admitted. "They've arrested Monty Montclair, who I evaluated for the court as part of his divorce proceedings."

She continued before Faye could ask the obvious question.

"And no, I don't think Monty is the killer."

She met Faye's curious gaze.

"He's a narcissist for sure," Bridget said. "He checks all the boxes and then some."

Her voice hardened as she began listing the traits attributable to the CEO.

"Monty Montclair's sense of entitlement is absolute. No one and nothing takes precedence over his own wants or his perceived needs," she said bluntly. "He's arrogant and overbearing, dominating all interactions and openly mocking and denigrating those around him who might try to speak up, and he has a well-documented habit of taking advantage of others to get what he wants, regardless of the feelings or needs of anyone else."

"He sounds a lot like my first husband," Faye said with a rueful expression when Bridget paused to take a breath. "Come to think of it, he sounds a lot like my second husband as well."

"As terrible as it sounds, Monty's behavior isn't that unusual," Bridget said. "Something like one out of every twenty people in this country is a narcissist."

She leaned back against the sofa with a sigh.

"But as obnoxious as he is, Monty's shown no signs of being violent or psychopathic, and he shows no signs of having anger issues or violent outbursts."

"So, he doesn't match your profile?" Faye asked.

Bridget shook her head.

"Based on the crime scene photos, we're looking for someone who has trouble controlling his emotions and his temper. Maybe even a lust killer. Perhaps someone who feels slighted and persecuted and wants to take out his rage on others. Not someone pampered and catered to and held up on a pedestal like Monty. The profile doesn't fit."

"It sounds like Monty's not your guy," Faye said. "Which is good, because Chase Grafton said he's already out on bail."

Bridget got to her feet, suddenly too worked up to sit still.

If Monty was out of jail, she would go and see him.

She would find out what he knew about the murders, and she would find out if he was hiding his daughter.

* * *

It was mid-afternoon by the time Bridget walked into the intimidating glass and steel building that housed the Montclair Biotech headquarters.

She'd already dropped Hank off at home, changed into a black tailored jacket, and tucked her Glock into her purse.

Now she was ready to confront Monty, and she was pretty sure she knew where to find him.

Men like Monty don't run home with their tails between their legs after a public take down.

No, Monty would want to show the world that he was still king of his own little hill. He'd want to prove to himself that he was still in control.

And Bridget was going there with only one objective.

She needed to find out what he knew about Cassidy. The likelihood that something bad had happened to the girl grew stronger with each hour that passed.

Bridget could no longer sit around and wait for the teenager to show up. Or for another body to be found.

If Cassidy's not with her father, I'll report her missing myself.

The thought was somehow comforting as she entered the stark lobby and crossed to the elevators.

Riding up to the tenth floor, she wondered if she should have asked Charlie Day or even Terrance Gage to go with her.

Too late for that now. I'm here, and I'm going in.

Her pulse quickened as the glass doors slid open to reveal an attractive young woman sitting at a reception desk.

"I need to see Montgomery Montclair," Bridget said, holding up her credentials. "I'm with the FBI."

She lowered her hand before the receptionist could make out the *Consultant* label stamped across her photo ID.

Motioning for Bridget to wait, the woman hurried down a wide corridor, her heels tapping out a frantic beat against the sleek marble floor.

Bridget hesitated, then followed the clicking footsteps, unwilling to give the CEO a chance to slip away before she could ask him about Cassidy.

She heard raised voices before she reached the open door at the end of the hall and quickened her pace.

By the time she'd stuck her head into the room, the receptionist was heading back out in wide-eyed panic.

"You can't go in there," she said but made no effort to stop Bridget from stepping into the room.

A man's voice accosted her as she moved toward a long table positioned in front of the floor-to-ceiling windows.

"What do you think you're doing here?"

Suddenly Erwin Sutler was standing in front of her. The lawyer's eyes flashed with hostility as he stared down at her.

Bridget recoiled as he lifted a big hand, but he only used it to push a strand of pale hair off his forehead.

"I need to see Mr. Montclair," Bridget insisted. "I need to ask him about his daughter."

Sutler opened his mouth to protest when a familiar voice spoke up behind him.

"Dr. Bishop? Has something happened to my daughter?"

Slipping past Sutler's bulky body, Bridget saw that Monty was seated at the head of a crowded table.

"Cassidy is missing," she said bluntly. "Didn't Scarlett tell you? She's been gone for three days without any word. I was hoping she was staying with you."

Monty frowned, then ordered the men at the table to leave.

As they gathered their laptops, folders, and coffee cups, Bridget noted that one man was holding a file labeled *Vixenzia*.

When he saw her staring at the name, he quickly covered it with one hand and scurried past her.

After all the men but Sutler had gone, Bridget turned back to Monty, who sat in a highbacked chair like a king on his throne instead of a suspected criminal out on bail.

Glancing down toward the floor, Bridget expected to see his ankle monitor, but the table was hiding his leg.

"I haven't seen my daughter or talked to her since I was released on bail," he said in a cold voice. "My wife is likely hiding her away somewhere. I wouldn't put it past her to try to ransom the poor girl."

Bridget shook her head.

"This isn't a trick or a con," Bridget said. "I went over to Scarlett's house the night Cassidy left, and I saw for myself that she was gone. She'd taken her phone and her backpack, but not much else."

The frown on Monty's face deepened.

"You think something really could have happened to her?" he asked, suddenly sounding worried.

Bridget noted the distress in his voice. Genuine narcissists don't usually worry about the safety of others. Not even their own children.

His next question cleared up the confusion.

"How will it look if my daughter is missing?" he asked, looking to Sutler. "Will they try to blame me? Will they think I'm involved?"

He turned to Bridget.

"Is anyone even looking for her?" he demanded.

"I am," Bridget said in a calm voice, reminding herself that the man couldn't help the way he was. "I'm also working with the FBI's Behavioral Analysis Unit to create a profile of the man who killed Harmony Baxter and Esme Dupree. It's possible your daughter's disappearance is related to their deaths."

Her words prompted a shout of protest from Sutler.

"This has got to be some kind of set-up," he yelled. "Why else would she come in here trying to get you to talk?"

Before he could continue Monty held up a hand.

"I want to know who went into *my house* and killed Harmony. And I want to know who has *my daughter*."

He glared at Bridget.

"I've seen the reports about you, Dr. Bishop," he said.

The words sounded like an accusation.

"And if you really can find this psycho, then I'll tell you what you want to know."

He gestured to Sutler.

"Leave us."

Erwin Sutler responded at once to the regal command. He stood and left the room, throwing a reluctant look over his thickset shoulder.

"Do you know who could have killed Harmony?" Bridget asked as soon as the door closed behind Sutler. "If you do, tell me now, before Cassidy or anyone else gets hurt."

Monty shook his head.

"I don't have a clue," he said. "All I know is that someone set me up to take the blame. And I'm going to prove it."

A cold gleam entered his eyes.

"I'm not about to spend the rest of my life in prison," he ground out, his jaws clenched. "I'm prepared to do anything, pay any amount, to make sure that doesn't happen."

Bridget stared at him in dismay, realizing Cassidy's father had already forgotten about his missing daughter.

CHAPTER FIFTEEN

Vic Santino hurried into his apartment, set the bag of groceries on the table, and shrugged off his coat. As he crossed to the coatrack, he suddenly stopped and stared around the room, viewing the space with fresh eyes.

What is Bridget going to think when she gets here? Will she like it?

The modern, loft-style apartment was spacious and neat, but Santino hadn't gotten around to putting much of a personal touch on the place, and he realized to most people it would probably be seen as cold and uninviting.

The fact that he didn't spend much time at home was a big part of the problem. As a deputy marshal with the U.S. Marshal Service, he was often on the road tracking down dangerous fugitives and bringing them into custody.

It was hazardous work, but he didn't mind.

He liked the thrill. He liked to be in the zone. The knowledge that a momentary distraction could prove fatal to him, or to an innocent bystander, required the kind of focus that tended to block out any thoughts of past or future.

That kind of focus also served to block out the regret and

loneliness that had become Santino's constant companions since Mirabel's untimely death.

Even when he wasn't working, Santino tried to stay busy, knowing that sitting around the quiet, empty apartment staring at his four walls wasn't good for his state of mind.

During warmer months he enjoyed going out in his boat and spending time on the water. And of course, lately, he'd been enjoying spending time with Bridget Bishop, too.

The thought of the psychologist brought a rush of guilty anticipation, and he checked his watch, then turned back to the bag of groceries.

He'd invited her over to see his home for the first time and stay for dinner, and he was feeling a little nervous.

Instead of carrying the groceries into the kitchen, he left them on the table and moved toward the bedroom.

Standing in the doorway, he looked toward the dresser, unsure what to do about the photo.

He crossed the room and studied the picture taken on his wedding day. He and Mirabel both looked so young and happy. Luckily, they'd been blissfully unaware of what lay ahead.

But I promised never to forget. I promised so many things.

Leaving the picture as it was, he turned away. Something inside him wouldn't let him move it or hide it away.

He walked to the kitchen and began to prepare the pasta, forcing his mind to stay focused on each step in the process, refusing to let himself get pulled down into the dark hole of depression that threatened to swallow him up if he let it.

His grandmother had passed on a simple recipe for a

spicy red sauce that he cooked on any special occasion, and he had stopped at the store earlier to pick up a fresh loaf of crusty bread and some green leafy lettuce and tomatoes for a salad.

Pulling out a pricey bottle of cabernet, he opened it and set it on the counter to breathe, then turned back to the stove to stir the sauce.

The meal was coming together nicely when he heard a soft knock on the door announcing Bridget's arrival.

Santino swung open the door, taking in Bridget's flushed cheeks and bright blue eyes.

He looked behind her.

"No, Hank?"

She smiled and shook her head.

"It's past his bedtime," she teased as she stepped through the door and looked around the living room with frank curiosity.

Although it felt strange having someone in the apartment with him when he was usually there all alone, he decided he liked it. Her presence made the place feel instantly warmer.

Taking her coat, he hung it on the rack, then led her into the kitchen. Pouring two glasses of the cabernet, he held one toward Bridget, but her phone buzzed in her pocket before she could take it.

"It's Charlie," she said with an apologetic grimace. "I really should answer this. Is there somewhere I can take it where I won't disturb you?"

Santino froze, then pointed toward the bedroom.

He waited, still holding both glasses of wine, as Bridget

went into the bedroom and pushed the door closed behind her.

Wondering if she would see the picture on the dresser, Santino carried the wine to the table and then sank into a chair.

His heartbeat quickened as the door opened and Bridget came back out holding the phone by her side.

She dropped it into her bag and took a seat at the table.

"Charlie thinks they know who the Jane Doe is in the Devil's Blade investigation," Bridget said, her voice no longer light or playful. "Argus Murphy was able to narrow it down to a temp who worked at Montclair Biotech for a few weeks. A woman named Irina Jensen. They're going to exhume Jane Doe's body tomorrow."

Her eyes fell on her wine glass, and she picked it up and took a long sip, and then another.

"Once they get her out of the ground, they'll compare her dental records with Irina Jensen's to see if they are a match."

Santino watched as Bridget took another drink.

"I told Charlie I want to be there when they take her out," she said, swallowing hard. "But that's not the big news."

"What do you mean?" Santino asked, confused. "What's the big news? What's happened?"

Finishing the wine left in her glass in one big gulp, Bridget set the glass back on the table.

"Monty Montclair is gone," she said. "Apparently, he cut off his ankle monitor and has gone on the run."

WHERE EVIL HIDES

* * *

Santino had been woken before dawn by the incessant buzzing of his phone and the news that he'd been assigned to the team responsible for bringing in fugitive Monty Montclair.

He now stood in Monty's opulent home near Embassy Row, looking around the house with a mixture of awe and disdain.

The multi-million-dollar home was filled with the finest furnishings and artwork money could buy, but there was no warmth or coziness to be seen. No personal photos or mementos on display. It was like stepping into a museum. All cold marble and high ceilings.

"What does someone need with all this...*stuff*?" Santino muttered to Special Agent Tristan Hale, who had arrived in a bad mood, looking slightly bleary-eyed. "Seems more than a little excessive."

"What else is he going to do with the billions he's earned by overcharging sick and dying people for their medicine?" Hale asked before turning and stomping out of the room.

Hearing the bitterness in Hale's voice, Santino decided he wasn't just making an idle comment. The agent sounded resentful, even angry.

Santino was tempted to go after Hale and make sure he was alright but decided he'd have to save the conversation for a later date. They had a fugitive to find, and the task would only grow more difficult with every hour that passed.

Searching the maze of luxurious but impersonal rooms

with increasing frustration, Santino found no clues as to where the CEO could have gone.

He was just about to give up and head over to the billionaire's corporate headquarters when he noticed a photo on the dresser in the sumptuous master suite.

It was one of the only personal photos on display.

Leaning down to get a closer look, Santino saw a younger Monty and a teenaged Teddy Montclair in heavy coats and hats standing on the deck of a yacht.

The name *Monty's Mojo* had been painted on the hull.

Santino squinted at the dock in the photo and made out a familiar-looking marina in the background.

"You find something?" Hale asked, coming up behind him.

"I'm not sure," Santino said. "But it looks as if Monty has taken his boat out in the winter before."

He gestured toward the photo on the dresser, then began backing toward the door.

"I think maybe he's done it again."

Jogging toward the exit, Santino headed to his Chevy, eager to get to the Shoreline Marina in Alexandria.

A half-hour later, he parked the truck in the nearly empty lot and looked toward the silent row of boats lined up along the wooden pier.

He'd called Detective Quinn from the Charity Point PD on the way over, and she'd confirmed that Monty had claimed his forty-foot cabin cruiser had been docked at the marina for the winter months.

It was a popular choice for boat owners in the D.C. area

as Santino well knew. He'd rented a slip there for his own boat over the last few years to ensure it would be close at hand when he got the rare chance to go out on the water.

According to Quinn, Monty had paid the marina to winterize the yacht but had asked them to keep it in running order in the event he decided to take it out to Charity Point.

"We sent a crime scene crew to look over it since Mr. Montclair claimed the Devil's Blade knife we found on the kitchen floor had been taken from his boat, but the boat wasn't there," Quinn had told him.

"Did anyone at the marina notice when the boat cast off?" Santino asked.

"No one who we spoke with," Quinn had said. "We interviewed the dockmaster and an attendant who'd been on duty the afternoon Harmony Baxter was killed, but neither one claimed to have seen any activity around the boat. In fact, they seemed surprised it wasn't in the Montclair's slip when we arrived."

Now Santino walked toward the marina office carrying a slip of paper with the Hull Identification Number he'd gotten from Quinn.

Pushing open the battered wooden door, he saw a young female attendant leaning on the counter staring down at the phone in her hand.

She looked up with a guilty start when she saw him standing in the doorway and quickly set down the phone.

"Deputy Marshal Santino," he said, flashing his credentials at her. "I'm looking for one of your tenants. A

Mr. Montgomery Montclair. His boat is the *Monty's Mojo* and I have the HIN number. I just need to know what slip he's in."

The attendant stared at him with wide, scared eyes.

"I'll go get Wally," she said, backing toward the door behind her. "He's the dockmaster."

Santino nodded impatiently as she knocked on the door and stuck her head into the tiny back office.

"Can't these people leave me alone for five minutes?" a gruff voice bellowed from behind the thin wooden wall.

Heavy footsteps stomped across the floor, and then Wally Truman appeared in the doorway.

"What is it now?" he growled, wiping at his lips with the back of his hand. "I've already told the police and the FBI everything I know. Which is nothing."

"I'm not with the police or the FBI," Santino said in a hard voice. "I'm a U.S. Deputy Marshal, and I'm searching for a wanted fugitive who happens to be one of your tenants. His name is Montgomery Montclair, and I need to know what slip his boat, the *Monty's Mojo*, is in."

Studying Santino's stony face, the dockmaster sighed and turned to an ancient computer.

He turned the monitor toward Santino and punched in a few keys, calling forth a list of the slips in the marina, sorted by an assigned number.

The record for each occupied slip included the renter's name, along with the boat's official hull identification number.

"What's the HIN?" Wally asked.

As Santino recited the information Quinn had given him, the dockmaster used his thick, calloused fingers to type the letters and numbers out on the grimy keyboard.

He punched the *Enter* key and grunted, then pointed to the smudged screen.

Santino looked over the big man's shoulder, seeing at a glance that the HIN was registered to a boat owned by Mr. Montgomery Montclair in slip N32.

A *Paid in Full* status showed next to Monty's name.

"No way to track when the boat was in dock?" Santino asked. "No notes as to comings or goings?"

"As long as a tenant is paid up, I don't bother them," Wally said. "I don't go nosing into their business and they don't update me as to where they're going."

Santino nodded his thanks and backtracked down the pier until he reached slip N32.

It was empty.

He cursed under his breath as he studied the boats surrounding the empty slip.

Most of the boats had been tightly covered from bow to stern, their owners content to wait until spring to get back on the water.

Some boats had even been shrink-wrapped with clear material that allowed Santino a blurred peek at the deck.

Continuing down the pier, he noted the name on each boat hull as he went, wondering how some people came up with the names.

While he liked the names *Serendipity* and *Wanderlust*, he rolled his eyes at *Aquaholic* and *Nauti-Bouy*.

As he looked across the rows of boats filling the eerily silent marina, his phone buzzed in his pocket.

He turned away and headed back to his car, failing to see the boat softly bobbing in slip S23 with the name *Lucky Devil* freshly painted on its hull.

"Hey Bridget," he said, feeling deflated. "*Monty's Mojo* isn't here, and there's no sign of its namesake, either. Looks like Monty's taken the boat and sailed off into the sunset. For all we know, Cassidy is with him."

CHAPTER SIXTEEN

Monty forced one eye open, then quickly closed it again, wincing against the splitting pain in his head. A moan escaped his dry lips as he tried to lift a hand to shield his eyes from a shaft of light that was shining down on him. His arm wouldn't move.

Squinting down at the offending limb, he saw the white dock line wrapped around his wrists and was instantly awake.

"What the hell..."

The words emerged as a rough whisper in the silent cabin, tearing at his throat.

He knew he was in his own boat. He could feel the slight roll of the water beneath him. But how had he gotten there? And who had tied him up?

Shifting his throbbing head, he looked around the small space, expecting it to be empty.

He gasped when he saw his daughter lying next to him.

"Cassidy?"

The girl didn't move at Monty's hoarse whisper.

She was so pale and still, that Monty decided she must be dead. Then he saw her chest moving gently up and down.

"Cassidy?"

This time his whisper was louder and more urgent, but still, she didn't respond.

She must be unconscious...or drugged.

Struggling to remember what had happened, and how he'd gotten into his current predicament, Monty forced himself to lower his head and close his eyes.

As he sucked in a deep, calming breath, he tried to think. What was the last thing he could remember? Where had he been? What had he been doing?

Slowly, it all started coming back to him.

Monty picked up the tumbler and drained the last of the twenty-year-old scotch Randolph Hildebrand had presented to him at the start of the Vixenzia trials.

Back then he'd been sure that the new drug would turn Montclair Biotech's flagging business around and make him a national hero. And back then, he'd been a married, family man who'd never seen the inside of a jail cell.

He grimaced at the thought of how quickly things could change.

And just because of a few little mistakes.

Rage brewed in his gut, mixing with the alcohol.

Looking down at the ankle monitor, he went to the kitchen, retrieved a large Devil's Blade knife from the knife block, and went back to the living room.

He studied the long steel blade with angry eyes.

Teddy had gifted each of the executives at the company a standard set of knives to celebrate the Vixenzia launch, saying that the blades were made out of ice-tempered, high carbon steel.

His son had included an extra special set of marine knives for Monty, assuring his father that they were the best that money could buy. The sharpest knives in the world.

"Probably the most expensive, too," Monty mumbled to himself.

Teddy's generosity made Monty suspect he was paying him too much, and his frown deepened as he realized his son probably expected to be running the company soon enough and was already spending his future inheritance.

Thinking that Randolph Hildebrand might have something to say about that plan, Monty decided that Teddy may be in for a surprise.

But what did it matter to him either way? Why should he care who would be running the company if he was stuck in jail?

With sudden resolve, Monty stabbed down with the knife, slicing through the ankle monitor with savage force.

He looked down at the destroyed device with a pang of panic. There would be no going back now.

Racing out to his Jaguar, he headed toward the Shoreline Marina. He would take his boat and sail south until he could figure out who was setting him up.

Someone wanted the police and the FBI to think he'd killed Harmony and the other women. Someone wanted to frame him and get him out of the way.

But who could it be? There were plenty of people who were jealous of his success or angry at him for some perceived slight.

He'd long ago accepted the fact that having enemies was the price of being a successful, powerful man.

But who hated him enough to actually kill three women?

When he reached the marina, Monty parked the Jaguar in the nearly empty lot and ran toward the dock.

The wooden pier was slippery, and he almost went over the side and into the water below, before managing to regain his balance at the last minute.

His relief was short-lived when he saw that slip N32 was empty.

Monty's Mojo was gone.

Stomping down the pier to the dockmaster's office, Monty pounded on the door, but no one answered.

The dockmaster was nowhere to be seen.

Old Wally Truman was probably asleep in there. Probably plastered off his ass again.

Monty vowed to see to it that the useless old drunk was fired once he'd gotten himself out of his current mess.

The angry thought was interrupted by the hard shove of a gun in his back. Monty turned to see a man in a black balaclava and dark sunglasses standing behind him.

"Walk," the man commanded, emphasizing the order with another thrust of the gun. "Say a word and you're dead."

Monty's eyes dropped, and with a start of fear, he recognized the gray steel of a revolver.

Allowing himself to be propelled down the empty pier, he tried to plan some sort of escape. But the man was right behind him, prodding him toward a boat with the name *Lucky Devil* freshly painted on the hull.

He recognized his own cabin cruiser right away.

"What the hell-"

The words erupted before he could stop them, earning another sharp jab from the gun's muzzle.

Once he was onboard, the man pushed Monty toward the hatch leading down to the main cabin.

Panicking at the sight of the dark cabin below, he spun toward his assailant, intending to knock the gun from his hand only to see that it had been replaced with a hypodermic needle.

The sharp sting of the needle bit into the soft flesh of his neck, bringing with it all-consuming darkness.

Looking up through the hatch above him, Monty wondered how long he'd been unconscious.

He stilled his breathing and listened, hearing the engine rumbling softly, feeling the undulation of the water below.

We're on the water. He's taken us out on the Bay.

He struggled to break his hands free from the ropes binding him, then froze when he heard someone coming down the stairs.

The man in the balaclava stood looking down at him.

As if she could feel his glare, Cassidy began to groan and struggle against the ties.

"Who are you?" Monty demanded in a rasping voice that made him sound like an old man. "What are you going to do with me?"

"Shut up," the masked man growled, reaching down to wrench Monty up and off the bed.

Dragging him toward the stairs, the man spoke in a low, gravelly growl that Monty couldn't recognize.

"I'd like nothing better than to throw your sorry ass into

the Bay. But I've got other plans for you."

"But...what about Cassidy?" Monty called, looking back to see his daughter's eyes blink open.

The man ignored the question as he shoved Monty upward, then let him collapse onto the deck.

An icy gale of wind lifted Monty's hair and stole his breath as he looked around, trying to get his bearings.

The night was dark, but a sliver of moon hung in the sky, making it possible to see that the boat was docked behind Monty's house on Windwalker Way.

"Come on," the man said, half carrying, half dragging Monty down the dock. "Time for you to go home."

Hands still tied, and too weak to resist, Monty had no choice but to allow himself to be taken into the house, where he was dumped onto the hardwood floor.

Reaching into his pocket, the man held up a syringe.

"What is that?" Monty asked, shrinking back in fear.

"Something from the Montclair Biotech lab," the man told him, holding up the label so that Monty could see the name of a strong painkiller. "It'll get you so high, by the time the feds arrive to arrest you, you won't be able to remember your own name."

His hand shot forward, sinking the needle into Monty's flesh, and once again the darkness started to descend. But this time Monty struggled to stay awake.

As he faded in and out of consciousness, he saw the man leave the room, and then suddenly he was back, holding up a long, dangerous-looking knife.

It was a Devil's Blade.

The man forced the knife into Monty's hand.

Looking down, Monty saw it was a twin to the knife that had been used to kill Harmony Baxter. And it was covered in blood.

Is that Cassidy's blood?

Monty opened his mouth to ask what the man had done with his daughter, but his mouth wouldn't move.

The room swirled around him, fading in and out.

"Be quiet and stay still," the man muttered in his ear. "Someone will be here soon."

"I'll tell them…" Monty moaned.

"Go ahead," the man taunted. "Tell them you've been set up. Tell them someone forced you to cut off your ankle monitor and take too many drugs. I'm sure they'll believe you."

Laughter followed the voice as it faded into the night.

Minutes later Monty heard the boat engine come to life in the distance. He tried to get up, but he couldn't move.

The drugs were too strong, and he was too weak.

Just as he'd decided to let himself give in to the pull of the dark, a light flashed on somewhere in the house.

He stirred and tried to lift his head, but it was too heavy.

Footsteps sounded, and then a figure loomed over Monty.

As a familiar face came into focus, he sighed in relief and closed his eyes.

He'd be safe now.

CHAPTER SEVENTEEN

Bridget poured herself a cup of freshly brewed coffee and sat down at the kitchen table in front of her computer. She moved quietly, not wanting to make too much noise since it wasn't yet dawn and Hank was still fast asleep.

After waking up early, she hadn't been able to go back to sleep, too anxious about the exhumation of Jane Doe planned for later that day, and too worried about Cassidy Montclair.

The more she thought about the missing teenager, the more she doubted that Cassidy had simply run away, and had chosen to stay away, of her own free will.

Struggling to concentrate on the data reports Argus had emailed the previous evening, and unable to push away her growing sense of unease, Bridget closed her computer and tried to think.

If I were Cassidy, and I was in trouble, where would I go?

Images of the affluent homes she'd already visited flashed through her head. The girl hadn't run to Monty's big house in D.C., or to his vacation home on Charity Point, or even to Teddy's pristine townhouse.

No, Cassidy was probably looking for comfort, not luxury.

Bridget had a sudden memory of Roy and Shirley Lafferty standing beside Cassidy. She'd only had one chance to meet the teen's grandparents, but the couple had made a lasting impression.

Maybe Scarlett was wrong. Perhaps Cassidy has turned to her grandparents after all.

Bundling herself into a heavy coat and warm hat, Bridget ran out to her Explorer, armed with her trusty ice scraper and a thermos of hot coffee.

The early morning traffic was light, and she arrived at the modest ranch-style home on Newberry Street just after eight.

She knew it was early to show up unannounced but hoped to catch the older couple at home and didn't want to give Cassidy any warning that she was coming.

Her knock on the door prompted the barking of a small dog and the sound of slow, steady footsteps inside.

Shirley Lafferty opened the door wearing the same friendly smile she'd worn the last time they'd met.

"Why, Dr. Bridget, how wonderful to see you," she said, looking a bit flustered. "Although I'm not really dressed for company."

Raising a hand to smooth her white curls, she stepped back and waved Bridget inside, shushing the barking dog that pattered around their feet.

"Who's this?" Bridget asked, bending down to give the furry dog a scratch on his little head.

"That's Bingo," Shirley said with obvious affection.

"Cassidy loves the little guy, even though she doesn't get to see him often."

"He reminds me of that little dog on TV," Bridget replied.

She smiled down at the dog's eagerly wagging tale.

"You know, the one in all those movies?"

"Yes, that's what I thought when I saw him at the shelter. He's just a mutt, but I thought he'd be perfect for Cassidy."

Shirley's smile dimmed.

"I found out too late that Monty only allows purebred dogs in his house," she sniffed. "But we love having Bingo around."

She motioned down the hall.

"Roy and I were just eating breakfast," she said. "You're more than welcome to join us."

Bridget followed the woman's small figure into the kitchen, feeling awkward and a little foolish.

It was obvious the older couple wasn't hiding their granddaughter. She'd wasted her morning and had intruded on the Laffertys for no good reason.

"Roy, we've got a visitor," Shirley said, speaking loudly toward the man hidden behind the morning paper. "You remember Dr. Bishop, don't you?"

The man lowered the paper and stared at Bridget in surprise, before jumping up from the table and circling around to offer a wide hand that felt pleasantly soft and warm.

"Were we expecting you, Dr. Bishop?" he asked with a slight frown. "I sometimes get confused with dates and such, but–"

"No, I'm sorry to just show up," Bridget said, feeling her cheeks grow warm. "I'm here about Cassidy. And please...call me Bridget."

The frown didn't leave Roy's face. His eyes were wary as he put an arm around his wife's shoulders.

"I guess you're not here to deliver good news, are you?"

Bridget shook her head. It was best to be honest and straightforward with the older couple from the start.

"I'm guessing Scarlett hasn't told you," Bridget said softly. "But Cassidy is missing."

Shirley let out a gasp of alarm.

"What do you mean, missing? What happened?"

The question came from Roy.

"Cassidy had an argument with her mother Monday night," Bridget said. "She disappeared from her room soon after. It looked as if she'd gone out the window. Scarlett assumed she'd run away. Maybe gone to a friend's house or her father's."

Bridget suddenly wished she'd stayed home with Hank.

"It's been four days and she hasn't come home," she continued, knowing she had no choice but to tell the truth. "We haven't been able to locate her, so I was hoping she might be here with you."

She didn't add that she was beginning to suspect Cassidy had run into some kind of trouble. Maybe even a killer.

No need to worry them.

The theory was really just a hunch at this point anyway.

Lifting a small hand, Shirley covered her mouth.

"Not my sweet Cassidy," she whispered, shaking her head in denial. "On her own for four days? She's just a child."

Guiding his wife into the living room, Roy gestured for Bridget to follow them.

Framed family photos hung on every wall and sat on every spare surface. Scarlett featured prominently in most of them, along with various poses of Cassidy at every age.

"Scarlett was always mugging for the camera," Shirley said weakly as Bridget stopped to study a photo of Scarlett in a bright blue cheerleading uniform. "She has always loved being the center of attention. Not like our granddaughter…"

Shirley faltered on the words. She waved Bridget toward a comfortable-looking couch, then sank down beside her.

"So, you think Cassidy's in trouble?" Roy asked in a gravelly voice. "Do you have any idea where she could be?"

"We're working on it," Bridget said, wishing she could give them something solid. "But right now, we're just not sure."

She watched as tears formed in Shirley's eyes, which were the same emerald-green shade as her daughter's and her granddaughter's, but the older woman managed to blink them away before they could fall.

"I'm sorry to spring this on you," Bridget said, biting her lip. "I assumed Scarlett would have told you."

"Scarlett doesn't tell us much," Shirley replied, reaching for a tissue. "She's always been independent and headstrong. It's my fault really…"

Roy started to protest but Shirley stopped him.

"You know it's true, Roy."

She turned her red-rimmed eyes to Bridget.

"We didn't have Scarlett until late in life. She was an only child and...well, I let that girl get away with murder," she confessed. "I should have been harder on her growing up, but I just never did understand that child."

Bridget resisted the urge to remind Shirley that her daughter was no longer a child. Scarlett had been a full-grown adult for almost two decades.

And it was likely a personality disorder, not poor parenting, that had influenced Scarlett's behavior since adolescence.

But that was a discussion for another day, or perhaps even the focus of long-term therapy for the family.

For now, Bridget could best help the worried couple by finding their granddaughter.

"I'd better go," she said, getting to her feet and moving toward the door. "I'm sorry to have bothered you."

"You will find Cassidy, won't you?" Shirley asked as Bridget stepped out onto the porch. "You'll bring our sweet girl home?"

"I'll do my very best," Bridget agreed. "I promise you that."

※ ※ ※

The Eternal Rest Cemetery was located thirty minutes outside D.C. on a good traffic day. But it was Friday, and the roads were slick, so the drive took Bridget over an hour.

By the time she pulled the Explorer past the big stone gate, Opal Fitzgerald was already standing by the grave watching as a man maneuvered a small backhoe between two headstones.

The medical examiner's gray curls were covered by a thick white cap, and her short, solid figure was bundled in a heavy waterproof coat. Sturdy work boots completed the outfit.

Further down the path, Charlie Day and Tristan Hale stood speaking to a man with a camera.

Charlie saw Bridget and crossed toward her.

"You sure you want to be here?" she asked. "Have you ever witnessed an exhumation?"

Shaking her head, Bridget tried to look stoic.

"No, but there's got to be a first time for everything," she said. "And if this woman is Irina Jensen, from what we've learned about her so far, it doesn't look like she has anyone else to be here for her. No one to bear witness, so..."

"So, you thought you would?"

"I thought I *should*," Bridget said with a shrug. "After all, we're disturbing her eternal rest in the hopes she can help us find our unsub. The least we can do is pay our respects."

"Is that why *they're* here?"

She pointed to two men walking toward them.

One was tall, dark, and handsome, while the other was not.

"I didn't know that Gage and Argus were coming," Bridget said, trying not to show her dismay. "I guess they had the same idea as me."

Waving the men over, Charlie led them toward the gravesite.

The backhoe had cleared off the frozen topsoil and two men were down in the hole digging the coffin out with shovels.

Bridget noticed that a simple stone engraved only with the words *May She Rest in Peace* had been removed and placed safely under a large oak tree.

"How'd the body end up here?" Bridget asked, looking around the peaceful, rolling hills of gravestones. "I thought unclaimed remains were buried in shared graves at designated cemeteries near the city."

Charlie shrugged and turned to Opal, who had come up behind her to watch the gravediggers' progress.

"Local detectives working the homicide talked the M.E. into keeping the body for over a month in the cooler while they tried to ID her," she said. "When they were told she was going to be cremated and buried in a mass grave with other unclaimed bodies, they started a fundraiser. Ended up getting enough money to put her here."

The clang of metal on wood made Opal wince.

Bridget heard one of the gravediggers yell.

"Okay, we've reached the box. Let's bring her up."

"I guess they didn't raise enough for a metal coffin," Opal said, swallowing hard. "Which means you'll all want to stay back. The wooden ones aren't watertight, and they don't always stay in one piece when they're taken out of the ground."

The M.E. looked past Bridget and frowned.

"Is he okay?"

Bridget followed her gaze and saw Argus staring at the open grave with wide, unblinking eyes.

"Argus, are you alright?"

A bead of sweat dripped down his face despite the cold breeze as he shook his head. Turning away, he stumbled back onto the path.

"He just needs some air," Gage said.

But Bridget had seen the analyst's face and she wasn't so sure. Going after him, she put a hand on his shoulder.

"I'm...sorry," he gasped, leaning over to put his hands on his knees. "This hasn't...happened before."

"It's okay," Bridget said, handing him a tissue from her purse. "It happens to us all sometimes. And from what I can tell, this kind of stuff never gets easy."

She suspected Argus had just realized Irina Jensen was a real person, and not just a name in a database. And from the glazed look in his eyes, it had hit him pretty hard.

The smell of decay hanging in the air couldn't be helping either.

Wiping his mouth, Argus straightened and glanced over at her with a pained expression.

"I need to go sit in the car," he said, holding both hands to his stomach. "I don't want to see her come out of there."

He dropped his eyes and turned toward Gage's Navigator.

Bridget stopped him before he walked away.

"You know, you did a good thing...finding her, I mean," she said, glancing toward the grave. "Thanks to you, the woman in that grave might finally get the justice she deserves."

CHAPTER EIGHTEEN

It was late afternoon by the time Charlie got the call from Opal Fitzgerald. Seeing the medical examiner's name on the display, she snatched the phone off her desk and held it to her ear, eager to get confirmation that their Jane Doe had finally been identified.

"It's our girl," Opal said triumphantly. "Irina Jensen's dentist back in Memphis called. He confirmed her dental records match that of Jane Doe."

Charlie felt a rush of adrenaline as she realized they finally had a name, which would surely lead them to a suspect, and to the truth about what had happened to Irina Jensen.

Opening the file Argus Murphy had given her, she scanned through the data the behavioral analyst had collected on Irina Jensen during his investigation.

The temp worker had made a hasty move from Memphis to D.C. after a messy break-up. The disturbing details had been included in the woman's petition for a restraining order, and a photocopy of the petition was included in the file.

Argus had also managed to find Irina's last known

address, which Charlie saw was only a quick drive away.

Looking over at Hale's empty desk, she checked her watch, not sure how long he might take for lunch, and decided not to wait. She would interview Irina's landlord on her own.

She wasn't familiar with the rundown apartment complex listed in the file, but there was something about the long, low building that gave her the creeps as she pulled up outside.

With the high cost of rent in the city, Charlie figured the depressing place had been the only option Irina could afford.

As she parked in front of the leasing office and stepped out of the Expedition, she instinctively put a hand on her Glock.

But the little man sitting at the desk inside seemed relatively harmless, despite his leering grin.

"You looking for an apartment?" he asked hopefully.

"I'm looking for information," Charlie replied, holding up her badge and pushing back her jacket to reveal her holster. "One of your renters went missing months ago, but no one reported it. Turns out she was the victim of a homicide."

The man's grin vanished.

"I don't know anything about it."

Holding up a photo of Irina Jensen that Argus had found online, Charlie cocked her head.

"You remember her?"

The man nodded slowly.

"Oh, yeah, she was a real hottie," he said, scratching at his stubbly chin. "But she skipped out on the rent. After no word for thirty days, we evicted her and cleared out all her stuff."

Charlie frowned.

"Cleared out her stuff?" she asked in dismay. "Don't tell me you threw it away?"

"You're in luck," he said. "She didn't have much, so I put it in a few boxes and shoved it in our storage unit."

Opening a drawer, the man produced a small set of keys.

"I figured she may come back for it at some point and be grateful if you know what I mean."

He wiggled his eyebrows and produced another grin.

"Help yourself," he said, leaning forward to hand her the keys. "The storage unit is at the back of the property."

Charlie recoiled as his fingers brushed hers, and she hurried out of the stuffy office, sure that she'd smelled alcohol on his breath even though it was barely noon.

Striding back to the dented door of the storage unit, Charlie forced the key into the rusty lock and wrenched it open.

She'd expected it to be packed with boxes and bags of unwanted and confiscated items, but there were only a few rows of flimsy cardboard boxes propped against the left wall.

Two boxes were labeled *Irina Jensen*.

A dull anger began to stir inside Charlie as she sorted through the meager remains of Irina Jensen's life.

Such a senseless, pointless death.

Her heart jumped when she saw the laptop and charger.

Underneath the computer, she found a thin photo album. She opened it and scanned through a dozen pages of family pictures. The last picture was a headshot of Irina.

Charlie wasn't sure, but she thought it was a graduation photo. Whatever the occasion, the young woman had been stunning, with a soft fall of blonde hair skimming her shoulders and bright eyes framed with long lashes.

Dramatic eyebrows, sharp cheekbones, and full lips completed a face that would have appeared at home on the cover of any fashion magazine.

Deciding to take both boxes back to the lab, she closed and locked the storage unit behind her, then carried the boxes to the Expedition and loaded them into the back.

She stopped by the leasing office, returned the key, then headed back toward the highway, her mind full of the images she'd seen in the photo album and the details she'd read in the restraining order petition.

Charlie figured she'd seen enough to piece together the dead woman's entire life story, including her tragic end.

First, a simple childhood in Memphis marked by birthday cakes, Christmas lights, and July Fourth fireworks.

Then, her first fairytale romance ended when her dream man turned out to be a nightmare.

And just as she was starting a new life in a new city, she'd lost her life altogether. And that was the end.

"Oh no, that's not the end at all," Charlie muttered under her breath as she merged into traffic. "Not by a longshot."

* * *

Charlie was still fuming when she got back to her office and set the box with Irina Jensen's laptop on her desk.

She didn't speak as Hale entered the office carrying a cup of coffee. His dark hair was disheveled and his five o'clock shadow had spouted into a starter beard.

"What's in the box?" he asked cautiously as if sensing her lingering anger.

"That's what's left of Irina Jensen's earthly possessions," she said darkly. "I got them from her old apartment."

Hale raised his eyebrows but didn't reply as he peered into one of the boxes.

"A laptop?" he said, sounding impressed. "You want me to take this over to Vivian Burke at the lab? I bet she can get it expedited to the front of the line with the cyber techs for us."

The mention of the attractive forensic technician did nothing to improve Charlie's mood.

"You two still buddies?" she asked sourly.

"Why wouldn't we be?"

He frowned at her as he took a sip from the steaming mug.

"I don't know," she snapped. "One minute you're all buddy-buddy and the next you're barely talking."

She sighed as her anger drained away.

"I guess I can't keep up with your social life."

Charlie tensed for a sharp reply but was relieved to see a

grin appear on Hale's face as he grabbed the laptop and beckoned her to follow him.

With a pang, she realized how much she'd been missing his roguish sense of humor lately, and by the time she and Hale arrived at the Quantico campus, she was feeling slightly better.

Walking into the impressive building that housed the state-of-the-art FBI lab, she saw Vivian Burke was already waiting for them in the lobby.

Her thick red hair was pulled back in a loose French braid, and she wore a crisp white lab coat over her street clothes.

"I've arranged for you to meet Luis Cortez," she said, leading them down a maze of corridors. "He's the cyber tech who worked on Esme Dupree's laptop, and he's absolutely brilliant."

She pushed through the door to a small conference room where a young, handsome technician was waiting.

"Cortez, this is Special Agent Charlie Day and Special Agent Tristan Hale from the Washington field office."

The technician gave a friendly nod, but his eyes were on the laptop in Charlie's hands. He reached for it before she'd gotten all the way into the room, quickly plugging in a power supply, and booting it up.

He tapped a few keys, then looked up at Charlie.

"I'm in," he said with an easy smile.

"How did you find the password so quickly?" Charlie asked.

Turning the laptop toward her, he pointed to a small

post-it stuck to the screen.

"She made it easy," he admitted with a lopsided smile. "Although I have a program that will crack most passwords if given enough time. Most people use weak passwords they can easily remember, so..."

His voice trailed off as he turned the computer around and started typing and clicking. After a few minutes, he looked up.

"I think you'll want to see this."

Charlie leaned forward to read an email sent to Irina Jensen's Montclair Biotech email account. It included only a single line with no greeting or signature.

I'm watching you.

Her pulse jumped when she saw the sender's name.

"Who's LuckyDevil13?"

"I'm not sure," Cortez admitted. "But similar messages from the same user were also sent to Esme Dupree and Harmony Baxter before they were killed. I found them when I went through their computers and emails."

Cortez opened a laptop on the table and tapped the touchpad to wake up the screen.

"This is Monty Montclair's computer," he said. "He received messages from LuckyDevil13 as well. Only his were a little different."

Sinking into the chair next to Cortez, Charlie read the email message on the screen aloud.

"If you don't want me to spill the details about your dirty little secret to the police and the press, wire $50,000 to the account below within the next 24 hours. Otherwise, get ready for the

whole rotten company to come crashing down around you."

She silently read the message again.

"We've already checked the account details," Vivian said, taking a seat on Cortez's other side. "The bank is in the Cayman Islands. As far as we can tell, no transfer was made from Monty's personal accounts in the U.S., but he could have used an offshore account to send the wire."

"What about the company accounts?" Charlie asked. "Have you checked the Montclair Biotech corporate accounts?"

Vivian shook her head.

"Not yet, but we have a forensic accountant ready to go through the corporate accounts as soon as a warrant is issued."

Studying the sender's name, Charlie looked to Luis Cortez.

"So, how do we go about tracking this LuckyDevil13 user account back to whoever sent the messages?"

The cyber tech sat back and ran a hand through his hair.

"The IP address used to send the messages belongs to the Montclair Biotech servers," he said. "So as far as I can tell, it looks like the messages were sent from an unidentified laptop on the corporate headquarters' network. Most likely someone within the building. But that's pretty much all I've got."

Charlie's mind was still spinning as she thanked Cortez for his help and followed Hale back outside.

"What do you think Monty's dirty little secret could be?" she asked as they drove toward the highway. "Could it be the women he'd been harassing at the office?"

"I'm not sure that was much of a secret," Hale said. "It seems like pretty much everyone in the company already knew about that, so it would be unlikely to cause a public uproar and bring down the whole company."

Charlie thought about the possibilities as she fought her way through traffic, wondering what else Monty could be hiding.

When they made it back to their office, Hale jumped out and headed straight for his car, already tapping something into his phone. Beatrix must be waiting.

Watching him walk away, Charlie took out her own phone and tapped in the main number to Montclair Biotech.

When the operator answered, she cleared her throat.

"May I speak to Cliff Finley in Compliance, please?"

After a few minutes, she heard the man's deep voice.

"Mr. Finley, this is Agent Charlie Day," she said, not sure he would remember her. "I was wondering if we could meet."

"Of course," he said, sounding surprised but agreeable. "When and where were you thinking?"

She was momentarily lost for words. She hadn't expected him to be quite so cooperative.

"The sooner the better," she finally said. "Although I'm thinking it may be best to meet away from your office. I have questions to ask about the company that could be sensitive."

There was a short silence on the other end of the connection, and then Finley cleared his throat.

"So, this is about your investigation?"

He sounded disappointed, and she wondered what he'd imagined. Did he think she'd called to proposition him rather than interview him?

Of course, he was a good-looking man. He was probably used to having women come on to him all the time.

And if she was honest with herself, she had been quite friendly with him the first time they'd met, if only in an attempt to get him to talk, so perhaps she couldn't blame him for his presumption.

And if we'd met under different circumstances...

She shook the idea from her head.

Dating someone I'm investigating would be even worse than dating a coworker. I need to get a grip.

"I'm sorry if I was unclear," she said, softening her tone. "But I'd like to interview you."

When he didn't respond, she decided to take a chance and explain what she was really after.

"You see, I've received a tip suggesting Mr. Montclair is holding back damaging information related to Montclair Biotech that could be used against him. I was hoping to ask you about that. It's extremely important."

"I can't discuss anything like that," Finley said, suddenly sounding nervous. "It goes against all regulations. If Monty found out, I would be out on my ear."

But she could hear the hesitation in his voice.

"Look, I wouldn't let anyone know the information came from you," Charlie assured him. "And this really is a matter of life and death."

Finley lowered his voice as if not wanting to be overheard.

"I don't know all the details, but there's a problem with Vixenzia, the new drug in trials now. If you want to get the whole story, you'll have to ask Randolph Hildebrand or Erwin Sutler," he said, speaking quickly. "The two of them are handling the situation. But please, don't tell him you've spoken to me, and..."

He faltered as if considering his next words.

"And what, Mr. Finley?" Charlie prodded as she wrote down the name of the drug.

"And just....be careful."

She opened her mouth to ask Finley what he meant, but he'd already disconnected the call.

Looking down at the phone, she considered going around to Montclair Biotech's corporate headquarters and speaking to Finley in person, then looked at her watch and decided it was too late.

She'd done all she could do for the day.

It was Friday evening and there would be no weekend off. Not with Monty Montclair on the run and the Devil's Blade murders still unsolved.

No, it was best to go home and get some rest.

It was going to be a busy weekend.

WHERE EVIL HIDES

CHAPTER NINETEEN

The Saturday morning sky hung gray and heavy over Lucky's head as he stood in the cabin cruiser's cockpit. Studying the ominous clouds and the snow-covered shore with satisfaction, he was confident they would encounter few other boats on the Chesapeake Bay that weekend.

Sunny skies and warmer weather would have derailed his plans, bringing out all the weekend boaters who hadn't stored away their vessels for the winter. But the forecasted snow and cold winds would act to keep most people inside, off the Bay, and out of his way.

Safely anchored in a quiet cove just north of Charity Point, Lucky went below deck and took a seat at the teak dining table in the main cabin.

Opening his laptop, he searched the morning news feed to see if there was any mention of Monty Montclair's escape and recapture. He clicked on all the local sites, then frowned.

There were several stories referring to what the police and press were now calling the Devil's Blade investigation, but there was nothing new about Monty Montclair's attempt to jump bail, or his subsequent recapture.

Leaning back in his chair, Lucky tried to think.

Did something go wrong with the plan?

Taking out his phone, he tapped out a number and held the phone to his ear.

"Yes?" a guarded voice said.

"I delivered Monty as agreed," Lucky said. "I expected to see his face splashed across the news. What happened?"

"Don't worry, I took care of him."

Lucky hesitated.

"You took care of him? Does that mean-"

"That means I took care of him," the voice snapped.

A tense silence followed.

"That wasn't in the plan."

"Neither was killing those women," the voice said. "But that didn't stop *you*. Looks like we've both gone rogue."

Sensing the challenge in the words, Lucky gripped the phone tighter in his hand.

"What about Cassidy?" he asked.

"Do what you like," the voice said. "And do it soon."

The phone went dead before Lucky could reply.

Staring down at the dead phone for a long beat, he dropped it on the table and turned back to his laptop with a surge of anticipation.

If we're both going rogue, then we might as well go all the way.

Remotely accessing the Montclair Biotech network, he logged into Monty Montclair's email and clicked *New Email*.

He smiled as he began to type.

WHERE EVIL HIDES

To: Scarlett Montclair
From: Monty Montclair
Subject: About Cassidy

Scarlett - I didn't kill Harmony Baxter or Esme Dupree. You know it and I know it. But the truth doesn't appear to matter anymore. The FBI is determined to frame me, which is why I've decided to leave the country.

Cassidy is with me, and she wants to come along. But I don't know where I'll end up or what will happen to me, so I've decided to leave her with you, regardless of everything that has happened between us.

This doesn't mean I've forgiven you. This nightmare is as much your doing as it is mine.

We have both been unfaithful and dishonest. (Yes, I know all about your affairs.) But I'm making this decision for Cassidy's sake.

I am planning to leave as soon as possible. You can meet me this afternoon at the marina – you know the one - to pick up Cassidy.

Come alone and don't tell anyone where you're going. Not your parents, not the police, and especially not the FBI.

If you tell anyone, I will know about it and will be forced to take Cassidy with me. If that happens, you'll never see her again, and you'll never see another dime of my money.

Make the right decision for once in your life and come alone to the marina at 2:00 p.m. sharp.

Monty

Lucky pictured Scarlett's reaction and smiled as he clicked *Send*, imagining her panic and outrage.

His pulse began to race at the thought.

The beautiful but unstable woman often lost control when she got angry. He'd witnessed many of her tantrums firsthand.

She'd never properly learned how to control her temper, but he was looking forward to teaching her.

It would be a hard lesson.

But he'd been patient long enough.

Lucky's careful surveillance of the entire Montclair family had proven Scarlett to be disloyal, unstable, and immoral, but he had to admit she'd managed to get under his skin, unwittingly casting a dangerous spell.

And as often happened when he focused on a new subject of surveillance, his mission had grown into an obsession. In this case, his fixation had extended to both Scarlett and her unfaithful husband.

He'd infiltrated every part of their dysfunctional lives, gaining access to their accounts, their emails, and even their security devices for their houses. Gaining control of their security systems and locks.

And now that Monty was out of the way, Scarlett would be his. At least for a little while.

But a soft moan reminded him that he had another problem to solve first. Moving back toward the sleeping berth, he peered in to verify that Cassidy was still asleep.

He stood for a long moment watching her pale, still face as her thin chest rose up and down in small shallow breaths.

The voice on the phone came back to him.

"Do what you like...and do it soon."

Lucky rested his hand on the sheath at his waist and moved closer to the sleeping girl. Close enough to touch her.

I can end it here and now. Take her out quickly and painlessly.

Of course, it wouldn't be like the other times. There would be no release. No thrill of satisfaction when the deed was over.

But he could do what needed to be done.

He'd been trained for just such a moment.

Still, his hand didn't reach for the knife as he tried to think.

Maybe I should hold on to her a little bit longer.

Perhaps, Cassidy would prove to be his insurance policy. His get-out-of-jail-free card.

If anyone did discover who he was and what he was doing, he could use the teenager as a hostage to secure his escape, or even ransom her off for a sizable amount if it came to that.

After all, if the FBI figured out who he was and what he'd done, he would need enough money to speed off into the sunset in Monty's cruiser and never be seen again.

CHAPTER TWENTY

The cold front had tightened its grip on Wisteria Falls as Bridget backed her Explorer out of the driveway and onto Fern Creek Road. Hard-packed drifts of snow lined the street as she headed out of the neighborhood, turning left onto Landsend Road.

Looking back at Hank, who had taken up his usual post by the back window, she shook her head.

"It's too cold for open windows today, Buddy," she said with a shiver as the SUV's heater rattled and hummed, emitting only the slightest hint of tepid air.

She headed east, slowing as she approached the sharp curve leading to the Shenandoah River.

Beaufort Hollow lay to her left, and she eased the Explorer onto the dirt road that wound through the hilly terrain.

Stopping next to a cluster of cars parked at the end of the road, she stepped out onto snow-covered ground which sloped down toward a small, frozen stream.

Excited voices echoed through the frigid air as Bridget watched a swarm of children dragging sleds up to the top of the snowy hill so that they could come careening back down amidst shouts of laughter.

Their parents stood huddled by their cars in warm coats, looking considerably less excited than their children to be up so early on a cold Saturday morning.

"Bridget!"

Turning at Ginny Finch's high-pitched squeal, Bridget saw the six-year-old running toward her. The little girl was pulling Daphne Finch along after her.

"I wasn't sure you were coming," Daphne said, trying to catch her breath.

Bridget released Hank from the backseat, and the Irish setter ran through the snow in circles, energized and ready to play, eliciting a new round of squeals from Ginny.

"Mom sent some hot chocolate." Daphne held up a thermos. "Better get a cup before Ginny finishes it off."

"Thanks, but I'll have to pass," Bridget said, shaking her head. "Hank and I can't stay for long."

But Daphne was no longer listening. Instead, she was chasing after Ginny trying to pull a fuzzy ski cap over her daughter's unruly blonde hair.

The little girl wiggled away, intent on carrying a neon pink plastic sled up the long gentle slope ahead.

"Let's go sledding, Hank!" she called over her shoulder.

The Irish setter raced after the girl, forcing Daphne and Bridget to trudge along behind them.

They stood together at the bottom of the hill, watching as Ginny and the dog scampered through the snow, their exuberance undampened by the cold.

Only when the little girl reached the top of the hill did

her smile falter and fade. Confused by her sudden change in demeanor, Bridget followed Ginny's gaze toward the dozen or so cars parked nearby.

Her stomach dropped when she saw a bearded man in a red beanie standing by her car.

"What in the world is Chase Grafton doing here?" Bridget asked, turning to Daphne.

But her friend had also spotted the podcaster and was already plowing through the snow to greet him.

Bridget turned back to see Ginny sliding toward her, but there was no accompanying laughter as the girl got to the bottom and looked for her mother.

"Could the Devil's Blade Killer be out here in the snow?" a familiar voice said from behind her. "Is that why you're here?"

Turning around to face Chase Grafton, Bridget grimaced.

"I'm here to spend time with Ginny and Daphne," Bridget said. "I'm guessing you can't say the same."

Chase produced a mocking frown.

"Just what are you suggesting, Dr. Bishop? That I came here to see *you*?"

"I think you came here trying to get information for your next episode," she replied in a low voice before turning to Daphne. "Did you tell him I would be here?"

Daphne hesitated, then gave a reluctant nod.

"I told him I was meeting you, but I didn't know he would show up like this," she said, throwing Chase an annoyed look.

"That's okay," Bridget assured her, unwilling to let

Chase ruin the morning for Ginny. "It's no big deal."

She smiled down at the little girl, who had appeared next to her mother looking worried.

"You go with your mom and take another turn on the hill, and I'll take Hank back to the car. His paws are getting cold."

Ginny hesitated, then nodded and ran back to the other children with Daphne reluctantly following behind her.

Once they were gone, Bridget headed toward the Explorer.

"Hey, wait up," Chase called, trailing after her. "I wanted to ask you a few questions about-"

Whirling around before the podcaster could finish his sentence, Bridget stuck a finger in his face.

"If you ever bother me or my friends again, I'll report you to the police for stalking and harassment," she said, not sure why she was so angry.

Maybe it was the disappointment she'd seen on Ginny's face, or maybe it was the fact that the podcaster was treating a series of vicious homicides like a game. Whatever it was, she was sick of Chase Grafton and his meddling.

She turned and called to Hank, then continued striding toward the SUV, aware that Chase was walking a few paces behind her.

"Looks like you've forgotten something called *freedom of the press*," he called out. "The public has a right to know if there is a killer going around slicing up women. Even if that killer is a high-powered billionaire."

Bridget ignored Chase as she ushered Hank into the

backseat. She turned to find Chase standing right behind her, his handheld recorder in hand.

"Dr. Bishop, can you give my listeners an update on the investigation into the homicide of Harmony Baxter? She's the woman who was killed at Montgomery Montclair's vacation home on the Chesapeake Bay, am I right?"

"I'd say you're very *wrong*, Mr. Grafton. Wrong for thinking you can use my friend to get to me, and wrong to think I would ever provide confidential information on a case to you."

She attempted to move past him, but Chase leaned back against the driver's side door, blocking her exit.

"My next episode is called *Devil in Disguise*."

He crossed his arms over his chest.

"Want to know what it's about?"

"I have a feeling you're about to tell me whether I want to know or not," Bridget said with a sigh.

Producing a mocking grin, he rubbed at his beard as if deep in thought.

"The episode exposes Monty Montclair's secret life as a serial killer," he said. "I plan to make the case that he's gone around for years pretending to be a model of virtue when in reality he's a murderer. A *devil in disguise* you could say."

Bridget cringed and grabbed for the doorhandle, forcing Chase to move to the side.

Losing his balance, he fell to one knee in the snow as Bridget climbed into the driver's seat and started the engine.

"The episode after that will focus on the Jane Doe who was exhumed in Eternal Rest Cemetery yesterday," Chase called out, as Bridget slammed the door shut. "I'm still trying to verify her real identity. But I bet she worked for Monty Montclair. Like his other two victims."

As she drove back toward Landsend Road, Bridget looked in the rearview mirror. Chase still stood in the snow staring after her, his red beanie askew.

"I don't know what Daphne sees in that man, Hank," she said, glancing back at the Irish setter. "But I don't trust him."

* * *

Santino's unexpected call came in before Bridget had made it back home. She hadn't expected to hear from the deputy marshal while he was conducting a manhunt for Monty Montclair.

"Did you find him?" she asked hopefully.

"Not yet," he admitted. "Monty Montclair is still on the run, and still considered a high-priority fugitive. Which is actually why I'm calling you."

Bridget remained silent, sensing she wasn't going to like what he was about to say.

"You see, we've notified all airports, train stations, bus stations, ports, and highway patrols to be on the lookout. But I got a call from the BAU saying that they believe Monty and Cassidy might both be on Monty's private yacht."

"You got a call from the BAU?"

She wrinkled her nose, not sure she'd heard him correctly.

"Yes, I guess Argus Murphy is an analyst now and he said he's analyzed the data on–"

"Hold on, Argus called you directly and told you he thinks Monty and Cassidy are on the *Monty's Mojo*?"

The fact that she'd heard nothing about Argus' theory before he'd notified the U.S. Marshals irritated her, even though she knew Argus didn't report to her.

But we're supposed to be working together on this, aren't we?

Swallowing back her annoyance, Bridget tried to focus on what Santino was saying.

"Yes, Argus pulled up the history at all the marinas in the area. He confirmed that Monty has rented a slip for a forty-foot cabin cruiser at the Shoreline Marina in Alexandria each winter for the last three years."

"The same boat has a reserved slip at the marina this year, too, but it's empty," Santino said. "And *Monty's Mojo* isn't docked at the house in Charity Point either. We had someone go out and check first thing this morning."

Bridget frowned.

"Okay, and you think there's something I can do to help?"

"We need to know where else Monty might take the boat, and I thought, since Scarlett trusts you, maybe you could go talk to her and ask her if she can think of anywhere else Monty might hole up."

She winced at the idea of trying to get useful information out of Scarlett Montclair while Monty was on the run and

Cassidy was missing.

According to Charlie, the poor woman had been calling several times a day wanting an update on the search for her daughter, and she was likely even now spiraling into a fog of drink and depression.

"Will you do this for me?" Santino asked. "It would save me from having to drive all the way over to Wisteria Falls."

Bridget hesitated.

If this is Argus' bright idea, why doesn't he go talk to Scarlett?

The prickly reply stuck in her throat, refusing to come out.

Santino needed her. And Gage had asked her to partner with Argus, which meant supporting his theories.

"Okay," she said. "I'll go over there now, but don't hold your breath. I doubt Scarlett will tell me anything useful."

She ended the call and steered the Explorer toward Coventry Lane, deciding she might as well get it over with.

But as she pulled up outside the charming house with the graceful columns, she looked down at her wet boots and wished she'd gone home to change first.

Going up to the front porch, she knocked on the door with a gloved hand. When there was no response, she stepped back and looked over at the window.

Someone moved behind the blinds, and Bridget thought she saw a flash of Scarlett's red hair.

"Scarlett! I need to ask you a few questions."

The door cracked open, revealing half of Scarlett's face.

"Don't worry, I don't want to come in," Bridget said, pointing to her boots. "My feet are pretty wet, and my dog is in the car. But I do need to ask you a question."

"I don't have time to talk," Scarlett said, sounding serious and sober. "Come back later."

Before she could close the door, Bridget impulsively stepped closer and stuck her boot between the door and the frame.

"The U.S. Marshals are searching for Monty, and they think he might be on his boat," she said. "They think you might know where it would be moored, or where he might take it. They thought of the Shoreline Marina-"

"No, he wouldn't take it there," Scarlett said quickly. "He would go south to Cape Charles. If he was on the run, he would try to get to the Atlantic."

Bridget nodded and removed her boot.

"Okay, is there a special place he'd stop at along the way? Somewhere he'd feel comfortable? Where he'd take Cassidy?"

"I'm not sure," Scarlett said, her eyes wide and scared behind the crack in the door. "But I've got to go."

Before Bridget could react, she slammed the door shut.

As she headed back to the car, Bridget pictured the fear in Scarlett's eyes, and a thought popped into her head.

Scarlett knows something. She may even know where Cassidy is.

CHAPTER TWENTY-ONE

Gage bent over and scooped up another shovelful of snow as Russell shouted for him to watch. Looking up, Gage saw the teenager lob a snowball toward the basketball hoop he had purchased as soon as the boy had moved in. The snowball missed its mark, splattering against the frozen net, and dislodging an icicle hanging from the rim.

"You need to work on your shot," Gage teased.

He turned as a white SUV pulled onto the driveway behind him. Thinking at first it must be Bridget, he did a double-take when he saw Argus behind the wheel.

"You and Bridget drive the same type of vehicle?"

Gage circled around the SUV as Argus stepped out.

"For people with such different personalities, it seems strange you'd have such similar taste in cars."

"Actually, I don't really like the car," Argus admitted. "But a white SUV is statistically the safest vehicle on the road, so..."

Gage laughed.

"I doubt Bridget used the same logic," he said. "I bet if

you asked her, she'd say something like the car *just felt right*."

Watching as Russell threw another misdirected snowball at the hoop, Argus handed the thick folder under his arm to Gage and picked up a handful of snow.

He packed the snow into a perfectly round sphere and lobbed a clean shot through the basketball hoop.

"That was awesome!" Russell yelled. "Can you do it again?"

"It's all about getting the perfect entry angle and depth."

Argus couldn't suppress a small smile.

"Do you play basketball?" Gage asked, sounding doubtful.

"No, not really," Argus admitted. "Managing a perfect arc is a lot harder when you're running and someone's sticking a hand in your face. But I do like to shoot around when I'm brainstorming a problem. It helps me think."

As Russell began to pack more snowballs, Gage handed back Argus' folder and gestured to the shovel.

"Did you come by to help, or was there something else?"

"I've been trying to figure out where Monty Montclair could be," he said, holding up the folder.

Gage cocked his head.

"I thought the Marshals were working on that."

"They are," Argus said. "But I figure the Bureau should be helping since Monty's a suspect in an open investigation. Charlie and Hale have already put out an APB on Monty's car, and they've been working with Homeland Security to make sure he doesn't get on a commercial plane, train, or boat."

Starting to shovel again, Gage listened as Argus continued.

"They told me Deputy Santino with the Marshals Service has been working with private airports and chartered flight services," he said. "But I called him up and told him I thought he should focus on Monty's yacht."

"You did what?" Gage asked, freezing in place. "You called the U.S. Marshall Service with a theory without talking to me and Bridget first?"

The harsh disapproval in his voice caused both Argus and Russell to stare at him with wide eyes.

"I guess I thought-"

"I know you want to catch this guy...so do I. But you can't just start communicating to other federal agencies on your own without consulting me and the rest of the team."

Argus lifted his chin.

"You mean Bridget, right?" he asked, his eyes suddenly blazing. "Cause you think she's the *real* profiler and I'm just a data geek. You'd rather have her than me any day."

"That's not true," Gage said, taken aback by the analyst's outburst. "But I'm glad you let me know how you're feeling. Because if we're going to be a team, we have to act like one. And more than that, we have to *feel* like one."

He pinned the analyst with another hard look.

"I told you from the beginning the BAU needs the skills that both you and Bridget bring to the table. But it can only work if you're playing as part of the team."

"That's what my coach says, too."

Both Gage and Argus turned at Russell's comment as if they'd forgotten he was there listening.

"Coach said there's no *I* in team."

Gage smiled at the earnest expression on Russell's face.

"That's right, son," he said, then swallowed hard, hoping the boy didn't mind him using the word. "Your coach must know that winning the game takes the whole team."

Glancing at Argus, he saw the analyst was smiling, too.

"I guess I'm a little too eager to prove myself," he said. "I'll remember Russell's advice from now on."

Russell looked pleased as he went back to preparing his pile of snowballs and Argus turned back to his folder.

"Anyway, I came here to say that I've mapped out all the locations between D.C. and Charity Point where a boat could dock and get supplies."

He pulled out a nautical map scattered with red dots.

"Now we've got to see if any of the marinas have rented a slip to a boat matching the HIN for *Monty's Mojo*."

"What's a HIN?" Russell asked.

The boy's question seemed to startle Argus.

"It's the Hull Identification Number," he said. "You do know what a hull is, don't you?"

The teenager shook his head.

"A hull is the body of a boat," Argus said. "And a HIN is a unique number that is affixed to the boat. It tells you where and who made it, and how old the boat is."

He cocked an eyebrow at Gage.

"You should teach this young man a thing or two about boats. You never know when it could come in useful."

"Yeah, sure," Gage said, rolling his eyes. "But I still don't know why you've interrupted our Saturday."

He crossed his arms over his broad chest.

"I thought we could start checking out these marinas today," Argus explained. "If Monty is on the boat, eventually he'll need to put in somewhere to get supplies and gas, so I thought I would talk to the dockmasters."

When Gage just stared at him, he continued.

"We could find out if they've noticed anything odd in the last few days. Anything that struck them as unusual or out of place," Argus said. "And we can ask about the pattern of activity at the marinas during winter. That way I can add the data to my algorithm."

"I thought you didn't like to conduct interviews," Gage said. "You told me you prefer to work behind the computer."

Argus shrugged.

"I'll do what needs to be done to find Monty Montclair."

The analyst's resolve surprised Gage.

"Bridget is convinced Monty isn't the Devil's Blade Killer," Gage reminded him. "She says he's a narcissist, so he doesn't fit the profile. Besides, Scarlett Montclair claims Monty wasn't the one she saw kill Harmony Baxter."

"I know that."

Cocking his head, Gage frowned.

"Then why are you in such a big hurry to bring Monty in?" he asked. "Are you saying Bridget is wrong...that

Monty *is* dangerous?"

"I don't think Monty Montclair is dangerous at all," Argus said, shaking his head. "But I do think he may be *in* danger. I think whoever killed Harmony Baxter may have planned to kill Monty, too. Either that or he wanted to set him up."

The words hung in the air between them.

"So, you want to find Monty in order to protect him?"

"Of course," Argus said. "But my main objective is to find the man responsible for the Devil's Blade murders and stop him from hurting anyone else."

He met Gage's eyes.

"The killer clearly has some sort of connection to Monty, his family, or his company. I believe that once we find Monty, and determine what that connection is, we'll find out who our killer is."

"Makes sense to me," Gage said, nodding his approval.

Plucking a snowball out of Russell's hand, Gage threw it toward the basketball hoop.

It smashed against the garage door and then slid to the ground, leaving a wet streak behind it.

"The arc...it's all about the arc," Argus said primly.

"You in the mood to see some boats?" Gage asked Russell, ignoring the teenager's bray of laughter at his miss. "Maybe grab some lunch on the way back?"

The boy nodded, still smiling.

"Okay, Argus," Gage said, straightening the knit cap on his head. "Let's go find *Monty's Mojo.*"

CHAPTER TWENTY-TWO

Scarlett Montclair gripped the steering wheel with shaking hands as she turned the white Mercedes into the Shoreline Marina parking lot. Leaving the engine running, she stared over at the pier, wondering if Cassidy really was on one of the boats floating in the choppy water.

In preparation to face Monty's wrath, she took a long swig from the slim, stainless steel whiskey flask she always carried in her purse, then shut off the engine.

Time to go get my little girl.

She climbed out of the car, tightened the belt of her expensive red woolen trench coat, and surveyed the area, making sure she wasn't being watched.

No one was in sight.

Walking toward the dock, she nearly slipped as she stepped up onto the slick wood. Looking down at her boots, Scarlett realized the four-inch heels probably hadn't been a good idea.

A gust of wind blew her coat against her legs and started her moving again. She needed to get Cassidy and get out of there.

She'd just have to take whatever crap Monty wanted to

throw at her and leave. As long as he let her leave with her little girl, she didn't care what he said.

And once Cassidy was with her, Monty would sail off into the sunset and she'd never have to deal with him again.

The only problem was she couldn't really remember where Monty parked his boat. All the docks and slips looked alike, as did most of the boats in the marina.

Spotting the marina office, Scarlett considered stopping in to ask for directions, then decided it wouldn't be a good idea to go in and announce her arrival. She didn't want anyone to know she was there, or that she was planning to meet Monty.

As she made her way further down the pier, she heard quiet footsteps on the wooden dock behind her.

Scarlett spun around to face Jagger Yardley.

His tall figure blocked out the sun as he loomed over her.

"What are you doing here?" she gasped, unable to step back without going into the water.

"That's what I was about to ask you," he said.

He reached out and grabbed hold of her wrist.

"I saw you leave the house and-"

"And you just thought you'd follow me," she said, wrenching her arm away. "I'm not paying you to spy on *me*."

One of her heels slipped off the edge of the pier and Jagger again grabbed her arm to steady her.

"You're an accident waiting to happen in those things."

He glared down with disdain at her boots.

"And I wasn't spying on you. I was coming to check on

you. You wouldn't answer my calls. I was worried something had happened to you."

"Nothing has happened to me," Scarlett insisted, lowering her voice. "But Monty called and said Cassidy was with him. He said if I met him here alone, he'd let her come home with me. He's planning to go on the run."

Glancing around the marina as if he'd just remembered where they were, Jagger began propelling her toward her car.

"He's playing you for a fool," he said, gripping her arm tighter as she tried to pull away. "He's laid an ambush I'll bet. Probably plans to abduct you, too, before taking off to God knows where."

The thought had never occurred to Scarlett. As she looked around the quiet marina, she saw no signs of an ambush.

"I think you've watched too many movies," she said as he steered her back to the Mercedes and opened the door. "And Monty isn't interested in taking me anywhere. Besides, he's not a violent man. That's probably the one good thing I can say about him."

"Just sit there and wait while I check it out," Jagger ordered. "Keep the doors locked. Don't move until I come back."

Slamming the door against her protests, he marched away down the pier, leaving Scarlett to fume on her own.

She was tempted to go after him, then decided she'd give him five minutes.

If he can't find Monty by then, I'll get out and do it myself.

The thought was followed by a familiar craving, and she

reached into her purse and pulled out the stainless-steel flask.

Unscrewing the top, she took a long sip and sighed as the liquid warmed her throat. Resting her head against the seat back, she closed her eyes.

* * *

Scarlett wasn't sure how long she'd been out when her eyes fluttered open. It took her a few minutes to remember where she was and what she was supposed to be doing.

Checking her watch in panic, she saw that it was already well past two o'clock and Jagger was nowhere to be seen.

What if Monty is already gone? What if he's taken Cassidy with him? I might never see my little girl again.

Jumping out of the car, she hear a thud and looked down to see the whiskey flask had fallen to the ground.

Golden brown liquid spilled onto the icy asphalt as she turned to see an old man walking down the pier toward her, his face weathered and creased into a deep frown.

"Excuse me!" she called out, deciding she didn't have time to be discrete. "I'm looking for Monty Montclair."

"So's the rest of the world," the man snorted without slowing his pace. "He rents slip N32. But he's not there."

Scarlett stopped in dismay.

"So, he's gone already?" she asked, her heart dropping.

"Looks that way," the man said, crossing to a battered van parked in the space marked *Reserved for Dockmaster*.

His eyes flicked down to her boots.

"Be careful, lady, you don't want to end up in the water today," he said. "It's cold enough to kill you."

As she watched the old man drive away, Scarlett reached for her phone. She'd have to call the police. Maybe even the FBI.

Her eyes widened as she saw the message from Jagger, then she sighed in relief.

Everything's okay. Meet me at Slip S23.

Looking down at the slip numbers stenciled on the wood, Scarlett precariously made her way over to the far dock, quickly reaching Slip S23, where a large, partially covered boat bobbed on the water. She didn't need to check the name on the other side of the hull to know it was the right boat.

She stepped onboard, her boots teetering on the snow-slicked deck, and crossed to the companionway steps.

"Monty?" she called. "Jagger?"

As she climbed down into the cabin, she immediately recognized the teak table and the furnishings she had helped Monty pick out several years before.

But no one was sitting at the table. The cabin appeared to be empty. Had she gotten the message too late? Had they all gone off somewhere without her?

Hearing a noise coming from the sleeping berth, she moved forward and opened the little door that separated the space from the main cabin.

A square of light from the overhead hatch fell on the bed. Scarlett gasped as she saw the small form on the bed.

"Cassidy?"

Her daughter didn't respond. As Scarlett started to move forward, a familiar voice spoke from the shadows.

"She'll be fine. She's just sleeping."

Before she could turn around, a muscled arm encircled her slender neck and yanked her back against a hard chest.

"I can't say the same for you."

Scarlett felt the cold steel of a blade against her throat. It pulsed in time with the blood pounding through her carotid artery and sent adrenaline coursing through her veins.

Wondering why he hadn't slit her throat already, Scarlett sucked in a deep breath, lifted her left leg, and stabbed her four-inch heel backward into her attacker's knee.

When his hold loosened, she dropped to the floor, then scrambled toward the companionway stairs.

She was halfway to the deck when she felt the knife whistle past her. Screaming in terror, she ducked to the side, continuing up the stairs and clambering onto the deck on her hands and knees.

A figure loomed over her as she stumbled to her feet.

Turning just as the knife plunged toward her, Scarlett instinctively lifted her hands to block the blow.

Pain ripped through her arm as the sharp blade easily cut through her coat sleeve to slice the tender flesh beneath.

The knife slashed down a second time, sending a hot squirt of blood onto the deck. She wheeled backward in a frantic attempt to escape the blade, realizing too late that she'd reached the end of the aft deck.

Her stomach lurched up into her throat and she emitted a high-pitched screech as she plunged into the icy water.

As she sank downward, a state of cold shock took over her body, making it impossible for her arms to move.

Finally, she got enough control of her arms to struggle toward the surface. As her head emerged above the water, she sucked in a deep lungful of air, then began to hyperventilate.

Struggling to catch her breath, she tried to kick her legs, desperate to get back on the boat, but her foot was stuck.

A dock line had wrapped itself around her leg.

Fear knifed through her as she heard the engine start.

As the boat began to move, she tried to scream, but the ice-cold water had frozen her lungs.

CHAPTER TWENTY-THREE

Bridget followed the server to a table by the window. Pulling off her coat, she hung it over the back of a chair and took a seat facing the door. Santino should be joining her any minute for a late lunch, although she didn't have much of an appetite.

Her mind kept replaying the disturbing encounters she'd had that morning. Serving up images of Roy Lafferty trying to comfort his wife. Of little Ginny Finch's small, worried face. Of Scarlett Montclair's fearful eyes behind the crack in the door.

Looking out the window, Bridget saw no sign of Santino or his red Chevy. She knew he was busy with the ongoing search for Monty, but she'd convinced him that he still had to eat, and he'd agreed to meet her at the café near his apartment.

She picked up the menu, then set it down again, deciding to call Charlie while she waited. She needed to tell someone her suspicions about Scarlett.

"Bridget, how are you?" Charlie said, sounding

distracted. "I'm just going in to meet with Vivian Burke to review the forensics from the Esme Dupree crime scene. Now that we know she was involved with Monty Montclair, we're taking another look at all the evidence."

"I still don't believe Monty killed Esme," Bridget said, unable to stop the words from spilling out. "I know you have to follow where the evidence leads you, but it doesn't make sense. Monty doesn't fit the profile."

Charlie cleared her throat.

"Is that what you were calling to tell me?"

"No, actually," Bridget admitted. "I was calling to let you know that I saw Scarlett Montclair this morning."

She spoke quickly, knowing Charlie didn't have much time.

"Santino asked me to find out if she knew where Monty could be, or if she had any idea where he might go in his boat."

"And did she?"

Charlie was suddenly interested.

"She said she didn't, but she seemed nervous. It was almost as if she was scared," Bridget said. "She pretty much slammed the door in my face. Once I left, I started thinking, and I'm pretty sure she knows something."

"You think she knows where Monty is?"

Bridget hesitated, wondering if she'd read too much into Scarlett's behavior. Borderline personality disorder could cause sudden intense episodes of anxiety or even panic attacks.

Her fear might have nothing to do with Monty.

But something in her eyes suggested she'd been lying.

"She didn't ask me about Cassidy," Bridget said aloud, suddenly realizing what had been niggling at her. "She has been looking for her daughter for days, calling you for updates nonstop, but this morning, she didn't even mention Cassidy or ask what was being done to find her."

"So, you think Scarlett already knows where Cassidy is?"

Bridget saw the flash of Santino's red Chevy pass by the window as she nodded.

"Yes, I think she knows something," Bridget said. "And whatever it is, it has her scared."

"We have been tracing her phone ever since Monty went on the run," Charlie said, sounding thoughtful. "Nothing's come up so far, but I can check to see where she is. Maybe that'll tell us what she's up to."

The door to the café opened and Santino strode in. Looking around, he saw Bridget sitting by the window.

"Santino's here," she said. "We're meeting for lunch. But if you need me to come over-"

"Have your lunch," Charlie insisted. "I'll check on Scarlett's whereabouts and let you know."

Dropping her phone in her pocket, she smiled as Santino sank into a chair with a weary exhale.

Bridget waved over the server to order soup and sandwiches, and then they filled each other in on the morning's activities.

According to Santino, there was still no sign of Monty or Cassidy. Based on the BAU's theory that Monty would be on his private yacht, they were preparing to start an official search on the Chesapeake Bay.

The server had just brought over a tray with two steaming bowls of soup and set them on the table when Charlie called.

"It's kind of weird," she said as soon as Bridget answered the phone. "Scarlett Montclair's phone went quiet within the last hour. We aren't picking up a signal at all."

Disappointment flooded through Bridget at the news. But before she could convey the information to Santino, Charlie continued.

"We think she must have turned the phone off or the battery may have died," she said. "But we can track where she's been. The last time her phone was on, she was at the Shoreline Marina in Alexandria."

Bridget's eyes widened.

"The Shoreline Marina? That's the place Argus predicted we would find Monty," Bridget said, raising her eyes to meet Santino's. "I asked Scarlett about it, and she specifically told me that Monty wouldn't go there."

"We'll maybe she decided to check it out," Charlie said.

Shaking her head, Bridget remembered the panic she'd heard in Scarlett's voice when she'd mentioned the marina.

"Maybe she knew he was there and wanted to keep us away for some reason," Bridget said. "I think we better get over there quickly and find out what's going on."

Santino was already getting to his feet as Bridget ended the call and stuck the phone back in her pocket.

Laying two twenty-dollar bills on the table to cover the uneaten soup and sandwiches, he headed toward the door.

"You can ride with me," he said, pointing to his Chevy, which he'd parked along the curb.

"Do you want me to look up the directions to the Shoreline Marina?" Bridget asked, noticing he hadn't entered the destination in the truck's navigation system.

He shook his head.

"I know the way," he said, easing the Chevy into traffic. "The Shoreline Marina is where I dock my boat. I was just out there on Wednesday looking for *Monty's Mojo*. It wasn't there."

As Bridget sat back in her seat, her stomach rumbled.

She tried not to think about their untouched lunch still sitting on the table as Santino merged onto the George Washington Memorial Parkway and sped toward Alexandria.

Twenty minutes later they pulled into the marina's parking lot and parked next to a dark gray SUV.

"Is that who I think it is?" Santino asked.

As he spoke, the door to the Navigator beside them opened and Terrance Gage emerged. Seconds later Argus Murphy climbed out of the passenger's seat, followed by a tall, thin teenager Bridget recognized as Russell Malone.

Santino was already striding forward as Bridget unbuckled her seatbelt and climbed out.

"You guys sure got here fast," he said, offering Gage a hand. "When did Charlie Day call you?"

"Nobody called us," Gage said, pumping Santino's hand and nodding at Bridget. "Argus' algorithm has us driving around to all the marinas in the area."

He threw an affectionate glance in Argus' direction.

"He's convinced Monty Montclair must have taken off on his boat, and we're going down the list."

"Well, Argus may be right," Santino said. "According to Charlie, Scarlett Montclair's phone was here within the last hour. We think she must have come here to meet Monty."

Santino waved them all down the pier, pointing to a boat in the water as they passed by.

"That's mine right there," he said without slowing down.

Bridget looked up just in time to catch the name on the hull.

Maribel.

CHAPTER TWENTY-FOUR

Santino felt Bridget's eyes on him as he continued walking down the pier toward slip N32. His heart squeezed as he moved past the *Maribel* floating in the icy water, feeling like a traitor for not stopping. He'd named the boat in memory of his late wife and always felt as if he were in safe hands on her deck.

But he'd come to the marina in search of Scarlett Montclair, the wife of a wanted fugitive, and he needed to focus on the task at hand. There was no telling what or who might be waiting for them up ahead.

Cornered men, especially the ones who had already killed before, were the most dangerous kind.

Resting one hand on his holster, he tensed as he neared the slip reserved for Monty's boat, then relaxed.

Slip N32 was still empty.

Monty's Mojo was nowhere to be seen.

Santino turned to Gage and Argus, who were only halfway down the dock, bringing up the rear.

"Nothing much to see here, guys," he called out. "The whole place is pretty much deserted. If Monty or Scarlett were here, they're gone now."

Bridget stopped next to him, looking down at the restless water below with a solemn expression.

"Could he have stored the boat in dry dock over the winter?" she asked softly.

"Not a forty-foot cabin cruiser," Santino said. "If she was smaller, like the *Maribel*, he'd have the option to keep her in the water or haul her out and put her in dry storage."

Bridget glanced up at him.

"Why do you keep your boat on the water?"

"It's not always this cold," he said, not quite meeting her eyes. "I guess I'm always hoping I'll get some time off on milder days so I can take her out."

When she didn't reply, he shrugged.

"It rarely happens, but I keep hoping."

He nodded over toward the marina office.

"Might as well check in with the dockmaster and see if he's seen Scarlett," Santino said, wanting to change the subject. "The guy's a real character. A modern-day Captain Ahab straight out of Moby Dick."

Waving Argus and Gage toward the office, he moved along the dock, scanning the boats as he passed.

"Why is that one all wrapped up?" Bridget asked, pointing to a shrink-wrapped speedboat.

"The wrap keeps out condensation," Santino said. "Some people actually live on cabin cruisers throughout the winter, although they usually have to rely on the marina's electrical and water hook-ups during the coldest months."

Bridget shivered at the idea as he tried to open the office door and found that it was locked.

"I guess Captain Ahab has already gone home for the day," Bridget said, putting her hands on her hips.

She turned and headed toward Argus, who appeared to be checking each slip against a document in his folder.

"What's he doing?" Santino asked Gage, who was waiting with Russell at the end of the dock.

"You mean Argus? He's collecting data for his charts and graphs," Gage said. "He uses them to-"

Bridget's sudden scream tore through the air, causing Santino to jump in fright.

Without thinking he ran forward, his eyes searching the dock for an assailant, then moving to Bridget, scanning her body for any signs of an injury.

"Down there!" she cried, pointing toward the water. "Scarlett's down there!"

Racing to the edge of slip S23, Santino looked down to see a bloom of red hair floating around a stark white face bobbing just under the water.

"Oh my God, is she..."

Bridget's question turned into a gasp as Scarlett's eyes fluttered open.

"Call 911!" Santino shouted to Gage, who had run up behind them. "Tell them we have a drowning victim."

Kneeling on the dock, Santino looked over the side.

Before he could change his mind, he sucked in a deep breath and lowered himself into the water, knowing he only had a few minutes before cold shock would set in and he'd lose coordination in his limbs

Scarlett's body felt stiff and cold beside him as Santino

wrapped an arm around her shoulders.

Attempting to pull her toward the ladder at the end of the dock, he met resistance. She wouldn't budge.

He looked down to see her leg entangled in a white dock line.

The rope had trapped her in the freezing water, keeping her tethered to the piling but close enough to the surface to allow the occasional gasp of air as the water rose and fell around her.

Santino's arms were growing numb and heavy as he tried to tread water with one hand while he reached for the tactical stainless steel folding knife in his holster.

With stiff fingers, he released the blade and sliced through the dock line, then pulled Scarlett toward the ladder where Argus and Gage were waiting.

As he pushed Scarlett up, he struggled to draw in a full breath, feeling his lungs begin to close.

Gasping for air, he watched as Scarlett's red coat disappeared onto the dock before pulling himself onto the bottom rung of the ladder.

His legs felt as if they were filled with sand as he hefted himself onto the wooden dock and forced his body to move toward the unconscious woman he'd pulled out of the water.

"She's not breathing," Bridget cried out.

A siren sounded in the distance, but it was too far away.

"You need to start CPR," Santino managed to say between chattering teeth. "Gage, you take Russell back to the car and wait for the paramedics."

Bridget had already positioned Scarlett on her back, opening her coat, and tilting her head back.

She looked up at Argus.

"Come on Argus, you handle the compressions and I'll take care of the breathing."

Staring down at Scarlett's motionless face in horror, Argus hesitated, then dropped to his knees.

"We can do this together, Argus," Bridget said, her blue eyes urging him on.

Santino sucked in shallow breaths as they began to work on Scarlett. They didn't stop until the paramedics were there, swarming the dock, and pushing Bridget and Argus out of the way.

"Look...her arm," Bridget said, pointing as the paramedics loaded Scarlett onto a gurney.

A rip in Scarlett's coat sleeve revealed a deep gash in her arm. Santino recognized it as a defensive wound.

"It wasn't an accident," he said in a hoarse voice. "She was attacked. The Devil's Blade Killer was here."

CHAPTER TWENTY-FIVE

Cassidy woke to the faint, high-pitched honking of a flock of snow geese flying overhead. She kept her eyes closed, listening for the yacht's engine, but it was still. The boat must be anchored or docked now, although when she'd woken earlier, it had been motoring along at a fast clip.

Light footsteps alerted her to her captor's presence in the cabin. She tried not to move as she felt his eyes on her.

"I know you're awake," he said, standing over her. "I brought you something to eat. And some water."

Opening her eyes, she blinked up at him, startled to see his bare face. He'd worn some sort of ski mask the night he'd snatched her outside her house and had stayed in the shadows since then, although she'd been sleeping much of the time.

She wondered if he'd now removed the mask because he no longer feared she'd get a chance to identify him to the police.

Maybe he's decided to kill me.

The thought wasn't as scary as she imagined it should be. Perhaps whatever drugs he'd been giving her prevented her from feeling fear, or much of anything else for that matter.

"You can use the head if you need to," he said.

Cassidy frowned, confused.

"The bathroom...you can use the bathroom."

"I'm okay," she tried to say but produced only a whisper.

Leaning forward, he held out a thermos.

When she made no move to take it, he tipped the cold water into her mouth. She tried to swallow it, but her throat was sore and dry. Some of the water ended up trickling down her chin.

He closed the thermos and dropped it on the bed, then threw a small, vacuum-packed bag next to it.

"Rations for the day," he said, leaning a shoulder against the doorjamb. "We won't be stopping to resupply for a while, so we'll have to make do with what we've got."

She looked at the bag and nodded.

"Where are we going?" she said, her throat feeling better now that she'd had a drink.

"Don't you worry about that."

His eyes narrowed.

"All you need to know is that the water is cold out there. Cold enough to freeze your lungs up within minutes if you're dumb enough to jump overboard or try to escape."

Shivering at the image his words conjured, she could almost feel the dark, wintry water washing over her.

"Why are you keeping me here?" Cassidy blurted out before she could stop herself. "What are you going to do with me?"

"You're here because of your parents."

He spoke in a low, raspy voice Cassidy didn't like.

"You see, your parents made an enemy," he said, "And that enemy has been paying me to watch them. I've been watching all of you for a very long time."

Cassidy shrank back against the mattress.

"Your parents are no good," he continued. "You might as well forget about them. They don't care about you anyway."

Anger began to simmer in her chest at his words.

"Who are you?" she asked in a whisper.

She knew she'd seen the man before, but whatever drugs he'd given her had made her head foggy and she couldn't remember where.

Perhaps with her father. Maybe at his office, or even at one of the many parties he'd hosted over the years.

"You can call me Lucky," he said with a shrug.

Wondering what his real name was, Cassidy decided not to ask him. For now, if she wanted to survive, it would be safest to just agree with whatever he said.

She would have to play along until the time was right.

"You're right, you know, Lucky," she said, dropping her eyes. "My parents are no good. That's why I ran away. I don't even want to go back. You'd be doing me a favor to take me as far away from them as possible."

When he just looked at her with a cold stare, she continued.

"And you'd be doing them a favor by getting rid of me. The only reason they're fighting over me is to spite each other."

He cocked his head as if considering her words and lifted a hand to scratch at his chin, revealing the tattoo on his forearm.

"What's that?" she asked. "Is it a devil or an animal?"

"Both, I guess. It's a tattoo I got in the Marines."

He flexed his arm with obvious pride.

"You were in the Marines?"

She tried to sound impressed.

"Yep, I was in the recon unit. I was involved with amphibious reconnaissance, ground reconnaissance, surveillance...you name it."

Before she could respond, the man seemed to lose interest in the conversation.

He got up and crossed to the stairs.

"Lucky?"

He stopped and looked back at her.

"What are you really going to do with me?"

At first, she thought he wasn't going to answer.

"I'm keeping you as leverage," he finally said. "And maybe for ransom. If I get what I want, I may even let you go."

A glimmer of hope lit up in her chest. Maybe if her parents paid this man ransom, he would let her live.

Picking up the thermos, she opened it and took another drink, then pointed to the bathroom door.

"I think I will use the...the head," she said.

She slid off the foam mattress and stepped into the compact bathroom, pushing the door shut behind her.

As she stood in front of the mirror, she noticed blood

spatter on the glass shower door behind her.
    Turning around, she stared at it with sudden clarity.
    He would never let her leave there alive.

CHAPTER TWENTY-SIX

Bridget parked in the crowded lot outside Saint Agatha's Memorial Hospital and stepped out of her Explorer. Looking up at the box-like brick building, her eyes searched the long row of windows on the top floor, half-expecting to see Scarlett Montclair's fiery hair and green eyes behind the glass.

Instead, she saw only the reflection of the gathering clouds overhead and wondered if they were in for more snow.

Walking into the building, she headed toward the bank of elevators to her left, just past the hospital chapel.

As she waited for the elevator, her eyes settled on a bronze plaque mounted outside the chapel entrance.

The plaque had been dedicated at the time the hospital was built more than sixty years earlier. It included an engraved image of a nurse praying by a sleeping patient's bedside, along with a short prayer attributed to the hospital's namesake.

Lord of all, you see my heart, you know my desires. Possess all that I am. I am your sheep:

make me worthy to overcome the devil.
-Saint Agatha, 250 A.D.

A chill rolled down Bridget's spine. The woman she'd come to see had faced a real-life devil just that morning and was now fighting for her life.

There was still a chance she would overcome her injuries.

Perhaps St. Agatha's prayer will be answered, after all.

Stepping into the elevator, Bridget pressed the button for the fourth floor and inhaled deeply, preparing herself for whatever she might find in Scarlett Montclair's hospital room.

But as she walked into Room 428, she was shocked to see the woman unconscious and on a ventilator with an endotracheal tube inserted into her airway.

The bedside monitor beeped and flashed, displaying Scarlett's blood pressure, heart rhythm, temperature, and breathing rate while a probe attached to her finger monitored her oxygen levels.

"Dr. Bishop?"

Bridget jumped as Teddy Montclair spoke from a chair against the wall. As he stood, Bridget saw him wipe at his eyes with the back of his hand.

"Sorry," he said with a self-conscious sniffle. "I wasn't expecting any visitors, and..."

He swallowed hard as Bridget dug in her purse and pulled out a pack of tissues. Holding one out to him, she met his sad, red-rimmed eyes.

"This must be very hard on you," she said. "To have your

father missing and your stepmother...here."

Holding the tissue to his face, Teddy nodded.

"Everyone must think my father did this," he said, his voice cracking on the words. "But he isn't a violent man. He would never hurt anyone. At least, not physically."

He cleared his throat, looking over at Scarlett's unconscious figure in the bed with a pained expression.

"I know he can be cruel and selfish," Teddy continued. "In fact, I know better than anyone. I watched my mother go through hell with all his *philandering* before he left her to marry a woman young enough to be his daughter."

Bridget glanced over at Scarlett, worried that the woman might somehow hear his bitter words, but Teddy didn't seem concerned.

"My mother loved my father, and his infidelity was excruciating for her. Breast cancer was the official cause of death, but I think she really died from a broken heart."

"I'm sorry," Bridget said softly. "You've lost your mother and now you may lose your stepmother. It can't be easy for you."

He shook his head.

"It isn't me I'm worried about. It's Cassidy. How will I be able to break the news to Cassidy that her mother's gone?"

The anguish in his voice prompted Bridget to reach out a hand and rest it on his arm.

"Hopefully you won't have to," she said. "The doctors are saying Scarlett has a good chance to pull through this. Now, we all need to focus on finding your sister. Cassidy will want to be here when her mother wakes up."

She saw the hesitation in Teddy's eyes, and then he nodded resolutely.

"Yes, you're right. There's nothing I can do for Scarlett now. She's in the doctor's hands," he said, moving toward the door. "I need to focus on Cassidy. I need to find my sister."

* * *

Bridget paced outside Scarlett Montclair's hospital room replaying her conversation with Teddy, wondering where Monty's son had gone in such a hurry.

Does he know where Cassidy is? Could he be going to see her and tell her about her mother?

She was tempted to go after him and find out, but there was something she needed to do first.

Her stomach clenched at the thought of what was to come.

When Shirley and Roy finally stepped out of the elevator holding hands, Bridget forced a sympathetic smile to her face, pushing back the guilt that flooded through her at the memory of the last time they'd met.

Shirley Lafferty had begged her to help find their granddaughter, and she had promised to do her best.

But so far, her best hadn't been good enough.

Cassidy was still missing, and Scarlett was fighting for her life. Now she had to tell the poor couple that she may have been too late to save their daughter from the Devil's Blade Killer.

WHERE EVIL HIDES

"What's happened, Dr. Bishop?" Shirley asked, clutching Bridget's hand. "The hospital called and said Scarlett's in critical condition. But she is going to make it, isn't she?"

"We found her in the water at the marina where Monty kept his boat," Bridget said softly.

There was no easy way to explain the ordeal Scarlett had been through. No way to soften the blow.

"It looks as if she was attacked with a knife," Bridget added. "We don't know for sure how long she was in the water. The doctors will give you an update on her condition, but I wanted to be here to tell you what happened. I know it's a shock."

"Thank you for finding her," Roy said, his face sagging with worry as he led Shirley into the room.

Bridget inhaled deeply, then started toward the elevator.

When the doors opened, she was surprised to see Santino. He'd gone home to shower and change into clean, dry clothes.

Stepping out into the corridor, he took her hand.

"Are you doing alright?" he asked.

"I'm fine," she assured him.

He looked toward the door to Room 428.

"And Scarlett?"

"She's in critical condition," Bridget said. "Still unconscious and on a ventilator. Her parents are in there with her now."

Santino jumped and squeezed Bridget's hand as an announcement came over the hospital's loudspeaker.

"Code Blue in Room 324! Code Blue in Room 324!"

"I don't like hospitals," Santino said, releasing his grip on her hand. "It brings back bad memories."

Staring up at him, she cocked her head.

"Memories of Maribel?" she asked softly.

He shook his head.

"Memories of my father," he said. "After the accident, he was on life support for days before the doctors could talk my mother into turning it off. It was hard on all of us and ever since then…"

His words trailed off as two nurses rushed past them, pushing their way into the room.

"Has something happened?" Bridget called out, but the nurses didn't respond as the door closed behind them.

As she looked toward the room, Shirley came to the door and called out hopefully in their direction.

"She's awake," Shirley said. "My baby girl's awake."

CHAPTER TWENTY-SEVEN

Charlie strode toward Gage and Argus, who stood beside a gray Navigator in the busy parking lot of the Shoreline Marina. She motioned for them to wait as she stopped to direct half a dozen uniformed officers to cordon off the entire marina, and not to let anyone else on the pier.

"The only people on that pier should be agents and techs from the FBI incident response team," she called out.

Continuing on toward the two BAU agents, Charlie noted Argus' disheveled appearance, and the slightly stunned look on his pale, freckled face.

"I hear you found Scarlett Montclair," she said. "Could you tell how badly she was injured?"

She pointed to a dried streak of blood on Argus' jacket.

"I'm guessing that was from the victim?"

Argus looked down in confusion, his eyes widening with revulsion as he saw the blood.

Unzipping the jacket, he pulled it off and shoved it toward Charlie, already shivering in the frigid breeze off the water.

"You better get him inside and warmed up," Charlie said to Gage, motioning over a technician to take the offending jacket.

He nodded.

"Yeah, and I think Russell's had enough of this marina for one day," he agreed, looking toward the SUV where the teenager sat waiting in the backseat.

Hesitating, he glanced over at Wally Truman. The belligerent old dockmaster sat stubbornly silent at the end of the pier.

"Think you can handle that one on your own?" Gage asked in a low voice. "I can tell these two to wait if–"

"No, I've got this," she assured him. "Besides, Hale should be here any minute. He said he was on the way."

Charlie waited until the Navigator had pulled out of the lot before she walked over to the dockmaster.

"Wally Truman? I'm Special Agent Charlie Day with the FBI. I understand you were on duty today when a woman was pulled out of the water."

"I was on a break," he muttered.

He lifted a hand to scratch at his straggling gray beard.

"Did you see this woman at the marina today?"

Charlie held up a photo of Scarlett Montclair.

"Sure did," he said. "And I told her to be careful."

"Why would you tell her that?"

The dockmaster snorted.

"Cause she was prancing around on the dock in boots with a heel this high," he said, holding his fingers apart to indicate three or four inches. "I told her she was gonna fall in."

"And you think that's what happened?" Charlie asked.

Wally shrugged.

"How about this man. Have you seen *him* today?"

Charlie produced a photo of Monty Montclair.

Keeping his eyes on the photo, Wally shook his head.

"Nope. I know Mr. Montclair, and I haven't seen him for quite a while," he said, lowering his voice. "But some guy who worked for him came by about a week ago and took the boat. Said Mr. Montclair wanted to keep it quiet."

He exhaled and looked up to meet Charlie's eyes.

"The guy gave me a hundred bucks to keep my mouth shut if anyone came by asking about it."

A surge of adrenaline shot through Charlie.

"So, you did see a man take the *Monty's Mojo*?" she asked, forcing herself to hold back a rebuke about his lies to the police. "We're gonna need a new statement and a description."

Wally looked alarmed.

"I didn't see him that good," he stammered. "My eyes are old...and he had this hat and coat on."

"You'll do your best," she said tartly. "Especially since you lied to Detective Quinn the first time she asked you what you'd seen. I'm sure you're eager to clear this up."

Seeing Hale walking toward the pier, Charlie called over an agent from the response team and left the dockmaster to give his revised statement.

"Where have you been?" she called out to Hale, her voice

sharper than she'd intended. "Scarlett Montclair was attacked with a knife, and she half-drowned in the water. She's down at St. Agatha's Hospital now in critical condition."

"Yes, I got your message and came here as soon as I could," Hale said, not breaking his stride as he moved toward the pier and surveyed the dock at Slip S23.

He turned to Charlie.

"Has the team gone into the water to search for evidence?" he asked. "If she was attacked by someone with a knife and ended up going in the water, maybe the knife went in, too."

Charlie opened her mouth to reply, but Hale was already on his phone requesting a dive team.

Thirty minutes later she was watching a woman in a wet suit lowering herself into the water beside the dock.

The diver hadn't been underwater for more than a minute when her head popped back above the surface.

Pulling off her mask, she stared up at the waiting faces.

"There's something down there alright, but it's not a knife," she said. "It's a body."

She sucked in another breath.

"Looks like a man's body," she continued. "I'd say someone weighed it down and threw it overboard."

Charlie stood in stunned silence as the dive team worked to document the scene below and bring up the body.

Once they'd deposited the dead man onto the wooden dock, Charlie bent over to study the lifeless face.

"Jagger Yardley," she murmured to Hale, who stood

beside her staring down at the thick white anchor line wrapped around Jagger's throat. "Whoever threw him in the water wanted to make sure he never came back up.

* * *

Charlie and Hale arrived at Saint Agatha's Memorial Hospital just past dark, riding up in the elevator in silence.

When they stepped out onto the Critical Care floor, Bridget and Santino were waiting for them in the hallway, along with Scarlett's doctor.

Dr. Nimitz was a serious-looking woman in her mid-forties. She wore light blue scrubs and a cap over her hair, which had been pulled back into a tight ponytail.

"Earlier today Mrs. Montclair regained consciousness for a brief period," she said briskly after introductions had been made. "But she's on a ventilator and can't speak yet."

"When do you think we can question her?" Hale asked.

The doctor frowned.

"First we need to get her off the ventilator," she said.

"Ok, when can that happen?" Hale persisted.

Seeing the doctor's shoulders stiffen, Charlie spoke up.

"I'm sorry if we seem impatient," she said "But we believe Scarlett may have seen her assailant. We also believe the man who did this to her is very dangerous. And he's still out there."

Dr. Nimitz's face softened.

"If she continues to improve overnight, we may be able to take her off the ventilator as early as tomorrow," she conceded. "We'll need to make sure she's out of danger first."

Charlie nodded in relief.

"Of course, she may not be strong enough for a full interview right away," the doctor cautioned. "And neurological damage is a possibility."

Once Dr. Nimitz had gone, Charlie turned to Bridget.

"I'm not sure if you've heard yet, but we found another body in the water at the marina. Jagger Yardley is dead."

Before Bridget could respond, Charlie's phone buzzed.

She looked down to see that Luis Cortez was calling.

The FBI cyber technician had started tracking Monty Montclair's email account after his arrest, and he'd been conducting technical surveillance on the CEO's devices and applications ever since he'd gone on the run.

"An email was sent through Monty's email account earlier this afternoon," Cortez said. "I just forwarded it to you. You're going to want to read it ASAP."

Charlie lowered the phone and navigated to her email. Seeing Cortez's message, she tapped to open the attached file.

She scanned the message, then cursed under her breath when she read the recipient's name.

"Monty sent a message to Scarlett earlier today," she said, looking over at Bridget. "He told her to meet him at the marina this afternoon. He said to come alone. And he claimed he has Cassidy with him."

CHAPTER TWENTY-EIGHT

Scarlett tried to lift her hands and screamed as the knife sliced toward her, but she couldn't move, and no sound would come out of her mouth. Her eyes popped open in terror. Staring up at the unfamiliar hospital ceiling, she blinked the dream away as the memories came flooding back.

He tried to kill me...but I'm still alive.

Feeling groggy, she forced her heavy eyes to move around the room, taking in the ventilator, and the tubes and wires snaking around her body.

Looking to her right, she caught a glimpse of the sky through the window. The sun was rising.

Have I been in the hospital all night?

Her thoughts automatically turned to Cassidy. She'd gone to the marina to meet Monty and to get her daughter.

But Monty hadn't been there.

An image flashed into her mind. Her daughter in the sleeping berth. Motionless on the bed.

Cassidy was there. But where was Monty?

Had Jagger been right? Had Monty tricked her into going to the marina? Had he been behind the attack?

The thought of Jagger Yardley conjured another, more disturbing image. Scarlett tried to push it away but failed.

Closing her eyes, she again saw Jagger Yardley's open, lifeless eyes under the water. He was staring up at her.

She'd tried to untether the dock line around her leg, but her arms had been too numb. Too heavy.

The water had splashed up and over her face again and again. As she'd looked down to find the source of the line, she'd seen Jagger.

She'd opened her mouth to scream but had managed only a wet gurgle before her head was under the icy water again.

Not daring to look down again, too frightened of what she would see, she'd kept her face up and had waited for the end to come. Had waited for it all to be over.

But someone had come to save her.

Dr. Bishop was there, wasn't she? She came looking for me and for Cassidy. She didn't give up on us.

The thought calmed her, and Scarlett relaxed against the pillow, allowing her muscles to soften and her eyes to focus on the sunrise outside.

I need to get out of here as soon as possible. I need to tell them who attacked me. I need them to go find Cassidy.

Her heart quickened as she realized the man who had killed Jagger, and who had tried to kill her, now had Cassidy.

There was no telling what he might do to her.

She couldn't just stay in the hospital while a maniac with

a knife sailed away with her daughter.

No, I need to go find Cassidy. And when I do, I'll never let her out of my sight again. I'll be the best mother ever. I'll even go to therapy like Dr. Bishop recommended. If I can just get out of here...

Her eyes grew heavier and heavier as she made plans to find her daughter and start a new, better life.

She'd just drifted off to sleep when the door creaked open, and she heard soft footsteps on the tiled floor.

The nurse must be there.

Scarlett struggled to open her heavy eyes. She had to tell the nurse to take out the tube. She needed to get out of the bed.

Squinting toward the door, she saw a dark figure standing in the shadows, just beyond the reach of the light coming in through the window.

She waited for the nurse to step closer, or to turn on the light, but the figure didn't move.

What's the matter? Does the nurse think I'm asleep?

A stealthy, furtive movement in the shadow sent a shiver of fear down Scarlett's spine.

"You're awake," a deep voice said as a man stepped out of the shadows. "That's good. I'd hoped we'd get a chance to talk before it was all...*over*."

He moved toward the bed on silent feet, stepping into the streak of sunlight shining in through the window, and revealing his face.

Scarlett's eyes widened in shock and confusion as he reached down and took her hand.

"You see, I need to make sure you don't tell anyone what you saw yesterday," he said softly. "So, I brought a little something to ensure your eternal silence."

He held up a vial of clear liquid.

"Taken from the Montclair Biotech lab," he said with a sardonic grin. "I thought that would be appropriate."

Scarlett tried again to move her arm and knock the vial from his hand, but her arm remained still and useless beside her as he reached up to inject the liquid into her IV.

A burning pain lit up inside her as the drug began to seep into her bloodstream, working its way throughout her body.

Bending over, he whispered next to her ear.

"I've already killed Monty. And Cassidy is next."

CHAPTER TWENTY-NINE

Bridget woke early on Sunday morning after a fitful night of bad dreams. Instead of her usual nightmares featuring one or more serial killers from her past, her dreams had been flooded with dark, choppy water washing over open, lifeless eyes.

She jerked awake to the echo of her own scream, and Hank jumped up, too. The Irish setter was too spooked to go back to sleep, so Bridget got dressed and took him for a walk, trudging through the fresh snow on tired legs.

Once she'd given Hank his breakfast, she got into the Explorer and drove toward Saint Agatha's Memorial Hospital, hoping Scarlett had regained consciousness.

She wanted to ask the woman if she'd seen her attacker.

No matter what the evidence pointed to, Bridget still couldn't believe Monty was the Devil's Blade Killer.

But what about the email he sent? And the fingerprints and DNA?

The little voice in her head had a point.

Perhaps she was ignoring the data. Maybe Argus was right. Maybe her intuition and the psychological profiles she'd created were nothing but wishful thinking and conjecture.

But then again, someone else could have sent the email using Monty's account to lure Scarlett to the marina. Maybe he is being set up after all.

There was only one way to know for sure. She needed to ask Scarlett. Hopefully this time, the woman would be honest with her answers, even if she couldn't talk.

Bridget had already thought of the ventilator and the fact that Scarlett would be partially sedated and unable to speak.

She figured Scarlett might be able to find a way to answer a series of yes or no questions.

Maybe she can blink once for yes and two for no.

But as the elevator opened onto the ICU floor, Bridget saw a knot of nurses and doctors standing outside the door to Room 428 with downcast expressions.

"What's happened?" Bridget asked Dr. Nimitz.

"Scarlett Montclair is dead," the doctor said. "It appears she had a cardiac arrest. It happens sometimes with near-drownings. The water...."

Bridget wasn't listening. She was too busy thinking of Shirley and Roy Lafferty, and of Cassidy.

If Cassidy was ever found, she'd have to tell the girl they'd been unable to save her mother.

It just doesn't make sense. It doesn't seem fair.

Scarlett had been attacked and thrown into freezing water but had still managed to survive. They'd found her just in time. They'd been so close to saving her.

They were even planning to take her off the ventilator as soon as the doctor had given the okay.

So why would her heart just give out? Why would she suddenly have a fatal heart attack?

Bridget went into the room and stood by the bed, looking down at Scarlett. The ventilator had been removed, and her face had relaxed into a peaceful repose on her pillow.

Sunshine from the window illuminated her with an ethereal glow, making her delicate features appear strangely serene.

Troubled by Scarlett's untimely death, Bridget remembered what her father had told her at the start of her career.

"*Listen to your gut. It'll tell you if something doesn't feel right.*"

The simple advice had served her well over the years.

Soft footsteps sounded behind her, and she turned to see Charlie Day's grim face.

"We need to get blood work," Bridget said. "We need a quick autopsy and full toxicology screen. We need to find out what really happened here."

* * *

Bridget had just finished breaking the news about Scarlett's death to Shirley and Roy Lafferty when Opal Fitzgerald arrived on the fourth floor to collect the body.

"Don't you look nice today," Bridget said, taking in Opal's make-up, and the pink skirt suit visible under her lab coat.

"I came straight from church," Opal explained. "Didn't

want to take the time to go home and change."

The medical examiner pulled on gloves as she read Scarlett's chart and performed a brief external exam.

"Defensive wounds?" she asked when she saw the bandages on Scarlett's forearms.

Bridget nodded.

"We think she fought off her attacker and went overboard," she said. "And we aren't sure how long she was in the water. They had her on a ventilator and she came around. The doctor thought she'd be okay but then...*this*."

"Well, it could be a case of dry drowning," Opal said, cocking her head. "It happens sometimes when water is inhaled. The muscles can spasm and block the airway."

Checking inside Scarlett's mouth, she shook her head.

"But I don't see the usual signs such as bloody froth."

She looked back at Bridget.

"It could be a case of secondary drowning. Water inhaled into the lungs can cause pulmonary edema. But we won't know for sure until we open her up and look at her lungs."

"How soon can you do it?" Bridget asked. "How quickly can we get an autopsy?"

Opal studied Bridget's anxious face and sighed.

"I guess I could do it this afternoon," she said. "Cecil will probably be glad to have the house to himself so he can watch his basketball game without interruptions."

"That would be great," Bridget said, relieved. "And we want a full toxicology screen as soon as possible."

She watched as Opal and her forensic technician Greg Alcott loaded Scarlett's body on a gurney and rolled it to the elevator.

Charlie was waiting for her in the hall.

"Looks like Opal will do the autopsy today," Bridget said, riding with Charlie down to the lobby.

When they stepped off the elevator, Bridget was startled to see a swarm of reporters waiting outside the hospital doors.

A man's voice called out loudly as they approached the parking garage.

"I hear the Devil's Blade Killer has struck again," he said. "Rumor is that this time the victim was a man and that there could be a surviving witness."

Bridget looked up to see Chase Grafton, but Charlie stepped between them before Bridget could reply.

She looked back and met Bridget's eyes.

"It's time to get the public involved in the search for Cassidy," Charlie said. "We need all the help we can get."

Turning to Chase Grafton, she addressed the podcaster in a loud voice that carried to the press milling outside the lobby.

"The reports are wrong," she said brusquely. "There is no surviving witness to the latest attack. Jagger Yardley was killed at the Shoreline Marina yesterday and Scarlett Montclair died at the hospital this morning. Her daughter Cassidy is missing."

Avoiding Chase's eager eyes, Bridget stood quietly behind Charlie as she made a brief statement asking anyone with information about sixteen-year-old Cassidy Montclair's whereabouts to contact the FBI hotline.

"We believe Cassidy could be in danger, and that she may be with her father, Monty Montclair, a fugitive wanted by the U.S. Marshals Service and the FBI."

Charlie pushed the reporters out of her way and pulled Bridget behind her toward the parking lot.

"Are you going to be okay?" Charlie asked when they reached Bridget's Explorer. "I've got to go give Calloway an update and Hale has gone AWOL. He was with me when we got to the hospital, but he's disappeared again."

She took in Bridget's morose nod.

"Is Santino around?" she asked. "He'll cheer you up."

Bridget looked up at the gray sky and shook her head.

"He's with the search party looking for Monty and Cassidy on the Bay," she said. "He's taken *Maribel* out on the water."

CHAPTER THIRTY

Santino steered the *Maribel* along the snow-covered coast near Charity Point, searching for any sign of *Monty's Mojo*, convinced that the boat's billionaire owner would want to drop anchor somewhere familiar and close to home if he hadn't already managed to escape the area.

Several other boats were searching further up the shore, including a Charity Point PD patrol boat captained by Detective Peggy Quinn, who had access to the network of cameras and radar used by the various marine law enforcement agencies monitoring the Chesapeake Bay.

The search team had decided to keep a low profile. They didn't want to alert the press or the locals that they were looking for Monty or his boat, since it might lure people out on the water, impeding the search and putting lives at risk.

Feeling a soft vibration in his coat pocket, Santino pulled out his phone to see Bridget's name on the display.

"Scarlett Montclair is dead," she said bluntly. "I thought you'd want to know right away. Although, you may have already heard about it on the news after Charlie Day's impromptu news conference outside the hospital."

Santino raised his eyebrows.

"No, I haven't heard anything. What exactly did she say?"

"She said Scarlett and Jagger Yardley were victims of the Devil's Blade Killer, and that the FBI and the U.S. Marshals Service are looking for fugitive Monty Montclair and his daughter Cassidy."

Slowing the engine, Santino groaned.

"So much for being discreet," he said. "Now everybody on the Bay will be looking for Monty."

"Isn't that a good thing?" Bridget asked.

"Not if he really is the Devil's Blade Killer," he said ominously. "And not if he has more of those knives."

Bridget was silent for a long beat.

"I'm still not convinced Monty is a killer," she finally admitted. "Something doesn't fit. His psychological profile for one thing is all wrong. And then the neat way everything points to Monty just seems too staged."

"Are you suggesting Monty wouldn't be careless enough to leave his fingerprints on the murder weapon left at the scene?" Santino asked. "Or that he wouldn't target women he is known to be involved with?"

He had to admit it was hard to believe a man who'd been smart enough to build a billion-dollar business could be so foolish.

"I'm saying that we may have overlooked other possibilities because we had Monty in our sights since the beginning. He was a perfect suspect, delivered to us at the crime scene. He was practically tied up with a bow."

Hearing the frustration in Bridget's voice, Santino adopted a soothing tone.

"It's been a stressful weekend," he said. "Why don't you go home and get some rest and–"

"I'm going to attend Scarlett's autopsy," Bridget said. "Opal Fitzgerald's agreed to do it this afternoon. I've already asked my father to watch Hank for me tonight."

Santino heard the resolve in her voice and knew it would be futile to point out that she may be getting too emotionally involved in the investigation.

He'd come to accept that Bridget put her whole heart into every case. It was the only way she worked.

"Okay, I'll let you know if we find anything out here," he said. "Although to be honest, I'm starting to lose hope. There are thousands of miles to cover, and it'll be dark soon enough."

"Be careful out there," Bridget said, suddenly sounding very far away. "I don't want anything to happen to you."

She hung up before he could return the sentiment.

Bringing his mind back to the water in front of him, Santino kept scanning the horizon, even though he knew it might all be a waste of time.

Monty's Mojo could be anchored along thousands of miles of shoreline or docked at countless moorings along the way.

He was tempted to divert course to Sofia's by the Shore. If he went to the bed and breakfast, he could get out of the cold wind and have a hot meal.

He thought longingly of his mother's warm kitchen but knew that for now, food and comfort would have to wait.

Deciding to make another pass by Charity Point and Monty's vacation home on Windwalker Way, he pulled out his binoculars.

A few miles north he spotted a flock of turkey vultures circling low over a fallen tree in a marshy area along the shore.

The scavengers' long dark wings flapped slowly as they descended, lowering their small red heads to peck at something caught within the bare branches.

"What is that?"

Zooming in on the gruesome scene, he blinked, not sure he could believe his eyes, then put out a call for assistance as he steered the boat toward shore.

He threw anchor in the shallow water and, for the second day in a row, lowered himself into icy water.

The water was no more than four feet deep, and he held his gun up over his head as he waded onto the rocky shore and jogged toward the spot where he'd seen the vultures.

As he drew near, he scanned the area to make sure no one was in range, then let off a gunshot into the air near the birds.

The vultures scattered into the sky as Santino let off another shot, wanting to make sure they were gone.

Once the scavenger birds were out of sight he moved forward and looked down at their meal.

The search for Monty Montclair was over.

CHAPTER THIRTY-ONE

Gage looked over at Russell, who stared out of the Navigator's window, quiet and withdrawn after the emotionally draining afternoon. They were coming back from the women's detention center, where he'd gotten the chance to see his mother. The visits seemed to depress his foster son, but Russell insisted on going regularly.

Glancing over at the teenager, Gage caught sight of his own tired, worried eyes in the rearview mirror.

He hadn't been able to sleep the night before and had gone downstairs to find Russell asleep on the sofa as a mindless reality show played on the television.

Kenny's son deserves better. But all he's got right now is me.

Gage rubbed at his chest, trying to be discreet, wondering if he should make an appointment to see the doctor.

Maybe it's my heart.

He dismissed the idea. He was only fifty years old, after all, and he was still in pretty good shape.

And isn't fifty supposed to be the new thirty?

Turning the Navigator onto Mansfield Place, he saw a white SUV in the driveway. At first, he thought Bridget had stopped by unannounced, but when he pulled up next to the vehicle, he saw Argus' carrot-hued hair through the window.

The behavioral analyst didn't look up until Gage knocked on the window and beckoned him inside.

Argus emerged from the SUV with a bulky laptop bag slung over his shoulder and a thick folder clutched in his hands.

He hurried toward the door, holding up a hand to Russell, who gave him a halfhearted high-five. The teenager headed upstairs without his usual banter.

"He's got homework to do," Gage said by way of an explanation for Russell's quick exit.

Leading Argus into the kitchen, he flipped on the light to reveal Sarge curled up in the cat bed.

Snuggled into his new favorite spot, the tomcat lifted his tiger-striped head to give Argus a once over, then lowered it again in disinterest.

"You ever listen to the *Chasing Killers* podcast?" Argus asked.

"Not regularly," Gage replied with a shrug. "I've heard it a few times. Enough to know it's not my thing. Why?"

Argus took his laptop out of his bag, set it on the kitchen table, and opened it. He tapped a few times on the touchpad, then sat back as a man's voice filled the room.

"Welcome subscribers, this is the Chasing Killers podcast, and I am your host, Chase Grafton. Today's episode focuses on the investigation into the Devil's Blade Murders, and I give you fair warning that today's topic is not for the faint of heart. I will be discussing some very graphic content, so if you get queasy at the

mention of violence or blood, sign off now."

Rolling his eyes at the podcaster's melodramatic tone, Gage sank into a chair across from Argus.

"Now, anyone who has seen the news recently will know that the wife of billionaire pharmaceutical CEO Monty Montclair has succumbed to injuries sustained in a gruesome knife attack yesterday. So far, we haven't heard if a Devil's Blade knife was discovered near the scene of the attack."

Gage crossed his arms over his chest and sighed.

"But I believe the murder weapon used in previous killings is at the heart of this case. I believe the Devil's Blade is the key to catching our killer."

Before the podcaster could continue, Argus tapped again on the touchpad to silence Chase Grafton's voice.

"I won't make you listen to the whole thing," Argus said to Gage's relief. "But as I was listening to the podcast, I got an idea. I decided to put the Devil's Blade at the heart of my analysis, so to speak, and I think Chase Grafton may be on to something."

Turning the laptop, Argus gave Gage a view of the screen.

"I spent time this morning working with a cluster analysis algorithm to classify our killer based on his pattern of behavior and I came up with something interesting."

Gage rewarded the words with a blank stare.

"I proceeded with the assumption that the killer selected the Devil's Blade knives deliberately, and that his LuckyDevil13 username wasn't random. That it was all symbolic."

"Okay, so you think this guy is a satanist...maybe into the

occult?" Gage asked.

"No," Argus said. "Maybe that's what he wants us to believe, but the algorithm tells a different story."

Gage raised an eyebrow, growing impatient.

"Okay, why not just skip to the ending then?"

Argus gestured toward a data chart on his screen, but the pressure in his chest made it hard for Gage to concentrate.

"What is all this supposed to mean?" he snapped. "What does the data signify?"

"It defines key characteristics or behaviors of the person we're looking for," Argus replied calmly. "For example, someone with an affinity for the Devil's Blade knife brand, someone who uses a boat for transportation, someone skilled or experienced in violent combat."

He pointed to an image on the bottom of the screen.

"Once I plugged all the data into the algorithm, I got an unexpected result to add to our profile."

Gage made out a snarling dog with devil horns.

"What's that supposed to be?" he asked.

"It's a hell hound," Argus said. "Also known as a devil dog, which is a nickname associated with the U.S. Marines. They were given the nickname by enemy soldiers during WWI who claimed they fought as savagely as the hounds of hell."

Before Gage could respond, Argus clicked on his browser and opened the website for the Devil's Blade manufacturer.

"Plenty of Marines still wear devil dog t-shirts or get devil dog tattoos," Argus said. "You can see here that the nickname was actually the inspiration behind the Devil's

Blade company name. The founder had been a former Marine in the reconnaissance unit."

Looking up at Argus, Gage cocked his head.

"So, we're looking for a Marine?"

"Or maybe a former Marine," Argus agreed.

Gage nodded slowly as he processed the information.

"It does seem plausible that someone capable of that kind of violence and stealth would have formal training."

"That's what I thought," Argus said, sounding more confident. "So, I cross-checked the entire database of Montclair Biotech employees with the database of former Marines and came up with a small list."

Impressed with the analyst's initiative, Gage leaned forward with growing interest.

"You'll never guess who was at the top."

Gage shook his head.

"Theodore Montclair," Argus said.

"Monty's son was a Marine?"

Somehow Gage never thought a pampered millionaire's son would be Marine material.

"He enlisted right out of high school," Argus said. "He probably wanted to get away from his overbearing father. He made it through boot camp and lasted four years, so if he only enlisted to piss off his dad, he worked pretty hard to do it."

Argus referred to his notes as he continued.

"Teddy came home straight after he was honorably discharged because his mother was dying of cancer," he said, "Then after she died, he went to college. He joined the family firm once he got his degree. He's been under his father's thumb since then."

Rubbing a hand over his smooth head, Gage tried to process the information.

"So, you think he could be killing the women his father was involved with to get some type of revenge?" Gage asked. "But why take Cassidy? Would he harm his own sister?"

He felt a surge of concern for the teenager.

"I'm not sure all this makes a strong enough case to get a warrant to search Teddy's house."

Argus held up a hand.

"Hold on just a minute," he said. "I was getting excited, too, until I realized that Teddy Montclair couldn't have killed Harmony Baxter. Not according to the recorded minutes of the Montclair Biotech strategic planning committee held on the day she died."

Gage sat back in his chair, suddenly deflated.

"Based on the minutes, Teddy Montclair was in the company's boardroom on the afternoon Harmony was killed. Randolph Hildebrand chaired the meeting in Monty's absence."

"They were talking about possible legal issues to do with one of their drug trials and it got pretty heated," Argus said. "They ended up deciding to wait to discuss it until the legal team was available."

"And you're sure the meeting notes were legit?" Gage asked. "You're sure Teddy was really there?"

"Yep. I contacted Tariq Green, the IT guy who pulled all

the messages and emails off the server for us and asked him if they stored video or audio recordings of the meetings."

"Short version is they do, and he sent me the video for that meeting. I watched enough to verify that Teddy was there. I'm sending you a copy now."

Argus tapped frantically on the keyboard.

"So, what do you propose we do next?" Gage asked.

"I want to keep working through the list I've compiled of Montclair Biotech employees with a background in the Marines," Argus said. "If that doesn't turn up something I can move on to Monty's friends and acquaintances."

"It's worth a shot," Gage agreed. "And in the meantime, send me that video of the board meeting."

After Argus had gone, Gage clicked on the video to open it. As he adjusted the volume so he could hear what was being said in the crowded boardroom, his eyes widened.

As soon as the video ended, he reached for the phone.

CHAPTER THIRTY-TWO

Bridget stared down at Scarlett Montclair's smooth face, finding it hard to connect the spirited yet troubled woman she'd known with the motionless body on the table. Scarlett still looked peaceful, just as she had in her hospital bed at Saint Agatha's.

Even now, on the cold, metal table of the medical examiner's office, Scarlett looked surprisingly young and serene, and uncomfortably similar to her teenage daughter.

For a horrifying moment, Bridget imagined young Cassidy Montclair lying in Scarlett's place.

Shaking away the disturbing image, she turned to Charlie Day, who stood next to her, looking as if she was lost in her own unsettling thoughts.

"Are you okay?" Bridget asked quietly, not wanting to disturb Opal Fitzgerald and Greg Alcott as they prepared to begin the autopsy.

"I'm fine," Charlie assured her.

Bridget wasn't convinced as she studied the agent's tired gray eyes behind her protective mask, but before she could inquire further, Opal motioned to Greg to activate the voice recorder.

"The body is that of a well-nourished, white female measuring sixty-six inches and weighing one hundred twenty-four pounds. Her appearance is consistent with the decedent's age of thirty-eight years. Her eyes are closed."

Opal moved down Scarlett's body, conducting a thorough external examination, pointing out various contusions.

She stopped when she got to the deep cuts on her forearm and allowed Greg to take multiple pictures and measurements.

"The cuts appear to be defensive wounds. They're deep, but no vital arteries or organs were involved. We'll have a forensic expert in the FBI lab compare the injuries to the murder weapon used in the other Devil's Blade homicides. I'm confident it'll be a close match."

Looking up at Bridget and Charlie, she hesitated.

"We'll start the internal examination next. I'll look at her lungs and heart to see if this could be pulmonary edema, or maybe a cardiac arrest brought on by the stress of the attack, but I see no outer signs to make me think we'll find anything."

Bridget also had the feeling the medical examiner wouldn't find a simple explanation.

"And of course, we'll collect samples for a complete toxicology screening," Opal added. "If I don't find a surprise in the internal exam, I'll have to list the official cause and manner of death as undetermined for the time being."

Bridget nodded and went out to the changing room with Charlie to remove her protective coveralls, masks, and booties.

She found Vivian Burke pulling coveralls over slim black pants and a vivid orange blouse that clashed with her red hair.

"Opal asked me to collect all the samples and rush the tests through the Bureau lab," the forensic examiner explained.

"Thanks for your help expediting the tests," Bridget said. "Any idea how long it will take to get the results back?"

Tucking her hair under a blue paper cap, Vivian made a show of considering the question.

"We could have preliminary results as early as tomorrow," she finally said. "Now, I better get in there."

She started toward the autopsy suite, then stopped next to Charlie and pulled down her mask.

"Where's Hale by the way?" she asked with a small frown. "Is he with Beatrix today?"

At first, Charlie just stared at Vivian in confusion, but then her face hardened.

"I'm not Hale's keeper," she said with a shrug. "What he does with his own time is his business. I don't really care."

Vivian's eyes narrowed at Charlie's dismissive response.

"And everyone thinks *I'm* the cold bitch," she said in an icy voice before pulling her mask up and stalking out of the room.

"What was that about?" Bridget asked.

"Hale must be seeing someone new," Charlie admitted. "He's been hard to get a hold of and sending messages to this Beatrix woman every five minutes. But I'm happy for him."

Bridget raised an eyebrow and they both laughed.

"Well, I may not be *happy*," Charlie admitted. "But I'm not going to let myself get involved. It's none of my business."

"It is if you care about him," Bridget protested. "Why not just ask him?"

Charlie met her eyes, and Bridget could see the answer behind them. She hadn't asked Hale about the new woman because she was scared of what he would say.

Or maybe she was scared of her own response.

If she didn't ask about it, she couldn't get hurt.

"I just think it's best if we keep our work relationship and his personal life separate," Charlie said. "As it should be."

Bridget was about to object, then decided to drop the subject, at least for the time being.

Charlie had been through an unpleasant work relationship in the past. Things had ended badly, and she was likely reluctant to repeat the experience.

Who am I to tell her otherwise, especially when she hasn't asked my opinion? It isn't my business.

Bridget winced as her own words echoed in her head.

If you care, then it is your business.

"Listen, Charlie," she found herself saying. "I imagine what happened down in Florida has scared you off relationships at work, but I'm wondering if you should see someone, like a therapist, and talk about it? If you have unresolved issues that are stopping you from moving on, then-"

"That's what I'm trying to do. I'm trying to move on," Charlie said, holding up a hand to stop her from saying more. "I appreciate your concern, but I don't need a therapist. Right now, there's only one man I'm interested in finding, and that's the Devil's Blade Killer."

* * *

Bridget was exhausted by the time she stopped by her father's house on Maplewood Drive to pick up Hank.

Deciding to go through the back, she knocked twice on the kitchen door, then let herself in to find her stepmother washing dinner plates at the sink.

Hank jumped up and trotted over to Bridget as Paloma put down the plate she was holding and turned to stare at her.

"Are you working on the Devil's Blade Killer investigation?" she asked, smoothing back her curls, which she'd recently dyed a rich champagne blonde. "I've been listening to the *Chasing Killers* podcast every morning and I just can't believe what Chase Grafton has been saying."

Paloma gave an exaggerated shudder.

"Is it really true?" she demanded. "Were all those poor women sliced open?"

Bending down to rub Hank's fur, Bridget looked toward the door to the hall, worried her father would come in and overhear their conversation.

Bridget didn't want Bob Bishop to worry about her or her

involvement with another serial investigation.

"Yes, unfortunately, there have been several homicides committed with a Devil's Blade knife in the last few months," Bridget admitted. "But it's nothing for you to be worried about. The FBI is working on it, as is the U.S. Marshals Service."

Paloma looked intrigued.

"If the Marshals are involved it must be dangerous."

"What's dangerous?"

Bob Bishop stood in the doorway wearing a frown.

"And why didn't you tell me Bridget was here?"

Coming into the room, he pinned Bridget with a hard stare.

"Don't think you're fooling me, young lady," he said, in the same tone of voice he'd always used when she was a teenager coming home after curfew. "I know you're working on that case involving Monty Montclair, so stop acting like I'm too old and fragile to know what's really going on."

"I just don't want you to worry," Bridget said, going over to her father and giving him a placating hug.

He shook his head and sighed.

"That's one thing that'll never change," he said. "I'm always going to worry, so you might as well tell me the truth."

Bridget wasn't sure if it was that simple, but she didn't argue. Instead, she led Hank out to the Explorer and headed home, turning the heater on high against the dropping temperature outside.

She and Hank had just walked in the door when Santino called. She could hear the fatigue in his voice.

"We found Monty Montclair's body this afternoon," he said. "He washed up in some underbrush. The turkey vultures got to him before we could."

Bridget winced at the terrible image his words summoned.

"We're not sure yet how he died, but it looks like he managed to fight back. The responding M.E. said there's definitely blood and tissues under his fingernails, so at least we'll have some forensic evidence to go on this time."

"And Cassidy?" she asked, suddenly afraid of what he might say. "Was there any sign of Cassidy?"

"No," Santino said. "No sign of Cassidy or *Monty's Mojo*."

They both fell silent as Bridget absorbed the information.

"Teddy," she said. "Someone's got to tell Teddy."

"Can't it wait for tomorrow?" Santino asked.

Bridget wished it could, but she knew better. Next of kin needed to be told as soon as possible to avoid the news getting out to the press first.

"I'll do it," she said.

She looked down, realizing she hadn't yet removed her coat and was still holding her purse.

"I'll feed Hank and get him settled, and then I'll drive into the city. It's best if Teddy's told before he hears it on the morning news."

"I don't like the idea of you going to see him alone," Santino said. "But I've got to take care of the scene out here. Why don't you call Gage? Or maybe Argus? You two seem to make a good team."

CHAPTER THIRTY-THREE

Teddy Montclair stood next to the fireplace staring down into the flames as Randolph Hildebrand paced back and forth behind him. The CFO had insisted he needed to talk to Teddy about the latest drug trials right away.

Vixenzia was supposed to bring in record revenue and revive Montclair Biotech's sagging stock prices. But the drug they'd been touting as a wonder drug wasn't playing along.

While the drug was intended to shrink cancerous tumors, there were growing reports of serious complications.

"Several more sudden deaths have been linked to Vixenzia in the last week," Hildebrand said, sounding winded. "Your father managed to persuade the doctors in charge of the trial to hold off on sounding the alarm. But now that he's disappeared, they're beginning to make noise again."

"Persuade?" Teddy said with distaste. "You mean *pay off*."

He knew his father had been trying to hide the truth from the public and the shareholders. If made public, the news could bring down the whole company.

"Shouldn't you be talking to Sutler about this?" Teddy said irritably. "He's the lawyer. It's his job to come up with a legal strategy if a lawsuit is filed."

"Sutler's not available," Hildebrand said. "Besides, once the press gets hold of this news, we'll be out of business long before it goes to trial."

A knock on the front door stopped Hildebrand's pacing.

Crossing into the foyer, Teddy looked through the peephole and saw Bridget Bishop standing on the doorstep. A thin, redheaded man stood bundled next to her.

Teddy hesitated, then flung open the door.

"Sorry to stop by unannounced, Mr. Montclair."

Bridget spoke in a somber voice that indicated whatever news she'd come to deliver wasn't going to be good.

"This is Special Agent Argus Murphy with the FBI's Behavioral Analysis Unit," she said, gesturing to the man beside her. "Can we come in?"

Teddy stepped back and waved them inside, pretty sure he knew what the psychologist was about to say.

"You didn't have to come all the way out here to tell me about my stepmother," he said as they reached the living room where Randolph Hildebrand stood. "It's been all over the news. I hear my stepmother's death is even the subject of a podcast."

Hildebrand shifted nervously at the sight of the FBI agents.

"I listened to an episode of *Chasing Killers* on my way over," the CFO added in a pained voice. "The host was delighted to have material for another episode. It's just entertainment to him. It sounded as if he was enjoying the whole thing."

"Actually, we're not here to talk about Scarlett," Bridget said. "We're here about your father."

Teddy's stomach clenched at the ominous words.

"What about my father? Has he been found? Is he okay?"

"Your father's body was found earlier this evening," Bridget said softly. "The searchers found him on the shore a few miles from Charity Point. There was no sign of Cassidy."

Teddy nodded numbly, unable to speak.

"Are you okay, Teddy?" Hildebrand asked, putting a hand on the younger man's arm.

Shaking off his hand, Teddy turned back to the big fireplace, which was glowing with a cheerfully crackling fire that seemed out of place considering the grim news.

His eyes rested on a picture on the mantle.

It showed a much younger Teddy and his father on the deck of *Monty's Mojo*. They were both wearing fishing attire.

The sandy beach and weathered trees of a small island completed the idyllic scene.

"My father loved the Bay," Teddy said quietly. "I've always remembered the day this photo was taken. We didn't often spend much time together, but this day was special."

He tapped a finger on the glass over the photo, then looked back at Bridget with a wistful smile.

"He took me to Snakeroot Island. Have you been there?"

Bridget shook her head.

"I guess most people haven't," he said. "Which is probably why my father enjoyed it so much. Part of the island is a bird preserve, and the rest is usually covered with wildflowers, at least in the spring and summer months."

"It was one of the only places I remember my father laughing and forgetting about work and...well, everything. It was special for him. Then once I was out of the house and gone, he started taking Cassidy there, too."

Teddy thought of Cassidy and tried to compose his features. He needed to remain strong.

Now that both Scarlett and his father were dead, it would be up to him to take care of the girl.

His mind replayed Bridget's words.

There was no sign of Cassidy.

He thought back to the last time he'd seen her.

It was on Christmas Day at his father's house. She'd grown into a young woman, although she was still small for her age.

Where is she now?

"What are you doing to find my sister?" he suddenly asked, spinning to face the agents. "Who's looking for her now?"

"We've organized a search party and released a statement to the public asking for information," Bridget assured him. "But anything you can tell us would be helpful."

Staring into her blue eyes, he nodded grimly.

"I'll cooperate in any way I can," he said, swallowing

hard. "Now that both my father and Scarlett are gone, Cassidy is my responsibility. She's the only family I have left."

CHAPTER THIRTY-FOUR

Cassidy looked out at the sun rising over the bluffs that formed the tip of Snakeroot Island, hoping she hadn't made a terrible mistake. When Lucky had told her the previous night that they'd be heading south past Cape Charles and out to the Atlantic, she'd hidden her fear, but had allowed a small frown to appear.

"Won't they be looking for this boat at the Chesapeake Bay Bridge tunnel?" she said. "Shouldn't we find a place to hole up nearby until they give up the search?"

He hadn't responded right away, but she could tell that her words had put a kernel of doubt in her captor's mind.

"My father always liked to go to Snakeroot Island when he wanted to get away from everyone."

The island had been her father's favorite place to take her on their rare trips out in the boat together.

Explaining that there were no docks on the island but that it offered safe mooring, with deep, well-protected anchorage and a half-mile long beach leading to tree-covered bluffs, she had assured him that in winter they'd be alone except for the flocks of snow geese who flew south from Canada to spend the winter on the Bay.

Snakeroot Island would be deserted, making it their own private hideaway, she had promised, and he'd agreed it might be a good place to hide out for a while.

Now staring at the isolated shore, Cassidy watched as a trio of birds soared overhead, the black tips of their wings emphasizing their snowy white feathers.

Her gaze dropped to the barren land, searching for the white flowers that usually filled the island during the summer months, but they were nowhere to be seen.

She flashed back to a long-ago day when she'd been no more than five or six years old. Back to a time when she'd idolized her father, sure that he was the smartest, most handsome man in the world.

Cassidy followed her father through a field covered in the little white blossoms of the snakeroot plant.

She reached down to pick a flower, but he grabbed her wrist and held it tight. So tight it hurt.

"Don't touch them!" he scolded.

"But they're pretty!" she complained.

"The flower may be pretty, but it's poisonous," he warned. "Just like your mother."

Staring up at him in confusion, she wanted to ask him what he meant, but he dropped her hand and gestured around at the blanket of delicate white flowers.

"Just look...don't touch," he said. "Snakeroot contains a toxin that could get on your hands. Then it could get in your mouth when you eat your lunch or touch your face."

Nodding somberly, she followed him as he turned and

continued walking through the field toward the bluffs.

A small glow of contentment filled her little chest.

Even though his tight grip around her small hand had hurt, she reveled in the concern she'd seen on his face.

He must care for her after all to be so worried.

Even as they skirted along the edge of the crumbling bluffs, she felt safe. Her father was there, and despite his frequent absences, he loved her.

He would never let anything happen to her.

The memory faded as Cassidy felt a presence behind her.

She forced her body to remain still. If she jumped or recoiled, Lucky would sense her fear.

She'd managed to convince him that she was on his side. That she wanted to get away from her dysfunctional parents.

Now that his guard was down, it was only a matter of time before she'd get a chance to make her move.

If she could get him to the edge of the boat, she could push him over. She would leave him on the isolated island and go alert the police.

She knew how to operate the boat. Her father had given her a lesson only last summer.

"I'll prepare to anchor," Lucky said.

Studying her for a long moment, he turned away as a news report came on the radio.

"Happy Monday morning to all our listeners in the Chesapeake Bay area. We have breaking news this morning in the hunt for billionaire Monty Montclair."

Cassidy's body stiffened.

"The body of the billionaire founder of Montclair Biotech was discovered last night, only hours after reports that his estranged wife, Scarlett Montclair, had succumbed to injuries sustained in an attack the previous day."

"These shocking developments come after a woman's death in the Montclair's luxury home in Charity Point last week was linked to the Devil's Blade murder investigation."

Cassidy's head spun as the information sank in.

She thought she'd been fooling Lucky, when in fact he'd been lying to her. Manipulating her into staying with him while her parents both lay dead in a morgue somewhere.

She spun around to see him staring at her as the radio broadcaster continued speaking in a somber voice.

"A search is ongoing for Monty's boat and for the couple's teenage daughter, Cassidy Montclair."

Lucky switched off the radio and frowned.

"So, Monty and Scarlett are both dead," he said slowly, sounding bemused. "I wasn't expecting to hear that."

"Liar!" Cassidy shouted, unable to maintain her act any longer. "That's what you wanted all along, wasn't it? Both my parents dead? That was your plan."

The man's face hardened.

"Didn't you say that I would be doing you a favor by eliminating your parents?" he asked, taking a menacing step forward. "Or was that just a lie to get me to lower my guard?"

"I said you'd be doing me a favor by taking me away from them. I didn't want you to kill them!"

"I didn't kill them," he objected. "But I can't pretend it doesn't make things easier for me."

She lunged for the knife he wore in a worn leather sheath attached to his belt, but her hand had barely settled over the handle when a hard blow to the side of her head sent her reeling.

Falling back onto the deck, she looked up to see him extracting the knife from its sheath.

He brandished the Devil's Blade in front of her and took a step forward, moving slowly and carefully.

Cassidy slid backward toward the stern, her eyes following the gleaming steel of the blade, her heart pounding and her breath coming in short hard gasps.

Sucking in one last deep breath, she flung herself backward, plunging into the cold water and disappearing from view.

CHAPTER THIRTY-FIVE

Bridget woke up with the weak winter sun shining in her eyes and Hank's soft face snuffling over her. The Irish setter was usually nervous in a new place, and this time she couldn't blame him, considering her impulsive decision to join Santino after leaving Teddy's house the night before.

The search for Cassidy Montclair and *Monty's Mojo* had been suspended soon after dark due to low visibility and plummeting temperatures, and Santino had called to say he was stopping off at Sofia's by the Shore to thaw out and spend the night.

Knowing that he would be out on the boat again first thing in the morning, Bridget had decided to surprise him, determined to join the search party when it resumed.

She'd slept surprisingly well and was more determined than ever to assist in the search for Cassidy as she climbed out of the comfortable queen-sized bed and slipped on the complimentary robe which hung in the guest room closet.

Sliding her feet into matching slippers, Bridget crossed to the adjoining bathroom where she splashed her face with icy cold water and brushed her teeth with the travel-sized toothbrush she always carried in her purse next to her Glock.

She pulled on the same clothes she'd worn the day before and made her way down the stairs and into the cozy dining room where Sofia and Luna were sitting.

They had been welcoming the night before, and Sofia had quickly invited Bridget to stay overnight, setting her up in one of the guest rooms which would have otherwise remained empty until the B&B opened again in the spring.

"I can take Hank out for a walk if you like," Luna said, obviously smitten with the Irish Setter's friendly disposition.

"I'm sure he'd like that," Bridget agreed as Sofia waved her into a chair and offered her coffee and a selection of cereal, pastries, and juices.

"I hope you don't feel you have to treat me like one of your guests," Bridget said, suddenly embarrassed to have shown up at the B&B uninvited. "I really appreciate you letting me stay here last night, but I'm sure you enjoy having the place to yourselves during the winter, so I'll be out of here just as-"

"Don't be silly," Sofia protested. "I'm thrilled to have you here. And thrilled to see my son smiling again."

Reassured by Sofia's warm response, Bridget helped herself to a cream cheese pastry and a mug of milky coffee.

She'd just taken a huge bite when Santino bounded into the room, followed by Hank and Luna.

"Morning, sleepyhead," he called as he grabbed a mug and poured himself a cup of coffee.

Forgoing any sweetener, he took a sip of the dark liquid.

"It's not even eight o'clock," Bridget protested after she'd swallowed the gooey bite. "And I'm all ready to go."

"I've been thinking about that," Santino said as he grabbed a bagel from the plate. "Maybe you and Hank should stay here today and I'll-"

"Oh no!" Bridget interrupted. "You're not going to fob me off that easily. I'm the only one who knows Cassidy, and if you do find her out there alive, she'll need someone who can offer emotional support."

The previously cheerful atmosphere grew suddenly silent as everyone in the room seemed to remember what was at stake.

"I'll watch out for Hank while you're gone," Luna offered, softly rubbing the fur above Hank's forehead.

As if her words had settled the matter, Santino nodded and pointed toward the door.

"Well, alright then, we better get going."

They were already climbing into the Chevy when they heard Luna call out.

"Wait! You'll need this!"

She ran toward them carrying a thick pink jacket.

"Take my sailing jacket," she said, holding the garment out to Bridget. "It's waterproof and really warm."

Luna turned and darted back toward the big house, leaving Bridget to settle into the Chevy's passenger's seat.

"You sure you want to do this?" Santino asked as she snapped on her seatbelt.

"I'm sure," Bridget lied between jittering teeth.

Santino gave an unhappy nod.

"Alright then, I guess it's time to go on the water."

* * *

Bridget leaned forward and strained to see through the fog.

She was impressed with the scale of the search and rescue operation she saw as they pulled up to the base of operations in Santino's red pickup.

The Charity Point PD had set up the command post and Detective Peggy Quinn seemed to be in charge.

Bridget made out Charlie and Hale standing by the shore. As she walked closer, she recognized the two men with them.

Both Gage and Argus were bundled in thick parkas and heavy woolen hats.

"You guys look like you're ready for the Arctic," Santino called out. "Sorry to break the news, but I don't think you're going to run into any polar bears around here."

Gage rubbed his gloved hands together and gave a visible shiver as Bridget approached.

"I don't know how anybody stays out here for long," Gage said, shaking his head. "At least nobody in their right mind."

"I don't think we're looking for someone in their right mind," Argus said matter-of-factly as he studied a map. "If we're gonna find a madman, we'll have to think like a madman, and go where a madman would go."

Bridget nodded her approval as she tried to snuggle deeper into Luna's jacket. She watched as Argus held up the map and motioned to Santino.

"Deputy Santino? I've studied the current and used the tide patterns to determine where Monty's body might have been dumped based on when he went missing and where his body was found," Argus said. "Based on my calculations, I'd say he was dumped somewhere around here."

He used two fingers to tap on the map, trailing a finger along the Eastern Shore.

Staring down at the map, Santino turned to Charlie, who had come up behind him.

"The Marshals were leading the search for Monty because he was a fugitive," Santino said. "But now that he's been found, it's not my call where to start the search. Not anymore."

Bridget realized he was right.

Now that Monty was dead, they were looking for *Monty's Mojo* in order to track down his killer and hopefully find Cassidy. It was a job for the local police and the FBI, and Santino was now participating in a supporting role.

Looking around at the search team gathered on the foggy shore, she suspected most of the searchers were probably expecting to find a dead body.

She watched as Charlie looked toward Hale, who was staring down at his phone with an unhappy frown, then turned toward Argus, who was studying his map.

Moving closer to look over his shoulder, Bridget saw a

familiar name and tapped on the map.

"Snakeroot Island," she said, looking up at Santino. "That's the place Teddy Montclair told us about last night. He said his father had taken him and Cassidy there as children."

Argus studied the map with an uncertain frown.

"Based on my calculations, I think the island is too far from the spot where Monty's body was found," he finally said.

"But what if Monty took her there to hide out before he was killed?" Bridget asked. "What if she's still out there waiting to be rescued?"

She looked around, seeing the doubt on the gathered faces. Even Santino seemed torn.

"Could a teenager really survive on an island alone in this weather?" he asked.

"Maybe she's not alone," Bridget replied, suddenly anxious to get the search started. "And we won't know until we go to the island and find out if she's there."

Noting the stubborn set of Bridget's jaw, Santino lifted both hands in supplication.

"As I said, it's not my call."

"How about we split up?" Charlie suggested. "That way we can use Argus' calculations as well as Bridget's intuition. Maybe we'll get lucky with one of them."

Santino nodded.

"I can take the *Mirabel* out to Snakeroot Island," he offered, earning a look of gratitude from Bridget. "And the other search boats can head along the shoreline near the coordinates Argus calculated."

Once the plan had been finalized, Bridget climbed aboard the *Mirabel* without waiting for an invitation. She saw that Hale had followed her onto the boat.

Taking up a position on the aft deck, she wrapped Luna's pink jacket more tightly around herself, then double-checked that her Glock was still safely zipped in the coat's front pocket where she'd secured it on the drive over.

As the boat began to motor away from the shore, Bridget tried to distract herself from the icy spray and cold wind by turning to look at Hale, who sat just behind her.

The agent was looking down at his phone, and the worried expression on his face matched her own.

"I hear you have a new girlfriend," Bridget called back to him. "Is she in law enforcement or a civilian?"

Hale's forehead creased as if he didn't understand.

"Vivian Burke said you've been seeing someone named Beatrix," Bridget tried again louder, wondering if he could hear her over the motor. "How's that going?"

"You must have misunderstood," he called back, his frown deepening. "Beatrix Allen isn't my girlfriend."

Before he could elaborate, Santino pointed toward the shore.

"That's where I found Monty's body," he shouted into the icy wind. "The turkey buzzards led me straight to him."

Bridget felt ill as she looked at the marshy area.

Once they'd passed the spot, she remained quiet, her eyes searching the shore, her stomach filled with worry for Cassidy.

A gust of wind ripped back the hood of her jacket, sending her dark hair whipping in the wind.

Frantically pulling the hood back into place, she snuggled deeper into the jacket. After a while, she felt Hale move up to the seat beside her.

She was about to ask him about the mysterious Beatrix again, but he spoke up first.

"So, who is this Argus guy?" he asked. "He seems pretty green. Can we trust his calculations?"

"He's a new analyst at the BAU," she explained, surprised Hale hadn't encountered Argus before. "He helped out with the Backroads Butcher case, so when an opening came up, Gage brought him on board. He's done well so far."

Bridget wondered why Hale's question had irritated her, and why she felt the need to defend Argus.

"Charlie told me Argus has a theory that the Devil's Blade Killer is a Marine or former Marine," Hale said. "Do you agree with him?"

Her blank expression gave her away.

"He didn't tell you?" Hale asked, raising one dark eyebrow. "Apparently, Argus used some sort of algorithm to make a connection between the Devil's Blade knives and the nickname the Marines use. He said they call themselves devil dogs."

Bridget wondered if she was the last one to hear about Argus' theory as she tried to focus on what Hale was saying.

"The founder of the Devil's Blade knife company was a former Marine," Hale continued. "So, I guess it makes sense."

He scratched at his unshaven chin.

"Argus gave us a list with all the Montclair Biotech employees and executives who have been in the Marines," he said. "We've talked to most of them already."

Bridget was intrigued despite her annoyance.

"There is one employee on the list we couldn't get in touch with who I think fits the profile," Hale said. "I called to set up an interview, but he's not been answering his phone."

"Okay, so who is it?" Bridget asked, eager to have a suspect.

Hale pulled out his phone and navigated to the Montclair Biotech corporate website.

He clicked on *Corporate Bios* and zoomed in on a headshot.

As Bridget read the name beneath it, an excited shout caused them both to look up.

"There it is!"

Santino was pointing toward an island cloaked in light fog.

"There's Snakeroot Island," he said, slowing the boat.

"It looks deserted," Hale said, pulling out his binoculars.

Bridget had to agree. The small strip of beach that was visible appeared to be empty, as did the brown, overgrown terrain behind it. Even the toxic white blossoms that had given the island its name had vanished.

Only a handful of snow geese circled in the air above them.

"I'll go around to the other side," Santino called, steering the boat closer to the shore. "We can find a place to anchor."

Straining to see through the fog, Bridget could see no sign that anyone was on the island, or ever had been.

"Go past those bluffs over there," Hale said, pointing to a series of low, rocky cliffs that stuck out over the water. "There's probably a good spot to throw anchor on the west side of the island if we can-"

His words faltered as he adjusted his binoculars.

"There's a boat up ahead," he said, pointing toward a bank of trees and foliage. "But that's not *Monty's Mojo*."

He lowered the binoculars and looked at Bridget.

"The name on the hull is *Lucky Devil*."

CHAPTER THIRTY-SIX

Lucky crouched under the sparse cover of the barren trees that covered Snakeroot Island and waited. The former corporal in the Marine's elite reconnaissance unit shivered as he strained to make out the small figure darting through the underbrush.

After Cassidy had gone over the side of the boat, he'd had to waste time ensuring the boat was securely anchored before he'd splashed in after her.

He couldn't afford to lose the boat to the strong current and wind up shipwrecked on the godforsaken island.

By the time Lucky had made it onto shore, the girl had disappeared, but he'd been able to track her progress, quickly determining that she was heading for the sand-colored bluffs that jutted out over the choppy water of the Bay.

All he had to do now was wait and be patient. Eventually, she would make a move and he'd be right there waiting with his trusty Devil's Blade.

Resting a gloved hand on the sheath at his waist, he looked down at the knife within, realizing with a pang of regret that it was the last one in his Devil's Blade set.

Teddy Montclair had given him the set to celebrate the Vixenzia trial launch, and it had been useful, although not in the way Teddy had likely intended.

The thought was interrupted by a faint buzzing. He stopped and listened as it came closer.

Is that a motor?

Lucky forced himself to remain calm. Forced himself to continue taking deep even breaths as he concentrated on the familiar sound of the boat approaching.

Winding his way through a maze of brown scrub bushes and skeletonized trees with dry, crooked branches, Lucky moved back toward the shore.

When he had a clear view of the water, he lifted the small marine binoculars he kept on a sturdy strap around his neck.

Almost immediately, a sleek cruiser with the name *Mirabel* on its hull came into view, stopping short of the newly christened *Lucky Devil*.

Lucky focused the binoculars on the boat, and his eyes narrowed as he saw several figures on board preparing to make anchor near the shore.

He zoomed in on the face of a dark-haired woman on deck and paused. Bridget Bishop had found him.

Does that mean I'll be famous now, like the others she's caught?

Of course, the game wasn't over yet. He still had a chance to evade her and the men she'd brought with her.

Turning his gaze to the two big men preparing to throw out the anchor, he thought he recognized one of them as the U.S. marshal who'd been on the news the night before.

The one who'd been at the marina when they'd found Scarlett. The one who'd pulled Jagger Yardley out of the water.

The distinct sound of a dead branch snapping behind him brought his mind back to Cassidy, and the immediate task at hand. He needed to take care of the girl before he could move on to the new arrivals on the boat.

The odds of three-to-one didn't bother him.

He'd faced worse odds during his time in the Marines and had always gotten out alive. His willingness to kill or be killed without hesitation had served him well.

Relying on skills learned during eight years of training, Lucky once again began tracking the girl, following her trail through the underbrush as she moved toward the west.

He was just starting to think he'd lost his touch when he saw footprints in the dirt leading toward the bluff. His pulse quickened as he walked toward the edge.

Figuring she planned on ambushing him, he instantly braced himself, prepared for her attack, confident there was no way the slip of a girl would have the strength to send him into the water.

But all was quiet as he stood on the edge of the bluff.

Another possibility suddenly occurred to him as he studied the footprints, which seemed to disappear over the side.

Had she already jumped or fallen into the water?

Moving closer he looked over the edge, half-expecting to see Cassidy's red head bobbing above the small choppy waves.

Instead, he heard frantic footsteps pounding in the dirt.

He spun around just in time to see Cassidy swinging a thick tree branch toward him, her face pulled back in a fevered grimace of fear and resolve.

Lucky took the brunt of the blow full in the chest, having no time to lift his arms to block the branch. But the wood was dry and brittle, and it cracked in two as it struck his hard body.

Half of the branch fell at his feet as Cassidy swung the other half again, this time going for his face.

But this time Lucky was prepared. He lunged forward, grabbed the branch, and wrench it out of the teenager's grip.

He tossed the dead wood to the side as his other hand seized Cassidy by the throat.

Forcing her toward the edge of the bluff, Lucky reached for his final Devil's Blade.

CHAPTER THIRTY-SEVEN

Charlie Day stood in the enclosed cockpit beside Detective Peggy Quinn, who was at the wheel of the Point Charity PD patrol boat. The boat's equipment gave Quinn access to the network of cameras, radar, and other tracking devices used to watch over the Chesapeake Bay, but today they were no match for Mother Nature.

Snow-laden clouds had formed overnight as Arctic air plunged across the Bay, blowing a strong northwest wind over the water, freezing everything in its path.

And now a thick layer of fog was gathering over the shoreline reducing visibility.

As Charlie looked back to see Argus Murphy shivering on the deck, she waved for him and Gage to join her and Quinn in the cockpit's shelter.

"It's freezing out there," Argus said, rubbing his gloved hands together. "I like it much better in here."

The analyst cleared his throat.

"Have you and Agent Hale gotten a chance to go through my list of Marines?" he asked, sounding hopeful. "I hate to be a pest, but I do think that's our best lead."

"Actually, we've made good progress going through the

list," Charlie said. "But I'm not sure your theory is going to pan out. There's only one person left that we haven't been able to interview and eliminate as a suspect."

She frowned as she thought of the man they'd been trying to reach without success over the weekend.

"Cliff Finley is Montclair Biotech's compliance officer," she said. "I've talked to him on several occasions, but I don't know much about him, other than he was in the Marines, of course."

"And you haven't established that he has an alibi for the day Harmony Baxter was killed?"

Charlie hesitated, then shook her head.

She didn't want to mention the talk she'd had with Finley on Friday afternoon. She'd likely scared him off with her questions. Perhaps that was why he wouldn't answer her calls.

"We tried to reach him after we got your updated profile yesterday, but he didn't answer his phone," she said. "I even sent an agent to his listed address, but no one came to the door. I guess he could have gone out of town for the weekend."

She checked her phone, looking for any missed calls, texts, or voicemails.

"He still hasn't returned my call even though it's Monday. He should be back in the office by now."

Argus nodded and thought for a minute, then began scrolling through his phone.

"Based on the contact number I have for Mr. Finley, I think he has one of the company phones Montclair Biotech issues to executives," he said, looking at Charlie. "We can track someone's location by their phone, right?"

"Not without a warrant," Charlie said.

Argus cocked his head.

"But what if it's a company phone?" he asked. "Could you track a phone if you had the company's official permission?"

Charlie thought about it and shrugged.

"I guess obtaining the permission of the phone's legal owner would hold up if challenged in court."

Argus was already pulling out his phone.

He punched in a number, then activated the speaker.

The voice that answered sounded familiar.

"Mr. Montclair?" Argus said. "You may remember me from last night. I'm Special Agent Murphy with the FBI and I need to ask you for a favor."

Hearing the wariness in Teddy's voice, Charlie expected the grieving man to hang up. Instead, he cleared his throat.

"What kind of favor?"

"I need your permission to trace one of your company phones," Argus said. "It's assigned to Cliff Finley."

There was a moment of silence.

"Why Finley?" Teddy finally asked. "You don't think he had something to do with my father's death, do you? Or that he could have Cassidy?"

Glancing at Charlie, Argus hesitated.

"We're just investigating all possibilities, Mr. Montclair."

"It can't be Finley," Teddy said. "He's a buddy of mine from the service. He was the best guy in my unit."

He sounded incredulous.

"The guy re-enlisted after I was discharged. He went on to the recon unit, which is nearly impossible to get into. He came out looking for something less stressful. Not sure corporate compliance is less stressful, but he's done a fine job."

Argus waited for Teddy to finish.

"So, you're okay with us tracking the corporate phone you issued to Cliff Finley and viewing any content we find on it?"

"I guess so, although I really should check with Erwin Sutler first," Teddy said, starting to backpedal. "He's the legal counsel, and he should be the one to say."

"This could be a matter of life or death for Cassidy," Argus reminded him. "Any delay could have serious consequences."

Charlie held her breath as Teddy wavered.

"Well...okay, then, fine," he said, sounding miserable. "You have my permission to track Finley's phone."

By the time Argus ended the call, Charlie was already on her phone requesting a trace. Minutes later she looked at Argus with wide gray eyes.

"You were wrong."

"About Cliff Finley being a prime suspect?" he asked.

She shook her head.

"No, you were wrong about the currents and the tides in the Chesapeake Bay," she said. "Because right now, Cliff Finley's phone is somewhere on Snakeroot Island."

Argus gaped at her in disbelief.

"So, unless he's taken the day off to visit an unpopulated bird preserve, I'm thinking he's somehow involved in Monty's death and the abduction of Cassidy Montclair."

* * *

Charlie tried Bridget's number again as the Charity Point PD patrol boat sped toward Snakeroot Island, but once again the call rolled to voicemail.

"I pulled up Cliff Finley's military service record," Argus said, tapping on his phone. "It was clean. But his arrest record tells a whole different story."

He spoke loudly to combat the whine of the engine as the boat picked up speed.

"When Teddy Montclair was giving us his glowing review of Mr. Finley, he failed to tell us that his buddy has a felony record," Argus said. "He was arrested for stalking a few years ago. He reached a plea agreement and served no time."

"You think Teddy knew about that?" Charlie asked.

Argus shrugged.

"You never know," he said. "If they served together, he probably feels some sort of loyalty toward the guy, although you'd think he'd want to protect the company's reputation."

"I imagine most publicly traded companies wouldn't want a stalker on their executive team," Charlie agreed.

A deep voice spoke up behind Charlie.

"Maybe Finley knows too much for Teddy to turn him

in."

Spinning around, Charlie saw that Gage had crammed his wide shoulders into the cockpit beside Quinn. She'd almost forgotten the BAU agent was on the boat.

"What do you mean *Finley knows too much*?" Charlie asked.

She stared at Gage, noticing he had one hand resting on his chest as if preparing to say the pledge of allegiance.

"Based on what I heard in a recording from the company's strategic planning meetings, I'd say it's possible that Cliff Finley was involved in some sort of cover-up," Gage said.

He lowered his voice, moving closer to Charlie and Argus.

"Most of the other Montclair Biotech executives were involved in the cover-up as well, including Monty Montclair," he said. "Apparently, the Vixenzia drug trial went wrong. People died that shouldn't have. I've already notified the FDA."

Another piece of the puzzle fell into place as Charlie realized the Vixenzia trial must be the secret Hildebrand and Sutler had been trying to keep.

"Snakeroot Island is straight ahead," Quinn called back to them. "Radar shows there are two boats anchored on the west side. We'll make landfall in the next ten minutes."

Rushing toward the bow, Charlie looked toward the horizon with wary eyes. It was finally time to meet the devil.

CHAPTER THIRTY-EIGHT

A scream tore through the frigid, foggy air as Bridget stood on the deck of the *Maribel*. Looking up toward the top of the bluff, she saw Cassidy Montclair stumble backward, her arms cartwheeling wildly in the air as she tottered on the cliff's edge.

Unable to look away, Bridget watched in horror as the teenager lost her balance and plummeted toward the cold, gray water almost fifty feet below.

As she started to rush toward the side of the boat, Santino's hand gripped her arm and held her in place.

"Hale and I will go find Cassidy," he said, "The water's only four to six feet deep around the shoreline, so we'll be fine. But we're going to need you to stay here and call for help. I saw a man up there. Cassidy didn't fall. He pushed her."

Pulling his gun from the holster under his jacket, he held it out to her.

"Keep this for protection," he said. "And let off a warning shot if you see Cassidy's assailant."

"I've got my own weapon."

Bridget patted her pocket.

"But I'll keep yours safe."

Hale was already lowering himself into the water, his face a mask of determination as the icy waves reached his chest.

As he moved steadily toward the spot where Cassidy had disappeared, he looked back at Bridget.

"Call Charlie. Tell her we need help."

Bridget nodded and reached for her phone as Santino followed after Hale into the water.

Still holding his gun, she kept her eyes on Santino as he plowed through the water behind Hale, moving fast, his head and shoulders visible above the choppy waves.

Glancing down, she saw she had no signal on her phone. Immediately turning to the radio, she made sure the radio was turned to the correct channel, then pressed the *Talk* button.

"Mayday, Mayday, Mayday. This is the *Maribel*. We have a passenger overboard and need immediate assistance. We're positioned on the west side of Snakeroot Island."

As she repeated the distress call twice more, Bridget stored Santino's gun under the console and unzipped her pocket.

She reached in to put a hand on her Glock, assuring herself the gun was there if she needed it.

Turning away from the radio, she stared toward the bluffs, desperately searching the water for Cassidy.

The drop from the top of the bluff to the water below didn't look far enough to prove fatal, but the hard fall into freezing water was sure to have knocked the air from the teenager's lungs and could easily send her body into cold shock.

A shout from Santino started Bridget's heart racing as she suddenly saw a third head appear in the water.

With a surge of relief, she saw that the men were pulling Cassidy toward the shore, although the teenager's body appeared to be limp and unmoving.

Scanning the beach and the trees beyond, Bridget searched for any sign of Cassidy's assailant.

She was concentrating so hard that she didn't see the man come out of the water and over the port side of the boat until it was too late.

A flicker of movement caught her eye and she spun around to see a man standing on the deck in front of her.

Although she'd seen him in person only once before, she knew exactly who he was. He was the man on the Montclair Biotech website. The former marine in the headshot Hale had shown her less than an hour before.

Bridget's mind flashed back to the Montclair Biotech boardroom and the day she'd gone to ask Monty Montclair about Cassidy. The man had been there acting in his role as Montclair Biotech's compliance officer.

Without a word, Cliff Finley extracted a long knife from the sheath at his waist. Holding it up in front of him, he motioned for her to move toward the cockpit.

Bridget glanced toward Santino and Hale. The men were still working to pull Cassidy onto the shore.

"Stay quiet and I may let you live, Dr. Bishop."

Finley kept his voice low and threatening.

"Scream, and I'll slit you wide open."

Keeping the knife pointed in her direction, he moved to the console and started the engine.

A surge of panic rolled through Bridget at the thought of the killer escaping in the *Mirabel* with her as a hostage.

Unable to stop herself, Bridget screamed at the top of her lungs and lunged toward the side of the boat.

For a fleeting moment, her eyes found Santino on the shore as his head jerked around and he looked toward the boat.

Then Finley's arm was around her neck, and he was squeezing the breath out of her.

"That was a stupid thing to do," he growled as Bridget's fingers clawed uselessly against his arm.

Knowing the Glock was her only hope, she stuck her hand in her pocket and pulled it out, then realized she had little hope of shooting Finley from the position she was in.

She hesitated, trying to think.

If she raised her arm, he would see the Glock and take the gun off her. He might even use it to fire at Santino and Hale, who would undoubtedly try to come after her.

Sucking in a deep breath, she aimed the gun at the only part of Finley's body she could see and pulled the trigger.

The bullet went straight through Finley's boot and through the deck. As the shot echoed through the air around her, she heard Santino yell her name.

Finley convulsed in pain and lowered the knife, but instead of grabbing for his foot as she'd expected, he whirled around and gripped the Glock.

Wrenching it from her hand, he flung it overboard.

Free from his grip, Bridget dove for the side of the boat. She thought she'd made it until she felt a hand grasp the hood of her pink jacket and yank her backward.

Twisting away with another high-pitched scream, her heel came down hard on Finley's injured foot, earning a howl of pain as he lost his balance and stumbled forward, falling heavily onto the Devil's Blade.

His body gave a violent shudder, then went still.

Bridget backed away in numb horror as a hot stream of blood spilled out onto the deck.

Hearing voices shouting on the shore, she looked back to see Detective Quinn and Charlie loading Cassie onto the patrol boat where Gage and Argus were waiting to cover her with their warm coats.

Then suddenly Santino was standing over her, dripping wet and panting from his frantic rush to get back to the *Mirabel*.

Looking down at Finley's crumpled body, he quickly checked his pulse, then shook his head.

"He's dead."

Their eyes met in a moment of stunned silence, and then he was pulling her into a hard, cold embrace.

As he began to shiver against her, Bridget pulled off Luna's jacket and wrapped it around him.

"I'm sorry," she said, resting her head on his shoulder

"Sorry about what?" Santino asked.

"I shot your boat," she said, pointing to the bullet hole in the deck. "I shot *Maribel*."

WHERE EVIL HIDES

CHAPTER THIRTY-NINE

Charlie turned the big Expedition into the parking lot of Saint Agatha's Memorial Hospital and found an empty space. Climbing out into the brisk morning air, she headed toward the main entrance, assuming Hale would follow her up to Cassidy Montclair's room.

But when they stepped into the lobby, he motioned for her to go upstairs without him.

"You go on," he said with a faint smile. "I've got to take care of something. I'll follow you up in a few minutes."

The elevator door opened with a ding as Hale turned away, walking toward the gift shop.

Letting the elevator doors close behind her, Charlie stared after Hale, then impulsively ducked into the hospital chapel in case he looked back.

She waited a few minutes in the empty space, allowing the stillness to surround her as she studied the statue of Saint Agatha above the altar.

The gentle face of the young martyr reminded Charlie of the teenager she'd come to see. Luckily, unlike the saint, Cassidy Montclair had survived her ordeal, although there was surely a long road of healing ahead of her.

Charlie sucked in a deep breath, then stepped back into the corridor just in time to see Hale emerge from the gift shop carrying a small bouquet of flowers.

She frowned as she watched him head down the hall in the opposite direction, unaware that he was being observed.

Wondering if he'd gotten turned around and lost his way, she hurried after him, trailing behind him up a flight of stairs to the oncology unit on the second floor.

She stopped in surprise when she came around the corner and saw him disappear into Room 210.

"Can I help you?"

A man in white scrubs stood behind her pushing a meal cart.

"I'm just visiting a friend," she said, striding forward as if she knew what she was doing.

Knocking softly on the door Hale had gone through, she pushed it open and stepped inside.

Instead of seeing Hale's startled face as she'd expected, she saw a frail, elderly woman asleep in a hospital bed by the window. The woman's medical chart hung by the door. Charlie saw the name Beatrix Allen at the top of the chart.

"What the hell are you doing here?"

She turned to see Hale standing in the doorway to the adjoining bathroom. He held a vase of flowers in one hand as if he'd been filling it with water.

"I was worried about you," Charlie said, a hot flush of embarrassment flooding her cheeks as she realized what she'd done. "I followed you because I thought..."

The words stuck in her throat as he set the flowers on a

table against the wall, then crossed the room and took her arm, intent on leading her out into the hall.

"Tristan? Is everything okay?" a small voice called out. "I wasn't expecting you until later. Who's with you?"

Hale stopped and looked back, his hard face melting into an instant smile as he looked at the woman in the bed.

"I came to the hospital to visit a witness and thought I would surprise you," Hale said in an affectionate tone Charlie hadn't heard before.

He moved forward to stand beside the bed, then turned to Charlie, his face suddenly open and vulnerable.

"Bea, I'd like to introduce Agent Charlotte Day," he said, meeting and holding Charlie's eyes. "Everybody just calls her Charlie, though. We work together at the Bureau."

"Is she the one you told me about?" the woman asked as a small smile lit up her face. "The one you're sweet on?"

Hale's face reddened.

"Now, don't get any ideas, Bea," he cautioned. "The feeling isn't mutual. We're just co-workers."

"Nonsense," Bea said, keeping her eyes on Charlie. "She wouldn't be looking at you like that if she wasn't sweet on you, too. A woman can always tell."

Motioning for Charlie to come closer, Bea studied her face.

"He didn't tell me you were beautiful," she said softly. "I never was, even when I was younger."

A wistful tone filled her voice.

"But I managed to find my soulmate anyway. When it comes to love, it's what's in your heart that counts. It's what lasts."

Charlie nodded, not sure what to say.

"Tristan has a bigger heart than most," Bea continued, her small face growing serious. "And he's taken care of me better than most sons take care of their own mothers."

She glanced over at Hale with a sad smile.

"When I found out I had the cancer, well, he was beside himself. He's barely left my side. I don't know what I would have done without him."

Swallowing a sudden lump in her throat, Charlie thought she knew just how Bea Allen felt.

"We've got to go, Bea," Hale said, moving toward the door. "But I'll be back at my usual time."

The older woman nodded and lifted a small hand.

"It was good to meet you, Charlie," she called, sounding suddenly fatigued. "I do hope I'll see you again."

"I hope so, too, Bea," Charlie managed to say before Hale put a hand on her elbow to steer her through the door.

Without a word, he propelled her down the hall toward an alcove beside the elevators where a *Family Waiting Room* sign hung over a row of red vinyl chairs.

Sinking into a chair, Charlie stared up at Hale, her gray eyes filled with questions. He sighed and ran a hand through his dark hair, then lowered himself into the chair beside her.

"A young man got shot when I was working undercover on a trafficking case," he said in a low voice, his eyes on the floor. "He was just a kid really. A twenty-year-old kid who'd hooked up with the wrong friends and made some bad choices."

Hale glanced over at Charlie.

"The kid was Bea's son. Her only child. Dwayne died before the ambulance arrived, and I was with him."

Pain filled Hale's voice at the memory.

"He asked me to tell his mom that he was sorry," Hale said, his voice raw. "It was the hardest thing I've ever done."

"You had to tell Bea her son was dead?"

Charlie knew how hard it was to break that kind of news. She'd done it before, and it never got easier.

"Couldn't someone else have-"

"I insisted," Hale cut in. "And in doing so I broke my cover. After I admitted I'd been with Dwayne when he die, that I'd been working undercover for the Bureau, I couldn't go back."

He exhaled and leaned back in his chair, closing his eyes.

"After the shooting, and after my cover was blown, the Bureau required me to take time off and go to counseling. My therapist advised me to make peace with what had happened, but I just kept thinking of Dwayne's final words. His concern for his mother."

His broad shoulders sagged, and Charlie could feel the weight of the guilt and remorse he'd been carrying on his own.

"I knew Bea was alone. She'd been a single mother, and..." he paused, struggling to keep his composure. "Something about Bea reminded me of my own mother."

He opened his eyes to meet hers.

"I'd been deep undercover when my mom died. It happened suddenly and I hadn't been with her. Never got to say goodbye. Somehow that and Dwayne's death...it all just felt connected. Getting to know Bea and trying to be there for her felt like what I was supposed to do. It felt right."

"I'm so sorry you had to go through that," Charlie said, feeling sad and foolish in equal measures. "All this time I was thinking Bea was your new girlfriend and that you were slacking off. I guess that's what I get for jumping to conclusions."

Nodding in agreement, Hale produced a mock scowl.

"You're a special agent in the FBI. You should know better."

He held her gaze, then smiled.

"So, you were jealous of Bea?" he asked. "Does that mean..."

"It means I'm a fool," Charlie objected, unable to hold back a smile. "And it means I've been a terrible friend. I should have asked you what was going on instead of sulking and following you around."

Hale's face fell.

"A friend? Is that what we are? *Friends?*"

Charlie considered the question, her heart and her head fighting a battle as she formulated an answer.

The man in front of her had suffered more than his fair share of grief already, and she knew more heartbreak awaited him as Bea's illness moved toward its inevitable end.

Now more than ever, he would need a friend to lean on.

Lifting a hand to push back a dark curl that had fallen over his forehead, she sighed.

"How about we forget the labels?" she said, ignoring the voice of caution in her head. "Let's just do what you did when you met Bea. Let's just do what feels right."

* * *

Charlie cleared her mind as she stepped out of the elevator onto the fourth floor, having left Hale to seek out Dr. Nimitz and get an official report on Cassidy Montclair's injuries.

Walking down the hall to Room 428, she knocked quietly on the door, then pushed it open.

Cassidy lay motionless on the hospital bed, her thin body attached to an assortment of tubes and wires, her face peaceful in the soft light coming in through the window.

Looking toward the man sitting beside the sleeping girl, Charlie did a doubletake, momentarily mistaking Teddy Montclair, with his thick brown hair and patrician features, for his father.

She hadn't seen the younger Montclair since his sister had been rescued from Snakeroot Island, but Teddy looked remarkably calm and well-rested, considering everything that had happened in the last forty-eight hours.

"How is she?" Charlie asked, keeping her voice low.

"She just fell asleep," Teddy replied, looking down at his sister as if making sure she was still there. "The doctors say she's going to make it. I can't tell you how grateful I am to you and the others who saved her."

He stood and offered her a long, slim hand.

Before she could take it, a voice spoke from the doorway. Charlie looked around to see Bridget Bishop.

"May I speak to you privately, Agent Day?"

The formal request took Charlie by surprise. Telling Teddy she'd be right back, she stepped out of the room.

She frowned when she saw Argus Murphy standing beside Bridget in the hall, immediately sensing the analyst's tension.

"Scarlett Montclair's bloodwork came back," Bridget said quietly. "When Vivian Burke heard we were coming here, she asked us to pass the lab results on to you right away."

Looking down at the folder in Bridget's hand, Charlie felt her pulse begin to race.

"The lab found lethal levels of a synthetic opioid in her blood," Argus blurted out before she could open the file. "The same type of opioid recently patented by Montclair Biotech."

"So, Scarlett's death was caused by an intentional overdose?" Charlie asked, raising an eyebrow. "Who was in her hospital room? Who had the opportunity?"

Clearing his throat, Argus nodded to the folder in her hand.

"The test results from samples taken at Monty's autopsy are also in there," he said. "Vivian told us blood and tissue had been collected from under the fingernails the vultures left intact. Apparently, Monty attempted to fight off his attacker."

Charlie hesitated, then looked toward Bridget without opening the folder.

"Go on, Bridget. Tell me. I can see from the look on your face you know what's in here."

"The DNA profile wasn't a match for Cliff Finley," Bridget replied without hesitation. "It was actually a partial match to Monty, which means he was attacked by a close male relative. Most likely his own son."

Before Charlie could react, the door behind her swung open.

Spinning around, she saw Teddy standing in the doorway, a water pitcher in his hand.

"Cassidy's awake," he said, frowning at the trio gathered in the hall. "I was going to refill this."

A loud *ding* sounded behind her, and Charlie glanced back to see Hale stepping out of the elevator, followed by Dr. Nimitz.

Nodding at the new arrivals, Charlie turned back to Teddy.

"Theodore Montclair, I'm arresting you for the murder of your father Montgomery Montclair, and your stepmother, Scarlett Montclair."

Keeping one hand on her holster, she pulled out her handcuffs and handed them to Bridget, who immediately cuffed one of Teddy's wrists, then stepped behind him to cuff the other one.

"You have the right to remain silent," Charlie continued, not bothering to pull out her Miranda card. "Anything you say can and will be used against you in a court of law. You have a right to an attorney. If you cannot afford an attorney, one will be appointed for you."

Teddy gaped at Charlie in shock, then shook his head and looked toward Bridget.

"Dr. Bishop, this is crazy. You know I could never have hurt anyone," he insisted. "I loved my father and Scarlett, and now I'm the only family Cassidy has left."

Ignoring Teddy's protestations, Charlie motioned to Hale.

"Pat him down," she ordered. "Check his pockets."

Hale stepped forward, following Charlie's command without question, patting along Teddy's arms and legs until he reached his right suit pocket.

Reaching inside, he pulled out a small vial with a rubber stopper. He held it up to the light, gently swirling the liquid contents within.

"Call Erwin Sutler," Teddy said coldly, averting his eyes from the vial. "I want my lawyer."

CHAPTER FORTY

Bridget Bishop followed Terrance Gage into the gray concrete block building that housed Teddy Montclair as he awaited trial and sentencing. The judge had refused to grant bail based on the seriousness of the charges and the flight risk presented by the vast fortune the accused murderer had recently inherited from his late father.

"What do you think he wants to tell me?" Bridget asked as they waited in the interview room for Teddy to be brought in.

"Maybe he wants to confess," Gage said. "Or maybe he wants to thank you for helping out with his sister."

Bridget shook her head, doubtful Teddy had anything quite so gracious planned.

She wasn't sure why Monty had requested the visit, but she'd accepted the invitation in the hopes of finding answers.

"Argus sends his regards, by the way," Gage said. "He's already working on a profile of a suspected serial killer in Tennessee. But I think he's going to miss having a partner."

Bridget refrained from rolling her eyes, but she couldn't

keep the skepticism out of her voice.

"Partner? I thought partners shared their theories with each other. No, I think Argus likes to work alone."

Sitting back in his chair, Gage raised his eyebrows.

"Maybe he needs someone to show him how to be a good partner," he said. "It's always best to learn by example."

The rebuke stung, but Bridget knew he had a point. She hadn't exactly welcomed Argus into her world with open arms.

"Well, even if he didn't share his theories with me this time, it looks as if he'll be a valuable addition to the BAU," Bridget conceded. "Maybe we'll both be better partners if we get a chance to work together in the future."

"Statistically speaking, I think it's highly probable," Gage said. "Especially once you are back at the BAU full time."

Ignoring the teasing comment, Bridget shook her head.

"What I don't understand is why you never showed up at the hospital when we made the arrest. You missed all the excitement," she teased. "Argus just about had a heart attack when he came face to face with Teddy."

"Well, maybe he should have been the one at the Cardiologist's then," Gage said, dropping his eyes to his hands.

Bridget stared at him in concern.

"Were you having chest pain?" she asked. "Are you okay?"

"My heart's just fine. But the doctor referred me to a psychologist. He's thinking the chest pressure and shortness of breath are being caused by stress and anxiety."

"You mean, you've been having panic attacks?"

"More like anxiety episodes," Gage corrected. "So, looks like I'll be back to see Faye Thackery. Maybe she can help me figure out this whole foster parent thing."

"You think your anxiety is related to Russell?"

"It's not his fault," Gage assured her. "He's a good kid. I just feel like I'm doing all the wrong things. Russell's been through so much, I just don't want to screw him up. And I don't want to let Kenny down."

"You're doing a great job from what I can see," Bridget said. "And Kenny would be so grateful to know everything you've done. I'm sure Faye will set you straight on that."

A shuffling sound in the hall announced the inmate's arrival. Both Bridget and Gage looked toward the door as it opened, and Teddy Montclair shuffled in wearing leg cuffs over his prison uniform.

The guards sat him in the chair across from Bridget, attaching his leg cuffs to the table before exiting the room.

"You're probably wondering why I wanted you to come," Teddy said as he propped his elbows on the table.

"I'm assuming you want to set the record straight," Bridget replied. "And I'm interested in hearing what you have to say."

Nodding his head, Teddy exhaled.

"My lawyer says we can fight the charges, but I think the evidence against me is too much to beat."

He tapped his fingers nervously on the tabletop.

"Right now, you're the only one I trust with the truth,"

he said. "Everybody else will just try to turn my tragedy into profit or entertainment."

When Bridget didn't respond, he continued.

"You're a psychologist and a profiler, so maybe you'll even understand why I did it. I'm not sure I do," he said with a shrug. "I guess you know I've been charged with two counts of first-degree murder, but now they're accusing me of conspiring with Cliff Finley to kill those women."

Bridget now knew that Finley had stalked and killed Irina Jensen, Esme Dupree, and Harmony Baxter. He'd also attacked Scarlett Montclair and stabbed Jagger Yardley to death.

"What did you know about Finley's crimes?" Gage asked.

"I'm here to tell Dr. Bishop my story, not *you*," Teddy said, his face twisting into a petulant scowl. "You're only in here because *she* insisted you listen in."

Giving Gage a warning look, she nodded at Teddy.

"That's right. We're here to listen," Bridget said, keeping her voice neutral. "So, why not start at the beginning? When did you meet Cliff Finley?"

Teddy was silent for a long beat, then sighed.

"I'm afraid this story goes back further than that," he said sourly. "It all started when my dear old dad decided to dump my mother and marry that whore Scarlett Lafferty."

Clenching his hands into fists, he banged them down on the tabletop, causing both Bridget and Gage to jump.

"I couldn't stand to see them together. She was only six years older than I was. It was revolting," he added. "As soon as I turned eighteen, I joined the Marines."

Anger seeped into his voice.

"I would have signed up for another four years, but my mother was sick by then. I came home to take care of her, but it was already too late. She didn't have any fight left after what my father had done. His betrayal killed my mother's spirit long before cancer took her life."

He lifted a hand to wipe at his eyes.

"She died a heartbroken woman, and I was left to fend for myself. I had no option but to work for my father," Teddy said. "He showed me that in business he was just as ruthless and unethical as he was in his personal life. I figured that would be the way I could get my revenge for everything he'd done."

Hesitating, he met and held Bridget's eyes.

"That's where Cliff Finley comes into the story. We were in the same platoon. He'd reenlisted after I'd gone home, but once he was out, he looked me up."

Bridget could sense Gage was about to ask a question and put a hand on his arm to stop him.

"Finley told me he'd trained in deep ground reconnaissance and surveillance using all this leading-edge technology. I figured he'd be able to find all the dirt on my father."

"So, you hired Cliff Finley in as the Compliance Officer with the intent he would spy on your father?" Bridget asked.

Teddy nodded.

"Pretty much. I told him to collect as much information and dirt as he could. I wanted to use it to destroy my father and humiliate him just as he'd done to my mother."

Hate shone from Teddy's eyes.

"Dear old Monty fell right into the trap, too. Kept messing around with women at the company, so I started sending the evidence Finley found to Scarlett," Teddy said. "She'd known all along he was cheating, but with the evidence thrust in her face, she couldn't keep denying it, even to herself. That's when she left him."

He gave an ugly laugh at the memory.

"And when Finley found out about the Vixenzia drug trial cover-up, I knew I'd won. I knew it was the kind of scandal that would take my father down both personally and professionally, leaving me to swoop in and save the company."

"So, you're saying you didn't know about the women Finley was killing?" Gage demanded. "About the use of the Devil's Blade knives?"

The question seemed to irritate Teddy.

"Finley was really into that whole Marine devil dog crap."

Teddy pointed to his forearm.

"He even had a tattoo on his arm of a dog with devil horns," he said. "Everyone in our squad called him Lucky, short for Lucky Devil because he got away with everything. Never ended up getting caught for all the crap he pulled."

Sitting back in his chair, Teddy suddenly sounded tired.

"Finley's the one who told me about those knives. Said they were the best in the world," Teddy said. "So, I got all the executives a set to celebrate the Vixenzia trial launch, and an extra set for my father to use on the boat."

He shook his head, adopting an injured expression.

"I didn't have a clue what Finley planned to do with them. I didn't know he was killing those women until reports started showing up on the news," he insisted. "By that time, there was nothing I could do to stop him."

"Did you even try?" Gage asked.

Teddy frowned.

"Finley wasn't scared of anything," he said. "But I tried to convince him he'd get caught. I thought that might stop him. But he only said he was doing it to set up my father. That it was for me. He wouldn't listen to reason."

He turned his gaze to Bridget.

"You believe me, don't you, Dr. Bishop? You can see I'm not a serial killer or a psychopath, can't you? You can see I had good reasons for what I did."

"How did you end up killing your father, Teddy?" Bridget asked, holding her breath.

If he was going to backtrack or clam up, this would be the time to do it.

"When my father skipped out on bail, Finley grabbed him, drugged him up, and left him in the house on Windwalker Way," Teddy admitted. "I was supposed to notify the police. Make it look like I'd come to the rescue in an attempt to save Cassidy and do the right thing."

"So, what happened?"

Teddy dropped his eyes.

"The drugs didn't work as Finley had promised. My dad came to and picked up the knife Finley had left as evidence.

He began to fight me, and I struggled for the knife."

His voice hardened.

"I killed him in self-defense," he said. "After that, I panicked and dumped him in the Bay."

"Okay, then what about Scarlett?" Bridget asked, not buying his self-defense story. "You brought the vial with you to the hospital. So, you must have planned it out in advance. That makes it premeditated murder. What I don't understand is why you would kill your stepmother when she was already out of your way."

The question earned an angry laugh.

"Out of my way? Oh no, Scarlett was still married to my father, and she was Cassidy's mother. I knew it was just a matter of time before they'd find my father's body, and with him dead, and the divorce never finalized, Scarlett stood to inherit half of his estate."

He brought an angry fist down on the table.

"And Cassidy would get half of what was left, which Scarlett would control. My inheritance would be a pittance compared to what that woman would get."

"So, you killed Scarlett over money?" Gage asked. "Is that why you were going to kill your sister?"

"She isn't my sister!" Teddy exploded. "My father didn't know it, but Cassidy wasn't his biological daughter."

Bridget and Gage stared at Teddy in shock as he continued.

"Finley found an old friend of Scarlett's who said she was already pregnant when she met my father. That she married the old man because he was rich, and she was in trouble."

"I snagged Cassidy's toothbrush when she'd been staying with my father and Finley got a DNA test done. It matched the friend's story. Cassidy's not my sister and I wasn't about to let her take half of my inheritance."

* * *

Bridget pointed to the modest house on Newberry Street.

"There it is," she said, waiting for Santino to park his Chevy in the driveway. "Come on Hank, let's go see Cassidy."

Climbing out of the truck, Bridget had only made it halfway up the walk when Shirley Lafferty appeared in the doorway.

"Come on in," Shirley said, waving the trio inside and leading them out to the kitchen. "Cassidy and Bingo are taking advantage of the warmer weather."

Bridget looked through the window, smiling as she saw Cassidy curled up on a lawn chair reading a book with Bingo snuggled up beside her.

"Sure is a nice day," Roy said, coming into the kitchen.

The older man shook Santino's hand and turned to Bridget.

"Well, is it official?" he asked. "Can she stay with us?"

"That'll be up to Judge Kimble," Bridget said, softening her words with a smile. "But my report to the court highly recommends that Cassidy be placed with her loving maternal grandparents, so I'm pretty sure it's going to work out."

Giving first Bridget and then Shirley a hug, Roy quickly headed for the backdoor.

"I've got to go tell Cassidy."

He paused and looked down at Hank.

"You want to come, too?"

The Irish setter followed Roy out the door as Shirley watched with a sad smile.

"It's been hard on us all," she said as she sank into a chair. "With Scarlett gone, and all the stories in the news...well, I just hope Cassidy will be alright."

"She'll need time to heal," Bridget said, knowing firsthand the heartbreak of losing a mother. "But she's got you to help her. And in time..."

Shirley nodded and dabbed at her eyes.

"At least that lawyer of Monty's said that Cassidy's trust fund is safe from the creditors circling around the company," she said. "She's not a billionaire like her father was, but she'll have enough to see her through college and then some."

"Yes, and the other good news is that Teddy's confession means there will be no need for Cassidy to testify in court," Bridget said. "So, she can just focus on getting her life back together."

Once they'd left the Lafferty's house and were back on the highway, Bridget relaxed in her seat.

"You know, this is the first time in a long time I have no pending cases to work on," she said with a smile. "Now that the case of Montclair vs. Montclair is officially over, I have no responsibilities and no plans. I'm as free as a bird."

Santino grinned over at her.

"Actually, I told my mother we'd go over and spend the weekend helping her get the B&B ready to open for the season. I didn't think you'd mind."

"That's fine," Bridget said. "I don't mind a little hard work. But no boating. Not yet. At least not until spring."

The End

ACKNOWLEDGEMENTS

WRITING THE THIRD BOOK IN THE BRIDGET BISHOP series felt a little like writing about friends and family. I know some of the characters so well that it's a bit like coming home when I sit down at my computer. And I am immensely grateful to my real family for giving me the time needed to write.

Without the patience of my loving husband, Giles, and my five fabulous children, Michael, Joey, Linda, Owen, and Juliet, this book would never have been written.

I'm also blessed with a supportive and kind extended family, including Melissa Romero, Leopoldo Romero, Melanie Arvin Kutz, David Woodhall, and Tessa Woodhall.

And my mother's spirit lives on in me, providing inspiration for so much of what I write. I am so grateful to have had her in my life.

ABOUT THE AUTHOR

Melinda Woodhall is the author of heart-pounding, emotional thrillers with a twist, including the *Mercy Harbor Thriller Series*, the *Veronica Lee Thriller Series*, and the new *Bridget Bishop FBI Mystery Thriller Series*. In addition to writing romantic thrillers and police procedurals, Melinda also writes women's contemporary fiction as M.M. Arvin.

When she's not writing, Melinda can be found reading, gardening, chauffeuring her children around town, and updating her vegetarian lifestyle website. Melinda is a native Floridian and the proud mother of five children. She lives with her family in Orlando. Visit Melinda's website at www.melindawoodhall.com

Other Books by Melinda Woodhall

Her Last Summer	*Girl Eight*
Her Final Fall	*Catch the Girl*
Her Winter of Darkness	*Girls Who Lie*
Her Silent Spring	*Steal Her Breath*
Her Day to Die	*Take Her Life*
Her Darkest Night	*Make Her Pay*
Her Fatal Hour	*Break Her Heart*
Her Bitter End	*Lessons in Evil*
The River Girls	*Taken By Evil*

Made in United States
North Haven, CT
10 July 2022